AIR

Will Phelps

Printed in the United States of America

ISBN: 978-1-936510-36-8

AIR

Will Phelps

Acknowledgement

The writing of my first book has been an eye opening and rewarding experience. As is true with many things in life, one does not achieve success without help from others.

I must extend great thanks to my wife Lisa for the continued support and encouragement through the highs and lows of the process. She was also extremely key in the editing process. Her keen eye for details and helpful suggestions made a world of difference.

My son Adam took a very basic layout for the covers and turned it into a work of art. His patient listening and creative excellence achieved far more than I could have asked.

My son Cameron expressed continuous enthusiasm for the book and his personal pride for what I was doing. That encouragement from him made me want to finish the book and be a positive example.

My daughter Nicole expressed her support by "spreading the word" about the book I was writing to everyone! Apparently there was never any doubt in her mind that I would get it done!

I am blessed by a wonderful and loving family and am very thankful for each of them.

Introduction

It was a little after 3 a.m. Dr. Holmsby was hunched over the lab table playing with the controls on a laser generator. Behind him and several feet below were the objects of his attention - a dozen or so small orbs that were set up in a circular array. As he applied the subtle changes in the control settings, a minor miracle began to evolve. In the center of the array, a disc shape began to appear hovering in mid air. Beneath the hovering disc was the shadow of the disc directly under the hovering image. He turned and looked with pride at the image, and more importantly the shadow under the image. He had done it, he had really done it. The achievement had taken most of his career at MIT. He had written grants for funding and begged and pleaded the University for funding for laser research. Despite the fact that no one had paid much attention, he had published a number of groundbreaking articles about his research, and the University was satisfied about receiving an adequate return for his research. But now he had the *coup de gras* - this was new technology that had earthshaking implications.

Dr. Holmsby powered down his equipment and put on his top coat to head home. Tomorrow was another day, and would be a new beginning for him and his family. He turned off the lab lights, locked the door and started down the hallway.

Air

As he pressed the down button to call the elevator, Dr. Holmsby sensed a presence behind him and turned to see if he was seeing ghosts in the night. As he turned, he was startled by a figure that stepped out of the shadows. At the same time and from behind, a hand with a cloth and a pungent odor closed around his mouth. He inhaled to yell for help, and when he did, he inhaled a big gulp of the pungent odor. Immediately his periphery vision began to close and he lost consciousness.

Allison Stewart had stowed away on board the transport aircraft and was huddled down behind bundles of illegal drug cargo. Her back rested against a steel bulkhead, where she felt every bump and vibration in the airplane. The pilot was flying a low altitude route, twisting and turning through canyons and quickly up and over hills and small mountains in an effort to stay out of sight. The abrupt and severe change of direction and altitude was literally beating Allison to a pulp. She had a gash above her forehead, she was bruised, and her legs ached from squatting behind the bundles for hours.

She peeked above the bundles to see if she could at least stand up and stretch, and she was horrified to see one of the armed guards just three feet in front of her sitting on one of the bundles. As silently as possible, she slid back into place in her very tight spot.

The cut-off shorts and tank top Allison was wearing were not giving her any protection from the beating she was taking, courtesy of the airplane, and she was just about to the point where she couldn't take it any more.

Suddenly the aircraft banked hard and began a steep descent. The whine of the flap gear motors being actuated indicated that a landing was eminent. Allison's hiding spot would be revealed if the aircraft were to be unloaded.

There was no doubt that the people on board would kill her without hesitation and dump her body in the desert. She was also sure that rape and torture would be part of the treatment. With all of these thoughts running through her mind, she had to find a way to get off the airplane undetected.

As her mind raced through her options, an opportunity presented itself. The transport rear ramp began to open as the airplane leveled out for the final approach. Apparently this was the spot they were going to unload. The nearby guard had moved up to the front of the airplane to operate the ramp controls and prepare to unload the pallets of drugs.

Allison knew this would be a very quick stop. She also knew she had to get off before the unloading began. She began to slip her slim body between the bundles and the aircraft bulkheads to work her way towards the ramp. Her plan was to dive off the ramp while the airplane was still moving down the runway and take her chances.

Finally, she was on the ramp behind the rear-most bundles, waiting for the aircraft to slow up a bit. As the airplane began to taxi, Allison figured she could at least survive a tuck-and-roll landing if she dove off the ramp. She moved into place and jumped. Just as she leaped, the airplane hit a bump on the primitive runway, causing the loading ramp to propel her 10 feet in the air. She landed unceremoniously in the sage brush, gathering even more bruises and scrapes, and rolled to her feet to see if she had made it without detection.

Just as she stood up behind the sage brush, Allison heard a bullet whiz over her head. She had her answer and was off running for her life, zigzagging though the brush. She had no idea where she was or where to seek refuge, but knew she had to get clear of the immediate area if she was going to live another day.

Air

After five minutes of hard running, Allison stopped to look back and reassess her situation. Her evasion had taken her up a slight hill, and she was able to look behind her down the hill to the runway and aircraft all while staying hidden behind the sage brush.

The runway was nothing more than a very rough bulldozed strip in the middle of a desert that had no sign of civilization as far as she could see. She could see the transport aircraft she had jumped off of, as well as three smaller aircraft on the runway. The transport had pushed the pallets off the ramp as it taxied, and it was now turning around to prepare for take off. Armed men were pushing the pallets off the runway to clear it for the transport's departure. One other man was standing near the airplanes. He was holding binoculars and a rifle with a scope, and he was scanning the area looking for Allison. She quietly ducked down and began to move with more deliberation up the hill away from the runway.

Even if she escaped the group on the runway, Allison knew she was in trouble, what with no food, no water, very little clothing and being stranded in the middle of the desert. If she didn't die from exposure, she could be injured or killed by any number of desert predators.

Allison began to think about her survival training and next steps to prepare for a prolonged stay. Just as she was contemplating her situation, she stepped on the side of a rock. Her ankle folded and collapsed under her. There was nothing she could do to prevent her fall, yet she reached out to catch herself as she went down, hitting the ground hard. The last thing to hit as she fell was her head, but unfortunately it landed on a small rock. She rolled onto her back after she fell, looked up at the sun and realized that her chances of survival just took a huge turn for the worse. That was her last thought as her peripheral vision blacked out and she lost consciousness.

Chapter 1

J im finally struggled out of bed. It was a cold Monday morning and he needed to be at the airport for early patrol. The sun was just beginning to color the sky as he stumbled into the kitchen. He drank a large glass of water to rehydrate and went back to his bedroom to dress for a morning run. He pulled on running shorts, his favorite Phoenix Suns t-shirt, and laced up his running shoes over light socks. As he went through his stretching regimen, his brain kicked into gear and he began to think about work a bit.

Even though the western quarter had been heavily patrolled, the pressure was being kept at a high level due to continued drug smuggling activity by organized crime. Jim had been on contract with the DEA now for nearly a year, serving as chief pilot patrolling the western Hualipai Mountains south of Kingman, Arizona.

He walked out his front door, taking care to lock it. Like all of the DEA and law enforcement everywhere, he wasn't very popular with the local scum. His modest house, on 25 acres north of town, had been built by Jim, and designed to be added to in phases. The first building on the property was a metal barn-like building, which he lived in while he built the house. The barn now housed Jim's cars and toys (muscle cars from the 60s and 70s, as well as motorcycles, were his weakness) securely while he was away from home.

The high desert was cool and dry as he started down the street. He loped at an easy pace, giving his legs a chance to loosen up.

Even though he was only 32, and in better than average shape, Jim knew his body didn't respond like it did when he was 18.

The morning run was a habit. It felt good and he missed it when he wasn't able to get his daily three miles in. He was probably a little compulsive about it, and he took a lot of ribbing from his friends, but hey, whatever worked.

Jim returned home with just enough time to cool down a bit and get ready for work. He turned on the television - he liked to channel surf between Fox, ESPN, and The Weather Channel, just to get an idea of what was going on in the world.

He stepped from the brisk shower, shaved quickly and jumped into his flight jumpsuit. Even though he was on contract with the DEA, Jim was required to carry a sidearm, a Browning automatic 9 mm, which he now slipped into his shoulder holster after checking the clip and action.

Jim's regular assignment with the FAA had been suspended while working on a special project with the DEA and the INS, but he still had regular contact with his supervisor and many co-workers.

The FAA had been supportive in supplying navigational aids, aircraft and other pilots like Jim. This current effort in reducing drug traffic had been the most productive yet. The success of this campaign was due to more aircraft in the air, as well as increased use of radar and other high-tech electronic weaponry that identified potential smuggler aircraft and plotted their intended routes. It would seem the deck was finally stacked in favor of the good guys...but the runners looking for a quick fortune kept coming.

Even as promising as some of the new technology made the war on drugs seem, Jim wondered if it was truly a war that could be won over the long run. Much of what they accomplished seemed to do so little in the face of increasing demand for drugs.

Jim had a personal stake in winning every little battle he could though. His nephew lost his life from a stray bullet in a drug-related gang war two years ago. Another statistic in the growing number of innocent bystanders killed or maimed for no reason. He swore at young James's funeral that the loss of his life at just 10 years old would not be an empty loss. The image of that casket being lowered into the hole in the ground was an image that left an indelible mark in Jim's mind.

James's mother, Jim's sister, was doing better, but she would never be the same, and she also served as a constant reminder of the importance of his work.

The short drive to the airport was even shorter on his Ducati motorcycle. The early arrival gave him just enough time for a quick breakfast at the cafe on the field. Nat Jones had operated the cafe since the end of the Korean Conflict in the late 50s, and he now seemed to be everyone's friend and served a reasonable meal. Nat kept fresh fruit and bagels on hand for Jim...another source of ribbing from his friends. Jim had been eating a low-fat diet since his father died at an early age from a major coronary.

Jim's Cessna 185 had just been released from the annual inspection and was operating better than ever. The FAA had it outfitted with the latest GPS (global positioning system) receiver. The system received the signals from up to eight satellites simultaneously and gave him a read-out of his position plus or minus 60 feet. It also allowed him to electronically "mark" new dirt strips and abandoned roads used for illegal landings by latitude and longitude, simply by pushing one button on the receiver. Not coincidentally, this was the same system that was used in the Persian Gulf conflict. The system had a moving map display that depicted the aircraft position in relation to his intended course and all airspace boundaries and navigational aids.

All of this data, along with the HSI (Horizontal Situation Indicator) display, airspeed, vertical airspeed, tachometer, and manifold pressure was all projected on to a HUD (heads up display) on the inside of the windshield. This allowed Jim to instrument scan without having to look down at the instrument panel. When operating in high terrain at low altitudes, it was critical that he be able to keep his eyes looking out the window.

The Cessna had been fitted with a Robertson STOL kit that allowed a competent pilot to set the big skywagon down in incredibly short strips, as well as climb out quickly over obstacles.

He reviewed his pre-takeoff checklist as he walked up to the hangar. One of his last "wilderness" takeoffs had broken one of the electronic antennas off the belly. He reminded himself to check the attachment screws on the new one.

Just as he was starting the pre-flight, Jim's new partner walked into the hangar. Jim had heard that his reputation was one of being a bit of a cowboy in an airplane.

"Sam Brooks," he said as he ambled up and stuck out his hand. "I guess we're going to be flying together. Let me give you a hand with the pre-flight."

"Jim Mitchell. Heard a lot about you. Welcome aboard," Jim replied as they shook hands. "Don't know what you've been told about this assignment, but you won't be bored," Jim said.

"Yeah, I heard you've seen a little bit of action over the past year."

I guess you could call it action...my last partner is now flying metroliners for Southwest Airlines because of the action," Jim replied.

"Have you got many C-185 hours in your logbook?" Jim asked.

"The last time I checked, I think I had a little over 600 hours in skywagons with Idaho Fish and Game. Most of my time is in push-pull Cessnas in Columbia, though, as a forward spotter," Sam replied.

"I guess you're used to a tight spot now and then?" Jim queried. It had been more of a statement than a question, as forward spotters were always taking small arms fire. They had the unenviable task of flying low and slow over suspected enemy positions, and firing a marking flare rocket into the position, then loitering there until the choppers arrived with their spray gear. No wonder he's considered a cowboy, Jim thought to himself.

The men finished the preflight and pulled the big Cessna out of the hangar with a lug-a-tug aircraft mover. Once out onto the hangar apron, both settled into their articulating seats and hooked up the five-point safety harness. In the event of a rough or hard landing, this harness system would keep them secure to the seat, but with one slap of a palm on the central release they would be free of it. Contrary to popular opinion, fires didn't occur often, even in the hardest of landings, but there was always the possibility, and the last place one would want to be would be in the airplane firmly strapped in.

Sam checked with ATIS (Automatic Terminal Information Service) to see what the current weather conditions were at Kingman Airport.

"Kingman airport weather 1400 Zulu, clear, visibility 5 zero miles, altimeter 30.01, temperature 62, dewpoint 47, winds calm, caution for work crews on the west end of runway two five. Landing and departing runway 25. Ad-

9

vise on contact that you have information *echo*," reported the recording.

No wind and clear skies, with a forecast to continue this way all day; should be a great day for flying, Jim thought.

They went through the pre start checklist. "Clear prop!" Jim yelled through the open window. After they both were sure the area was clear, Jim cranked the 300 hp continental engine to life. It started on three turns of the prop and settled into a comforting growl at idle of 800 rpm.

The great thing about this assignment was that Jim was able to use his mechanic friend for all of the aircraft maintenance. He was always sure that the maintenance of the Cessna was nothing short of meticulous, as long as Desmond was turning the wrenches.

"Kingman ground, Cessna four three niner seven seven, hangar 7 with echo. We'd like to taxi to two five," Sam said through his headset boom mike to ground control on frequency 121.7.

"Cessna four three niner seven seven, cleared to taxi to two five. Caution the Sheriff helicopter is air taxiing to the fuel area north of your position," came the reply from ground control.

Jim marveled at the clarity of the new radio system in his aircraft. Even though it had been installed several months earlier, he was still amazed that the reception was clear enough to actually understand what the controllers were saying.

Jim slowly advanced the throttle and brought the Continental's satisfying rumble to a roar as the tachometer indicated 1200 rpm. The tail-dragger began to roll. Jim tested the brakes after a few feet of ground roll and used differential braking to swing the tail around.

They slowly taxied through the main taxiway, s-turn-ing as they rolled. The Cessna sat so nose high, that the only way to see ahead was by s-turning back and forth and looking ahead through the side windows. As they taxied, Jim rolled and pulled the yoke through all the range of motion to check freedom of movement of the ailerons, rudder, and elevator. Sam tuned in the necessary navigational frequencies and unfolded the sectional chart for the area.

The Sheriff's helicopter air-taxied across their path 100 yards ahead and settled to a soft landing at the fuel dump. The chopper pilots saluted the Cessna as it rolled by. The DEA and the Sheriff's Department frequently cooperated along with the FAA in the handling of arrests. Pending federal charges, the Sheriff's Dept. supplied holding areas and transportation of prisoners, as well as backed up the federal authorities during a bust. A friendly rivalry and cooperative spirit existed between the local and federal authorities. Jim and Sam saluted back as they rolled past.

Jim swung the Cessna around to face the runway in the run-up area. He set the brakes and advanced the throttle to 2,000 rpm and began the detailed pre-takeoff checklist. As he switched first the right magneto off, then the left one, he noted that in both cases he got about a 75 rpm drop, which is exactly what the book called for...thanks to Desmond, Jim thought. He cycled the constant speed prop three times. The gauge scan was in order and all systems seemed to be operating like factory new.

Sam switched from ground frequency to the tower and called, "Cessna four three niner seven seven, ready for departure. We'd like a left turn and departure to the south." Simultaneously, Jim released the brake and maneuvered the aircraft up to the runway hold line and swung it to the right to face the approach path. This kept him clear of the runway, but also gave him a view of potential traffic in-bound.

"Cessna four three niner seven seven, hold short, landing traffic," came the reply from the tower. Both pilots looked to the right just in time to see a Lear jet make a hard turn from base to final close in.

Sam said, "This guy must think he's in an F-16."
The Lear deployed flaps and spoilers, dropped the gear
and turned on their landing lights and began to drop like a
rock. Just at the runway threshold, the Lear pilot brought
the power up and arrested the sink rate and settled on
the runway in a smooth landing. Sam and Jim looked at
each other and shrugged...maybe the Lear pilot was lucky,
maybe he was good, or a little of both.

Jim put in one notch of flaps in anticipation of takeoff
clearance. A few seconds later, the tower called, "Cessna
four three niner seven seven cleared for takeoff, left turn
approved...good hunting."

"Kingman tower, roger, thanks have a good one yourself," Sam replied.

Jim powered up and the Cessna begin to roll towards
the runway. He kept it rolling as he lined up on the centerline, and advanced the throttle to the stops. The 185 began
to move to the left a bit as the centrifugal force of the prop
and engine tried to move the airplane in the direction they
were turning. Jim smoothly pushed in on the right rudder
pedal to counter the left drift. The tail came up within a
few seconds and although the main landing gear was still
on the asphalt, for all practical purposes the aircraft was
flying.

The roar of the engine was deafening, and without
headsets, it was hard to hear yourself think, much less hear
the radio. The mains lifted off the runway after just a short
500 feet of takeoff roll. Jim increased the climb attitude,
until he had Vx or best angle of climb or about 1300 fpm.
At this climb attitude, even though they couldn't see over
the nose of the airplane, they gained enough altitude in a
short time to set back down on the runway if they lost the
engine.

At 500 feet, Jim retracted the flaps and lowered the

nose until the airspeed indicator showed 90 knots and the rate of climb stabilized at 1,000 fpm. He cleared the area then rolled into a left turn with 60 degrees of bank. As he banked, he gently pulled back on the yoke to maintain the climb rate while in the bank. Just enough rudder to keep the ball centered, he thought to himself.

Sam had been fiddling with the transponder and the GPS, but had a big grin on his face as the Cessna rolled out of the turn and clawed for altitude. "I'm going to like flying with you," Sam said, "I like to push the envelope a bit myself."

"Well, given the kind of people we're dealin' with, I don't like to be a low altitude target, even around civilization, any longer than I have to," Jim replied.

"Couldn't agree more," Sam said.

Even though both were pilots, Sam served the purpose of radio, and navigation officer. Despite only knowing each other less than an hour, the two young professionals seemed to have settled into a comfortable routine and understanding of each other and the job at hand. Unknown to both was a conviction each felt about their mission. Both had lost someone to the drug culture.

Jim explained the routine for the day. "We're going into sectors three and four to check abandoned strips for activity."

Sectors three and four reached all the way into the wilds of the badlands of Bagdad, Arizona. This territory had been mined heavily in the late 1800s and early 1900s but had been largely abandoned for decades. Coyotes, vultures and wild burros had taken over the hot inhospitable desert. The only other activity related to occasional utility workers servicing and surveying the gas and power lines cris-crossing the area, and the hombres the DEA wanted to talk to. Sam had been pre-briefed by district command on the patrol areas, as well as his role in the right seat.

Jim had trimmed the Cessna for cruise climb with an indicated airspeed of 110 knots, while still maintaining a rate of climb of 500 fpm. They passed through 4,000 feet on their way up to 6,500 to clear any cumulous granite along the route.

The first of several intended stops or low passes was an unmarked strip just north of a recently closed copper mine near Bagdad. They passed through some momentary light turbulence as the aircraft bounced around penetrating the light chop. The mountains created areas that to heat up early, causing rising warm air, all of which created the light turbulence they felt.

Sam called Kingman flight service to open their filed flight plan. It wouldn't do to have to force land in this desert and not have rescuers know where to look. "Kingman radio, Cessna four three niner seven seven...," he called.

After a couple of moments, the reply came "Cessna niner seven seven, Kingman Radio, go ahead."

"Kingman radio, we'd like to activate our standard flight plan as filed," Sam replied.

"Roger, niner seven seven, flight plan open as filed, have a good flight," the controller answered.

Sam merely double clicked the mic button to indicate he received the transmission. Sam then switched frequencies and called Albuquerque center to request radar control for the area, and advise Luke AFB that they were operating in the area. The base near Phoenix regularly had F-16 jocks in the area, and meeting up with an F-16 at mach .5 unannounced could ruin even a great day.

It seemed like another routine mission on a great flying day - it almost seemed like it was just possible the bad guys decided to take a day off.

Chapter 2

The dusty Mexican village was at siesta. Nothing moved as the heat bore down at mid-day. A hot dry breeze puffed up little clouds of dust as it swirled around the sparse adobe buildings.

In a small cantina at the center of the village, one of the few buildings with electricity, an old air conditioner rattled away trying to fight back the heat of the day. Lorenzo Perez sat in the back of the cantina nursing a Dos Equis and waiting for his contact to show up.

Lorenzo had been undercover for the DEA for 16 months and had finally penetrated one of the more significant smuggling operations in the area. The slime he was working for ran drugs and people across the border with incredible regularity. Such regularity that it almost appeared to be a legal export operation.

The Mexican authorities were paid handsomely to look the other way, and with the law of large numbers in their favor, more contraband made it across than the efforts of the U.S. could stop.

There was a core of company pilots flying stolen aircraft, and many amateurs that just wanted to fly one load across for the quick payoff. The one load was a trap though...the cash was too good, it was too easy. One trip led to two, and soon they were depending on the regular flow of extra income, and they were hooked.

The waiter brought Lorenzo the lunch of chicken tacos

he had ordered. Despite the poverty, the small villages of rural Mexico produced amazingly good food in their small cantinas. It was part of the pride of the village to be able to set a good table for visitors. Lorenzo hungrily bit into one of the tacos just as the front door opened.

Two middle aged Norte Americanos walked in and looked around warily. Both were in their late 30s, Lorenzo guessed. One was a bit on the heavy side and the other average build, about 5'10". They both wore shiny new cowboy boots, denim jeans, western belts with big buckles, and cowboy hats. It was clear they were playing the part of cowboys. Neither had probably ever been on a horse, much less worked as a cowboy.

The heavier of the two leaned up against the bar and looked back over his shoulder towards the back of the cantina, while the other sauntered back towards Lorenzo's table.

"You Gomez?" he said to Lorenzo. Gomez was such a common name in this part of Mexico, that Lorenzo had adopted it as his cover name.

"Who's asking?" Lorenzo replied.

"I think you have need of my services if you're Gomez," the stranger dodged.

"Who's your friend at the bar?" Lorenzo pressed.

"Just a friend," came the surly reply. "Are you Gomez or not?"

"If you're Uncle Joe, then I'm Gomez," Lorenzo replied in his best accented English.

"I'm Uncle Joe," he replied as he sat down at the table. Just as he sat down, the waiter shuffled over. "I'll have the same as my compadre here, Paco!" he called to the waiter. The waiter turned mid stride and returned to the bar for the order.

"You down here on business or vacation?" Lorenzo asked.

"I come down five or six times a year for business and one or two times for a little fun, if you know what I mean," the stranger winked as he replied and laughed loudly. American dollars could buy more than a little bit of fun just about anywhere in the poverty stricken country. One could literally have whatever they wanted if they had enough money. This attracted all kinds, but it mainly attracted a very bad element completely devoid of morals.

This guy made Lorenzo's skin crawl; he was the type to do anything for a few bucks. Not smart enough to have any real business sense but clever and crafty enough that you had to watch your back around him. Lorenzo did some quick calculations in his mind. If this guy took a 100 kilo load each time, he could be responsible for millions of dollars of cocaine hitting the streets and schools of the inner city and suburbia, not to mention the death that would result.

This character was exactly the type to set up for a fall north of the border. He had to pick and choose who he set up. If all his setups got caught, he'd blow his cover and probably end up face down in a back alley. But this guy was one he couldn't let slide. A couple of 10 kilo hops to get him hooked and comfortable, then send him north with a big load to nail him with and he'll spend a long time behind bars.

"How do you cross the border Joe?" Lorenzo asked.

"Usually at about 200 feet!" he laughed, and his partner at the bar joined in on the joke. Lorenzo played along with a good laugh.

"Oh, you're a pilot, Señor?" he asked in mock awe.

"No, I'm Superman," the slimeball retorted sarcastically. "What d'you care how I cross the border anyway, all you care about is how effective I am, right?"

"We may have a sizable investment riding with you Señor, we have the right to ask questions."

"Listen beaner, as long as I deliver, you got no rights to anything of mine. You tell me when and where, and I'll take care of the rest!"

This guy wasn't going to be easy, Lorenzo thought. "Fair enough, as long as you understand the consequences of a lost shipment my friend," Lorenzo replied.

"I comprende´ Paco," the American sneered.

Lorenzo felt a certain weariness creep over him as he contemplated what he was doing. Despite the fact that he was setting this guy up, he knew that some of the stuff would have to be let through to set him up right. The stuff that had to be let through is what worried him. He'd seen first hand what it could do to a kid. Several years ago he had spent 18 months working in a drug rehab center as an intern for his degree in sociology at UCLA. He'd seen kids as young as eight years old come in all strung out. Many of them didn't make it. Every time it happened, he strengthened his vow to help rid the world of the people that would do this to children.

"Ok Joe, we'll give you a try with a small package. I'll meet you at the airstrip two days from now on the 17th at 10pm. Ten grand to deliver the package, five now and five when you deliver."

"Ten grand?!! I thought this was a big operation!" the American practically yelled.

"Please Señor, your voice. My bosses want to keep a low profile," Lorenzo pleaded. The waiter delivered the cervesa that caused both to pause for a moment in their discussion. "This is the way it works Señor, we try you on some leetle packages, then if you do ok, we geeve you the beeger ones...my bosses insist!" Lorenzo explained firmly.

The American let out a sigh of exasperation. "Alright damn it, but I'm not going to work for this penny ante shit for long! Either I get moved up quick or I find someone who'll make it worth my while. You tell your bosses that!"

The American grabbed the beer and stood up and turned on his heel and started for the door. As he stomped for the door, his sidekick fell in behind him and they disappeared the way they came. Lorenzo shook his head in shame that these people came from his country and were a big part of the problems he fought against. It was damned frustrating to think about, so he tried to not contemplate it for long. Emotional involvement clouded his judgement and could cost him his life.

Lorenzo knew he would see these two again around the village, and he knew his stomach would turn each time. The ugly Americans would be seen spreading dolleros around with the local whores, guzzling local mescal, and generally acting like the assholes they were. It was going to be a pleasure to know they were locked up.

He knew that these guys were the little fish. He still needed to get the honchos who ran the operation across the border so this operation could be shut down permanently.

Mexico had finally agreed to allow drug smugglers apprehended in the U.S. to be tried and sentenced and imprisoned there, regardless of their Mexican citizenship. The prospect of NAFTA and all of the American wealth it promised brought a lot of leverage on other issues. He had already documented enough of the operation to get them convicted in the U.S. If he could just get them across the border while they were carrying a shipment.

He looked at his watch. It was almost time to meet Carmalita. As much as he had tried to avoid local entanglements, he found himself enjoying the company of a local girl. Carmalita had been educated at UCLA, and had returned to help her family and people at home in general to improve their lives. Not a typical local girl, Lorenzo found her company irresistible, particularly considering the loneliness of the position he was in. It had gone beyond friendship, and he wasn't unhappy about it.

He threw some pesos on the table and walked out into the sunlight.

Chapter 3

J im rolled in a quarter turn of trim to compensate for the flaps. The Skywagon continued to descend at 500 fpm, slightly nose high in landing attitude. At 100 feet, Jim opened the throttle a touch to arrest the descent and hold a level attitude for a low pass over and to the north of the deserted dirt strip.

They would make several passes, video taping each pass from a different angle. Each pass was a specified altitude and relativity to the airstrip. The tapes were then compared to footage of the same strip taped two days earlier, visually inspected for obvious signs of traffic, and then were digitized, and fed into a mainframe computer in Langley, Virginia, via modem from Kingman.

Enhancement using color and infrared technology would then produce comparative analysis to clearly identify changes between the two time periods. The enhancement process would show an infrared trail of any activity in the past two days, including infrared tracks on the runway. The unimproved dirt strips they patrolled held almost infinitesimal changes that could be captured with infrared film for five days.

Sam toggled the camera switch as they did the fly-by. Jim held the aircraft nose high to keep the low pass as slow as possible.

Even without the analysis, they could both see signs of recent activity. Fresh tire prints in the soft desert silt were easy to spot. Given the almost daily winds in the area, these tire tracks were probably made within 12 hours.

As he neared the end of the 2,500 foot strip, Jim fire-walled the throttle and rolled into a 45 degree bank to the left for a terrain avoidance turn. The strip was nestled among several small hills, all of which could be deadly if not avoided. The big continental responded to the throttle with a thunderous roar as they climbed easily to 500 feet.

High tension transmission lines at the top of the hill at the end of the runway would make this next pass a little tricky. He'd have to set up for a short field approach. He'd come over the power lines at 300 feet then drop like a rock to 100 feet once he was passed the lines, open the throttle and hold the level attitude for another taping on the other side of the runway.

His two years as a spray pilot had been good experience for this kind of work. He loved flying low and slow in a good airplane and was mindful of the hazards of such a vocation. As he neared the end of the taping run, Jim began to advance the throttle in anticipation of the climb-out and turn. Their next pass would be at 2,000 feet, directly over the runway for a vertical shot from the belly camera port. From where Sam sat, he could toggle any one of three cameras, forward looking, straight down, and right side angled down at 15 degrees.

The 300 horse-power under the cowling responded to the throttle, as Jim increased power and rolled into a right turn across the end of the runway.

"Jim! Make another low pass. There's something down there in the sage brush just off the end of the runway...it looks like a body! Looks like a woman! Looks as though she may have dragged herself off into the desert by the looks of the trail behind her!"

Instead of continuing in a climbing turn, Jim brought his bird on around in a tight right turn to what he thought would be a downwind leg...no wind socks here to gauge the wind. From 500 feet Jim cranked the Cessna around on a final and set up for the approach. Full flaps and just the right amount of power brought the craft down steeply over the hills. The earlier passes had shown him that the strip was a bit bumpy and narrow, he'd try to use a soft field approach to keep as much stress off the landing gear as possible.

"Sam, are you sure about this? Are you sure it wasn't a dead deer or some other animal?"

"No question pal! I know a human body when I see one."

The Skywagon touched down and bounced just a bit. The oversized tundra tires took the shock of the rough strip in stride as the prop kicked up a cloud of dust behind them. Good thing we got most of the taping done, Jim thought to himself, because any evidence that was there is now gone, or will be after take-off.

He gently applied the brakes to slow the landing roll as the tail settled to the ground. As he approached the end of the runway, he swung the airplane around so it was facing down the runway. With the low altitude and the hills, Sam had been unable to get off a call to anyone before landing. They were on their own.

Jim closed the throttle, brought the prop control all the way back and leaned the engine until it coughed and sputtered and finally quit. They both popped their doors open at the same time, curious as to what they would find.

"From the air it looked like she was over this way two to three hundred yards off," Sam yelled as he started to jog into the desert. Jim grabbed a canteen and a first aid kit and trotted in the direction Sam had run.

The temperature was pleasant but jogging through the desert sand and zigzagging through the sage caused them both to work up a sweat quickly, despite their good conditioning. Jim could see Sam's head bobbing above the brush ahead of him as he ran and tried to keep him in sight while struggling to keep his footing. Silently he wondered about snakes. Rattlers liked to sun themselves on warm days like this...it just be my luck he thought to himself that I'd step on one.

A minute or so into the trek, Sam disappeared ahead. Jim zigged around a big bush and almost stepped on Sam as he was kneeling over a young woman face down in the sand.

At first glance she looked dead, but then he could see the slight up and down movement from her breathing. She was dressed only in a pair of cut-off jeans and a tank-top. Her legs and arms were badly cut and scratched, and her skin was sunburned to a deep crimson. She obviously was suffering from prolonged exposure.

Sam gently rolled her over. She grimaced and groaned as Sam carefully eased her onto her back. Her lips were split from sun, wind and dehydration, her face was caked with dirt and sand, and there was noticeable swelling under her left eye.

There didn't appear to be any other wounds or injuries as Jim did a quick examination. He unscrewed the lid of the canteen and carefully poured a bit of the cool liquid onto her parched lips. Her eyes began to flutter at the feel of the water. She seemed to be coming back to life. She groaned from pain and shock.

"Easy, take it easy, you're with friends now," Jim soothed. Her eyes fluttered open and she squinted into the sunlight and looked up at them with the deepest bluest eyes Jim had ever seen. Even with the dirt ground into her hair and face, it was obvious she was very beautiful.

"What's your name? Can you talk?" Jim asked.

"Who are you with?" she asked in a raspy voice.

"We work for the DEA." Sam replied as he pulled out his ID.

"Oh, thank God, I made it!" she cried as tears welled up in the her eyes. She quickly gathered her composure, rubbed the moisture from her eyes and tried to sit up.

"How about a drink of water?" Jim offered.

She took the canteen and took a long drink. The realization that she was rescued hit her all at once and her body seemed to collapse into itself. The canteen slid from her hands and she fell back from her sitting position and slumped back into unconsciousness.

"Lets get her back to the plane, Sam." Jim handed the canteen and first aid kit to his partner and easily picked her up into a cradle carry and started the hike back to the strip.

Halfway back, she came to again. Her beauty stunned Jim as she looked up at him and said, "I think I can make it on my own."

"You've been through a lot and you've got a lot of recovering to do, just rest for now."

Even though the rear seat had been removed to accommodate the camera gear, the normally cavernous cargo and seating area of the Cessna left room for a full sized adult to lie down. The special modified wide double doors allowed easy access to the back area. Sam unrolled an emergency tarp and spread it out on one side on the floor as Jim walked up. Jim lay her down on the tarp and spread a blanket over her. Shock was always a strong potential as the body struggled to heal itself in situations like this. Many victims had been rescued alive in reasonable condition only to die from shock. The obvious victim of some sort of foul play, Jim tried again to get some information before she lapsed back into unconsciousness.

"Hey, talk to me, what's your name? Who should we call for you?" Jim probed.

"Alison Stewart," she said in almost a whisper. "Call the Phoenix office of Treasury Department, ask for Dave Richardson," she mumbled. She was slipping away into sleep quickly.

While Jim was getting her settled, Sam had done a quick pre-flight, looking for any brush or other debris that they may have picked up in the landing. Giving his partner a thumbs up, Sam climbed into the back to tend to their new cargo. Jim pulled himself into the left seat and began the start sequence.

"Clear prop," he yelled out of habit. The Continental caught instantly. Jim checked the controls for free and easy movement, and lined up on the center of the narrow strip. He could feel a slight quartering headwind as it toyed with the right wing. The breeze swirled around the hills and changed direction frequently.

What was a headwind now could turn into a cross wind or even a tail wind without warning. He flipped the flap lever and prepared for a short, soft field take-off. Even though the runway was more than long enough, he had hills to contend with, and the temperature was increasing. He wanted as much altitude as he could get as early as possible.

Chapter 4

The flight into Prescott was a short 20 minutes. Love Field was a moderately active mid sized airport with a control tower, and ATIS. Jim clicked in the ATIS frequency to get the wind direction and runway in use. Ten minutes earlier, he had radioed the Prescott Flight Service Station (FSS) and explained their situation. An ambulance was en-route from the local hospital and would meet them at the airport sheriff's office.

With any luck, their passenger would hang in there until she could get medical help. Still unconscious, she had grown pale and her breathing was labored as her body struggled with the effects of the abuse she had suffered. Jim had also asked Prescott FSS to call the Department of the Treasury in Phoenix and have Dave Richardson standing by for a call. They couldn't risk discussing details over the radio. Air frequencies are listened to and monitored by many ears. With the life of Alison Stewart hanging in the balance, security was critical.

The mains chirped with a satisfying squeak as Jim touched down on runway two-four. As soon as he could, he took the high speed taxiway and headed for the ramp in front of the sheriff's office.

An ambulance was waiting with the emergency lights rotating. Jim taxied the Cessna up to the ambulance and shut the engine down while they were still rolling. The aircraft braked to a stop 20 feet away from the waiting emergency vehicle. Two ambulance attendants and one EMT ran to the aircraft with a gurney. Quickly Allison Stewart was loaded into the ambulance, and it sped off with the siren wailing.

"I think, given the circumstances, she should have a guard in her room," Jim said to one of the local deputies.

"I'll talk to the sheriff about it," the deputy replied, "I'm sure he'll agree".

Sam was already on the phone to the Treasury dept. telling the story.

"The Treasury boys have a chopper on the way, Jim," Sam said. "Apparently Allison Stewart has been missing for over six weeks. She's been undercover in Mexico and dropped out of sight without a word. They wrote her off for dead three weeks ago."

A quick call to their bosses with the DEA confirmed what they thought, that they should stick around until they debriefed with the Treasury dept. Forty-five minutes later, a Bell Jet Ranger appeared on the horizon, swooped in low over the field, and circled around the ramp. The pilot was visually clearing the area prior to setting down. The chopper came to an easy rest on the ramp in front of the sheriff's office. The chopper was a plain wrap, no markings whatsoever.

Odd, thought Jim.

As the engine spooled down, two men in suits, white shirts and ties and looking very out of place climbed out of the chopper and walked very purposely and looking very important over to the office.

Jim suspected they were from the East and hadn't yet learned the casualness of the West. The two anal-retentives strutted over to the office, obviously impressed with their own self-importance.

"Where do they find these guys?" Jim muttered to Sam. As if on cue, the two Treasury agents pulled their

badge wallets out and flipped them open for Jim and Sam
to see, as if landing in a federal chopper wasn't enough
proof as to who they were. They announced their names
and department and shook hands with both Jim and Sam.

"So, tell us what happened," one of the agents queried
as the four of them walked to the sheriff's office.

Sam and Jim briefly recounted the story in a few
minutes. "That's about it," Jim said, "Not too much to tell
really.'

"What was Allison involved with?" Jim asked.

"Sorry, can't tell you anymore than you already know
pal," one of the suits replied. "Official Treasury business,
you know." The other suit said, "I know it may be difficult,
but you need to just forget everything you've seen today,
and forget all the names and faces. This is way over your
pay grades, and all asking questions is gonna do is get you
or someone else hurt," he continued. On that note, the two
suits turned and walked to the helicopter.

"Where do they get jerks like that?" Jim just shook
his head, "I think there's a factory somewhere that just
keeps churning them out," he replied. They both laughed
and walked back into the sheriff's office.

"How about we take a run down to the hospital and
see how our friend is?" Jim suggested. "Works for me,"
Sam replied, "let's go."

Being with the DEA, they had no problem borrowing
a sheriff's vehicle. The two pilots took off in a borrowed
sheriff's Chevy Tahoe for the six mile drive to the hospital.

The short drive afforded them both time to think and
speculate about the events that had unfolded this morning.
They both wondered with some unease where this was all
headed. Although Jim had operated on the fringe of this
kind of thing, he had never encountered it face to face. He
didn't like the feeling of not being in control or at least having some answers.

At the hospital, the large, gruff head nurse growled at them to produce some sort of I.D. if they were going to be allowed into Ms. Stewart's room.

"It's ok nurse, I'll take it from here," a deputy called as he walked up the hallway. "C'mon back boys, I think she'd like to talk a bit. You the ones that found her?"

"Yeah," Sam replied.

They walked through the door single file, not sure what they would find. As they neared the bed, Jim was once again struck by the beauty of Allison Stewart. Her blue eyes were wide open and didn't appear to be affected by sedatives. She had been cleaned up and miraculously looked as though she could stand up and walk out on her own. She flashed them a brilliant white smile and melted Jim in his tracks.

"How can I ever thank you? If you hadn't come along when you did..." the tears welled up in those incredible eyes.

"Well," Sam replied, "how about some explanation about what is going on? We know this is official Treasury dept. business, as two of your co-workers told us."

Allison's already washed-out face drained itself of all color. "What do you mean, two of my co-workers?" Allison stammered. "I only have one co-worker in Arizona, and no one but me knows who that is."

"That wouldn't be Dave Richardson would it?" Jim asked slyly.

"Dave Richardson is a fictitious character. The call you made asking for him was actually answered by an answering service. When someone calls asking for him, it cues them to call Langley, Virginia. If immediate help is needed for an agent, it is dispatched from the nearest office as soon as possible. The nearest office to us is Los Angeles. No one could have responded this quickly."

By now, her voice had a tremor in it, and a look of

genuine concern was creeping into her eyes.

Jim and Sam exchanged a worried look. "You mean the two jerks we...," Jim stopped in mid-sentence as the realization hit him.

Allison finished the sentence, "That's right, they weren't Treasury, DEA, FBI, or anything else. They're part of the slime I was trailing."

"Ms. Stewart, if you don't mind, since we're involved at this point, tell us what's going on, bring us into the loop," Sam said. "We've got our backs to watch now, too."

The story that she recounted was like something out of a James Bond novel.

The President of the United States, in frustration over the lack of success in the war on drugs, had authorized the Secret Service arm of the Department of Treasury to build a plan to penetrate the top elements of organized crime, both domestically and their foreign connections.

The plan being carried out placed two dozen Treasury agents in various locations in the states, Central and South America, the Caribbean, and Europe, all of them are in various positions within organizations engaged in drugs, prostitution, counterfeiting, and the movement of illegal aliens into the U.S.

In support of those agents were another two dozen agents positioned as contacts in the primary agents locale. Allison was one of those secondary agents in Acapulco.

The entire operation was completely black. No one but the President and a number of top people in Treasury knew about the scope of the operation. Even individual agents involved in the operation knew little about the big picture. Over the past 18 months, the operation, named Mustang, had been highly successful, though sadly at the expense of some American lives, including the agent Allison was supporting.

"All I can tell you guys is that I've been living in the

Acapulco area posing as a wealthy American heiress for the past 16 months. I was supposed to network myself into local society. Cushy job, eh? Any more information than that will have to come from someone higher than me, I'm afraid. But do be careful."

Jim and Sam both knew what she had been doing was anything but "cushy".

"So how did you end up in the middle of the Arizona desert"? Jim asked.

"It's a long story. Let's just say I was trailing some killers. I stowed aboard one of their large transports in the cargo area. I rolled out of the cargo door as they taxied two days ago."

"You've been in the desert for two days without water?" Sam exclaimed. "You're lucky to be alive."

Allison could only nod her head as tears welled up in her eyes again...she had a very grateful look in those blue eyes of hers. She knew how close she had come to death.

Chapter 5

The Senatorial aide looked nervously over his shoulder as he entered the Treasury building. He had made many trips on behalf of his boss over the past months, but he had a growing, gnawing unease that he was being followed or watched.

His footsteps echoed through the polished marble hall. It was late, and most of the government employees had left for their commute home. The thin valise he carried was getting heavier by the second. He wasn't cut out for this kind of work. He was unsure if what he was doing was wrong. Why would Senator Jacobsen have him pick up these packages? He had done this six or seven times. Each time it was the same thing. He left the locked valise in the outer office of the Interior Secretary, picked up a department store plastic shopping bag from a major department store with a gift-wrapped package in it, and returned to the Senator's office.

He made the switch and started back out the way he had come. He was in a hurry, the sooner he got this over with, the sooner he could start the weekend. He had plans to spend the next two days in Hilton Head, South Carolina.

He hurried to his car on a side street adjacent to the government auxiliary buildings. It was quiet, and twilight was just starting to descend on Washington. He slid in behind the wheel and started the car. He looked in the mirror and cold fear gripped him like a giant hand. Two

Air

of the coldest eyes he had ever seen were looking back at
him. He started to reach for the door but his hand failed
him as piano wire sliced through his carotid artery and
trachea. Warm arterial blood spilled down through his shirt
as he looked out the car window and watched his assailant
disappear the way he had just come. Just as his periphery
vision began to close in, he saw the killer get in a sedan and
speed away. He looked at the seat next to him and his last
thought before he died was the Nordstrom bag was missing...he thought drowsily, I wonder where it went?

Chapter 6

S enator Jacobsen looked up from the brief he was reviewing and glanced at his watch. Peter should have been back by now, probably Friday evening traffic was the cause of the delay.

The phone startled him. He picked it up on the first ring. "Yes!" he said impatiently into the receiver.

"Senator Jacobsen?" a mechanized voice said.

"Who...what is this?" the Senator asked.

"Senator we've just been doing a little shopping."

The good senator slammed down the phone and hit the erase button on his phone recorder. He gathered up a few items, called his driver and was out his door within 10 minutes of the call.

Comfortably seated in the back of the limousine, he began to catch his breath and gain some of his lost confidence. He called Ronald Reagan Airport and had a Lear Jet, provided for him by his friends, readied for a flight. He'd tell the pilot the destination after they were in the air. With any luck they'd be in Arizona within a few hours.

Despite this minor setback from the competition, he knew his North-South consortium was as strong as ever. The movement of drugs into the states bothered him, but it was a necessary part of the bigger picture. The Secretary of the Interior, Stuart Holmsby, and he were part of a shadow group known as the Founders that were creating break-through technology. The new technology would change the

world in many ways and bring the Founders incredible resources from which they could perpetuate their controlling
and directing efforts. Then it would be over and he would
get out of the drug business once and for all. He didn't like
dealing with his South American partners - they were crass,
uncivilized, amoral, and completely without scruples...he
hated them. But, he needed them for just a bit longer. The
necessary components could be assembled within the next
few weeks, if he could keep the drug competitors at bay a
bit longer.

The Founders were in fact centuries old, and frequently its members were the sons and daughters of previous
members, creating a continuity through the years in terms
of purpose and direction. The Founders came together in
England in the 12th century. The purpose of the group and
even the basic structure had not changed for over 600 years.
The Founders were much larger today, and controlled much
more wealth, but they remained steadfastly dedicated to
their purpose of protecting the principles of freedom, even
when the government could not do so. They never met
as a group, the general membership did not know who all
of the other members, and it operated through a series of
interlocking committees that had a single member in each
that was also a part of the leadership committee. Initia-
tives were germinated from lower committees or from the
top committee, and received support and funding, or were
discarded by the leadership committee.

Peter Humes's body was discovered by Capitol Security barely before it had cooled. His apparent murder made
the front page of the Post, but the case became like hundreds of others, not enough evidence to even create the start
of an investigative trail. His boss, Senator Jacobsen, was
on a junket in Arizona and on to South America. When he
was contacted, he expressed sorrow at the loss, but unfortunately he would be unable to return for the funeral.

Chapter 7

J im and Sam rolled back into the Prescott Airport just
after 20:00. The high desert had cooled, and the winds
had settled, making for what should be an enjoyable
flight back to Kingman.

The big Cessna had been fueled and looked like it
was ready to leap into the air, as it sat on the apron in front
of the local fbo (fixed base operator). The fbo had long
closed, but the hangar door was open and a mechanic was
busy pulling an engine out of a Piper Cherokee Six to be
replaced.

"Jim, hang on a minute, I'm going to have a word with
the local mechanic." Jim shrugged and walked over the
Skywagon to begin the preflight. His new partner seemed
to have more than his share of curiosity.

"How ya doin'?" Sam called as he walked into the
hangar.

The mechanic nodded. "Not bad, how bout you?" the
mechanic replied.

"You worked here long?" Sam queried.

"Oh, about three years, why?", the mechanic replied.

"Did you see the Bell Jet Ranger around noon?" Sam
asked. The mechanic just nodded.

"Ever seen it before?" Sam pressed.

"Maybe a few times, why?" the mechanic asked.

"We need to talk to the two slicks that were in it today.
They may be part of an investigation."

Air

"I've seen the chopper a couple of times, but I didn't recognize those two guys. I don't think they're from around here. Didn't really pay much attention though," the mechanic replied.

"Ok, thanks. Take care," Sam replied as he turned and walked back through the hangar door out into the cool evening air.

Jim had completed the pre-flight and was sitting in the pilot seat waiting for his partner. Just as Sam climbed into the right seat, Jim yelled, "Clear prop!" out the window. The McCauley "Black Mac" prop swung through two and a half turns before the Continental fired and settled into a rumbling idle.

"Well, what'd ya find out, Dick Tracey?" Jim asked with a chuckle, as Sam put his headphones on.

"You know, something bothers me about this whole thing," Sam replied. "Those two guys in the chopper had too much class for the typical drug smuggling bunch. And, how are they intercepting information that quickly? There's more to this whole thing than just drug smuggling."

Jim taxied through the ramp and onto the run-up area. The tower had been closed for over an hour and the air traffic was non-existent. Jim set the brakes and advanced the throttle to 2,000 rpm and went through the run-up. As he flipped back and forth between the right and left magnetos, Sam's comments echoed through his mind. And then it occurred to him that Sam's curiosity and comments had him wondering about Sam.

The magnetos both checked out, as did fuel pressure, oil pressure, vacuum suction and the oil temp was coming up into the green.

Time to go. Jim advanced the throttle and esss'd up to the hold line   just as Sam announced their intentions over the common frequency to any aircraft that might be in the area. They both scanned the approach and departure paths for any other aircraft.

No strobes or marker beacons in sight. Jim eased out onto the runway and lined up on the centerline. Just as the tail swung around, he fire-walled the throttle and brought the rumble up to a roar. Within a few seconds, the Cessna was accelerating through 60 knots indicated and ready to fly.

Out of Jim's peripheral vision, he caught a glimpse of some movement. A split second later a black shape flashed in front of their path. It was gone as quickly as it had arrived.

"What the hell was that?" Jim yelled into the boom mic. They were too far down the runway to abort. Jim kept the Skywagon under control and soon they were in the air.

"That was a Bell Jet Ranger my friend!" Sam replied. "And I've got a funny feeling we're going to see it again."

No sooner had he said it and the chopper appeared again off the left side of the aircraft, keeping pace with them. Jim laid the Cessna into a hard right turn with 60 degrees of bank and simultaneously sucked up the take-off flaps. The Skywagon climbed despite the hard turn. Jim glanced to his left looking for the chopper. It was gone again.

Jim flipped off the strobes, marker beacon and take-off light, trying to blend in with the night sky. He leveled off at 300 feet and concentrated on getting his heart rate back under 120. His heart thundered in his ears. Jim glanced over at his partner. Sam's jaw was set and he was looking over his shoulder for the chopper.

"The Ranger's on our 6 comin up our left side, break right, break right!"

Jim headed for the only cover he knew of; the granite dell canyons east of town. The winding canyons and giant granite boulders were a labyrinth. Frantically, he worried about the power lines that wound back and forth across the

canyon just above the canyon floor. He had landed on remote strips in the canyon, he had a fair idea of where most
of the lines were. The sweat began to trickle down Jim's
back. His mind began to fill with images from his crop
dusting days. Throttle and stick, feel the terrain, watch the
altitude, watch for the power lines, keep the airspeed up,
and do it all in a split second. The giant granite boulders
loomed ahead.

The Ranger was matching the Cessna with every jink
and turn, with every rise and fall...but it was simple now...
wouldn't be so simple in the rocks. Jim pushed the throttle
forward as far as it would go, and the tachometer was
above redline. The Skywagon was vibrating like a tuning
fork, but it was a harmonized vibration of engine, cables,
and aluminum.

"Hang in there, baby, hang in there!" Jim said under
his breath.

As he approached the granite dells, he had a choice to
make: either enter the main canyon through a massive two-
mile-wide mouth, or climb up over the south ridge and dive
into a smaller parallel canyon. He chose the latter. As he
flew directly at the canyon wall, he held his altitude down
and kept the airspeed up. He kept s-turning and zigzagging
back and forth trying to throw the ranger off or at least keep
the chopper pilot guessing. More importantly, if someone
in the chopper had a gun trained on them, he didn't want to
be an easy target.

As the canyon wall loomed ahead, it stood giant
and ominously dark, several hundred feet higher than the
Cessna.

Got to time this exactly right, Jim thought to himself.
He guessed when to start the pull up...should be about 3/4
of a mile, he calculated at 160 knots to climb up over the
ridge and still carry enough airspeed to roll into the waiting
canyon.

"Jim... I think now might be a good time to pull up," Sam said quietly into the headphones. A split second later, Jim began to haul back on the yoke. The VSI needle jumped to 1500' fpm almost instantly. The Cessna groaned under the strain as it clawed for altitude. The canyon wall loomed closer and closer, and for a few seconds they both thought they were too late, but then the ridgeline rose in the windscreen and disappeared under the belly. The airspeed had bled down to 90 knots in 15 seconds, and Jim began to lower the nose to get the airspeed back up to maneuver into the yawning dark canyon maw.

Just as the ridgeline disappeared behind them, Jim began a 90 degree roll to the right and dove into the canyon. Sam quietly complimented Jim on his timing, and couldn't suppress a kind of crazy grin on his face.

"Jim where'd you learn to fly like that?" Sam said in a controlled voice and clenched teeth, as he held onto the edge of the seat.

"Where's our friend?" Jim replied. Sam looked over his shoulder, up through the windshield, and Jim did the same. At the same time, both said, "He's not over here." The chopper had disappeared just as quickly as it had appeared. Jim leveled out the wings and dropped below the canyon rim as they both scanned in all directions. It was clear, the attacking helicopter was no where in sight. The creek in the canyon bed sparkled from the moonlight as it wound through the canyon.

In an instant, the situation had gone from nearly catastrophic to almost idyllic. Both their heart rates began to drop as the effects of the adrenaline wore off. Both men were also instantly aware they were deeply involved in something beyond a small-scale drug smuggling operation. The attack by the Ranger had been a warning to back off, and one they wouldn't forget.

Jim rolled in some nose up trim ascended up above

the canyon walls. Two hundred feet above the canyon, he rolled into a turn to the northwest back towards Kingman and home.

It had been a long day. They made small talk on the flight back, but both were alone with their thoughts about what had happened. All of the questions were unanswered. Would they ever have the answers? Probably not.

Chapter 8

T he mains of the Skywagon chirped as the Cessna settled to the runway in Kingman. The moon was continuing its rise above the horizon as Jim taxied to the hangar. He swung the tail around in front of the hangar door and closed the throttle as he did. The engine died and the prop bounced to a stop. The only sound was the gyros winding down as they sat in the cockpit and completed the shut down checklist.

"How about a beer and some enchiladas?" Sam said.

"Yeah, that sounds good, especially the beer part," Jim replied. They pushed the aircraft back into the hangar and left instructions to have both tanks topped with 100 octane low lead.

Just as they were walking to the parking lot, they both noticed a sheriff's Tahoe pulling into the airport entrance with the overhead lights on. The deputy pulled up to them, stopped and left the lights on.

"You Jim Mitchell and Sam Brooks?"

"I'm Brooks, this is Mitchell," Sam replied.

The deputy handed them both a heavy 8 1/2" x 11" envelope with a DEA seal on it. Each envelope was identified with their names on the front.

"I'm supposed to wait and see if you need assistance after you read the contents."

Silently, and with some trepidation, they both slit open their respective envelopes. Both had identical instructions:

Air

Report to the executive terminal Sky Harbor
airport no later than 2300 hours 29 May 2003.
Expect transportation Washington DC departing
same terminal 23:30.

It was signed by the director of the DEA. Caught completely by surprise, neither knew what exactly to say.

Sam broke the silence, "That gives us three hours to pack and fly to Phoenix."

"I guess we don't have a lot of choice but to at least see what's up at this point," Jim said.

"I'm here to see that you get off the ground on time," the deputy said rather officially.

"I'll be quicker on my bike," Sam said as he walked over to his Harley Road King.

"Meet you back here in an hour," Sam said as he thumbed the starter button on the handlebars."

"Lets go," Jim said to the deputy.

Just as the deputy turned the Tahoe around, Jim heard Sam's Harley rumble out the airport exit. On the ride into town, Jim silently mulled over the events of the day. It was becoming increasingly apparent that he and his new partner had become a part of much more than the ordinary drug chase, maybe more than either had bargained for.

The flight to Phoenix was uneventful and quiet, as both Sam and Jim were lost in thought. In fact, it was completely quiet until they were 20 miles north of the Phoenix airspace. Only then, because they had to talk to the controller, did they break their silence.

"Fly heading 180 and squawk 3325," were the controller's instructions.

Sam complied by repeating the instructions back to the controller and setting the transponder code.

The silence continued until they were turned over to the tower controller. Again, Sam complied with the controller's directions and repeated the instructions to indicate he understood. As Jim rolled out of the close in base leg onto final, they both saw the government Gulfstream parked next to the executive terminal. Jim pushed the flap lever to full flaps as he rolled wings level onto final, and at the same time he closed the throttle to 14 inches of manifold pressure. With the prop set at 2500 rpm, he was set up for landing.

As the Cessna floated in the flare down the runway, Jim caught some movement in his periphery vision. He looked left just in time to see the plain wrap black Bell Jet Ranger air taxiing on an intersecting course.

"Sam! Isn't that our friend in the Ranger?"

Sam leaned forward and looked across in front of Jim. "If it's not, this is the biggest damn coincidence in history!"

The pilot of the Ranger applied power, dipped the nose of the chopper, and climbed over the top of the Cessna. A second later, the Skywagon settled to the runway for the short taxi to the terminal. Both pilots had an increasing feeling they were playing a game with the odds stacked against them.

As Jim taxied towards the terminal, a "follow me" jeep pulled in front of them, and the ground controller instructed him to follow. The jeep led them directly into a large hanger 300 feet or so north of the terminal. One of the hangar crew guided Jim to a parking place to one side of the hangar. As Jim shut the engine down, a lone man walked out of the hangar office towards them. He looked vaguely familiar at a distance, and as he walked closer both recognized him instantly. The director of the DEA himself was nearing the airplane.

"Gentlemen, James Worthington," he said as he stuck his hand out.

45

Air

"I'm Jim Mitchell..." Jim started to say.

"I know. And this is your partner, Sam Brooks," the director said. "I recognized you both from the pictures in your personnel files.

"Thanks for coming on such short notice," he said, as if they had a choice in the matter. "Grab your gear. We've got a schedule to keep. I'll explain what's going on after we're airborne." The director was an athletic 55 years old, and he set the pace towards the Gulfstream of a man 20 years younger.

Jim and Sam just followed along behind the director like the good bureaucratic soldiers they were.

Chapter 9

L orenzo Perez flashed his mini-mag flashlight twice at the approaching car. The beat-up 15-year-old Chevy braked to a stop, sending up a cloud of dust. The two he had met in the cantina climbed out of the car. As the taller one stood up, he leaned down and said something to the driver. As soon as he slammed the door, the driver turned the car around and headed out of the airport the way he had come.

There was even less to like about these two than he thought. "Hey Paco, let's get this show on the road," the taller of the two said.

As they walked up, Lorenzo caught a whiff of tequila.

"Señor, here is the shipment and half of the payment, as we agreed. The coordinates of the landing strip are written on the package," Lorenzo continued.

He tossed the two packages to them and turned and walked away.

As he walked towards his pickup he could hear the two of them laughing and talking loudly like the two jackasses they were.

He opened the door of his old Ford truck. The door groaned with age as he pulled it open. He started to get in, but even in the dark, he could see a large envelope laying on the drivers seat. He looked around quickly for who might have put it in his truck. No one was in sight.

As he tore the envelope open, he heard one of the

engines of the Smuggler's light twin turn over. It cranked several times before it caught. Even after it was running it sounded rough. Most pilots would have shut it down.

Probably dirty fuel, Lorenzo thought to himself, they'll be lucky if they make it all the way to the drop.

The second engine started turning over and finally caught with a roar. Lorenzo just shook his head at the incompetence of these two. The pilot obviously had the throttle opened too far while he was starting.

Good way to start an engine fire, Lorenzo thought to himself as he flipped on his mini-mag and pulled the single sheet of paper out of the envelope. It read:

> Break off all contacts. Return to home plate
> without delay.

Home plate was Langly, Virginia, and without delay meant within 72 hours. His initial reaction was one of anger. He had spent over a year, and a dangerous year at that, weaving himself into the role he was playing. The anger subsided as he realized how important this must be to sacrifice the work and expense that had gone into this operation. True, they had put a few smugglers in jail, but the bigger fish were still loose and operating with immunity.

As he started his truck, the smugglers started taxiing the twin Cessna towards the runway. Lorenzo backed out and headed down the dirt road that led into the strip. As he drove away, he saw a shadow of the smuggler airplane without lights lift off and turn north.

Lorenzo drove back to the small village to pack his few things. Even though this was a poverty-stricken area, he had become acquainted with a few of the locals, and there was at least one he would miss a bit. His relationship with Carmalita Trujillo had developed well beyond his intent. When this was finished, he thought he might come back for her.

Can't think about that sort of thing, Lorenzo said to himself. Within 36 hours, he needed to be on a flight and headed north.

As he forcibly changed his thoughts back to business, he wondered, what could be so important to throw all this work away. The realization of what he was being instructed and how significant it was began to sink in. He decided he would spend his last 24 hours with Carmalita. He steered the old pick-up to the area of town where she lived.

As he pulled up at the curb in front of her home, he knew something was not right. Her front door stood open, and only a faint light shown from somewhere in the rear of the small rented house. As he quietly slipped from his truck, he drew a .357 magnum from his shoulder holster. He stepped silently through the front door and knelt to lessen the target that a possible assailant might have. He stayed quiet in the shadows for a few seconds, listening intently. The apartment was too still, almost like it was holding its breath.

He began to move towards the rear of the apartment in a crouched position. His movements were as quiet as the creaky old building would allow. The floor groaned a bit under his weight.

He decided to move a little quicker and try to use surprise to his advantage. He stood up and stepped through the kitchen door leading with the big magnum. He quickly scanned the small kitchen and didn't see anything out of place. Just as he was about to continue the search of the rest of the house, he felt the cold steel of a gun barrel press up behind his left ear.

A familiar voice said, "Ease the gun down onto the floor and step back away from it."

With relief, he said, "Carmelita, it's me Lorenzo."

"Lorenzo, oh baby," she said with relief in her voice. "What are you doing here, and what's with the gun?"

"I should ask you the same thing," Lorenzo questioned.

Carmelita quickly tucked the gun into her purse. "It's a habit I picked up at UCLA. A girl can't be too careful."

Lorenzo took her in his arms and held her close without saying anything.

"What's wrong?" she asked. "I can tell something awful is wrong."

"Not now," Lorenzo whispered as he impulsively bent down and gently kissed her neck.

He knew that kissing her neck and ears had an arousing effect on her. She shivered as she reached for Lorenzo's belt buckle. Lorenzo pulled her blouse out of the waistband of her skirt and up over her head. She shook her hair loose as it fell back on her shoulders.

He cupped a breast and felt her nipple harden under his touch. Carmalita slipped to her knees and pulled Lorenzos jeans down as she did. Lorenzo stepped out of his shoes and jeans while he pulled his shirt over his head.

Carmalita was backing towards the bedroom as she loosened her skirt, leaving it where it fell in the living room. She kicked off her sandals and turned to walk into the bedroom, while she unhooked her bra and dropped it on the floor. Her breasts were white and soft, in contrast to her tanned, firm body.

As she stepped out of her panties, Lorenzo felt himself drawn uncontrollably towards her as though he was floating through space. All at once they were entwined with each other on top of the quilt. Carmelita pinned him on his back and straddled him and began kissing his chest, working her way down his body.

Their lovemaking was always furious and heated, and they both were always completely spent afterwards. After, they lay naked, quietly sprawled on top of the coverlet, with Carmelita resting her head on Lorenzos chest.

"Ok, now we got that out of our system, tell me what's wrong?" Carmelita asked.

"I have to go away, and I'm not sure when I can make it back," he replied.

"I knew it was something like that, but as it turns out I have to leave as well." Carmelita replied.

"I have to go to Washington D.C.," they both said at the same time. They both stared long and hard at each other for a few seconds.

Carmelita said, "I have to be there in the next three days."

"So do I," Lorenzo replied with wonder in his voice.

"Well, that's great, we can travel together then, let's pack and get going. I can be ready in 20 minutes," she said.

"I have to take a specific route from Mexico City to Phoenix and from there I will be on a government flight...so we can at least travel as far as Phoenix together," Lorenzo said.

Carmalita was on her knees in the middle of the bed without a stitch on staring at Lorenzo wide eyed. She looked as though a light bulb had just come on over her head.

"Lorenzo," she asked, "who do you work for?"

"I'm afraid I can't discuss it, I'm sorry, but I'm involved in a very discreet business."

"Is it legal?" she asked.

"Absolutely, very legal," Lorenzo replied. "In fact, I work for the United States government, and I've been ordered off my current project to be reassigned."

"I have a confession," Carmelita began, "that gun I had earlier was not really a hold-over from my college days. But before I continue, do you have any kind of government I.D.?"

Air

"I don't. I'm here on an undercover assignment," Lorenzo replied.

"Lorenzo, something tells me we are going to be working together, if not soon, then sometime in the future," Carmelita said.

"Let's just fly to Phoenix and see what happens," Lorenzo replied.

"I can live with that for now," she said, just as Lorenzo reached up and pulled her down on top of him.

Chapter 10

S enator Jacobsen was settling into his hotel room when the phone rang. No one knew he was there. It must be someone from the hotel, he thought to himself as he reached for the phone.

"Yes?" he said. Stewart Holmsby Secretary of the Interior said in a shaky voice, "Bob our schedule just got shorter."

"How did you know I was here Stew?" the Senator asked quickly.

"I had a phone message on my desk to call you at the Phoenix Hilton."

"Stew, I didn't leave a message," the Senator replied.

"Then who..." the Secretary didn't finish his question.

Both knew the answer. The illegal covert operation they were a part of had been infiltrated. The completion of this phone call was a clear easy way for the other side to confirm two more of the players. Their phone conversation was no doubt being taped. The Senator hung up the phone slowly and walked to the window. As he stared out the window, it occurred to him that he could be a target clearly outlined in the window. He turned, pulled the blinds and settled in for the night. He didn't always have to look over his shoulder, it was extremely uncomfortable and a feeling he wanted to end soon.

The covert development of a remarkable atmospheric

shield system the good Senator was a part of for an elite group was now at risk. The flow of drugs, through the Senator's network of connection now firmly established, was funding the development of the system. Theoretically, the system would have the capability of changing weather by shielding parts of the globe from the full impact of the sun. Desert temperatures around the world could be reduced by as much as 20 degrees. The strength of hurricanes could be reduced measurably by reducing the impact of the sun on the sea water and reducing the evaporative rate into the storm. The impact of the system to the world economy and survival was staggering.

The control of the system is not only strategically of significance, but the patents are worth billions to the interests that own them.

Global Exports Inc. had finished the development and testing of such a system just hours before. His facilitating the flow of drugs to supply capital was no longer needed, in fact he no longer needed his friends in Central America. Global Exports Inc. now had a clear road ahead.

Global's management in the Cayman Islands had been informed that their owners would continue the operation with a few changes in their marketing plan, but under a new name. It was now time for Global Exports to disappear. The research and development facility unknown to the employees would continue to operate as a manufacturing site for the new system. The quiet, clean technology required to manufacture the system was neither personnel intensive, nor was the product output particularly noticeable. As the daily export business continued to function, laser guided "brains" would be assembled and readied for deployment to the first country with the purchase price.

This technology was capable of energizing the cold war all over again.

Chapter 11

The training facility at Langley looked tranquil to the untrained eye. The lawns surrounding the facility were manicured meticulously, as were the trees and shrubs in the planters. Only someone looking closely would see the 12-foot chain-link fence topped with razor wire behind the shrubs, and the infrared sensors and cameras at various stations inside the fence.

Even the gate and the guardhouse blended in to the vegetation that surrounded the complex. The gate was completely invisible. It looked as though the entrance drive came to a dead end at the wall. The gate actually retracted into a well in the ground and was identical in thickness, height, color and material as the wall. While not unbreachable, it was certainly very formidable to anyone trying to get in uninvited.

The guardhouse was hidden thoroughly to the side of the drive by shrubbery and constructed of both bullet proof and "bug" proof material. Contained in the guardhouse was an array of electronic equipment that would search and photograph any vehicle with a variety of cameras and sensors. Security at this facility rivaled Fort Knox. The equipment located there and training that took place were just as valuable as what Fort Knox held.

The facility went by a variety of names by the agencies that shared it. To the Department of the Treasury, it was two facilities in one, record keeping and computer center for the whole dept. and an agent training facility for the

Secret Service. The DEA, FBI, and even the armed forces also used it for similar purposes.

The 300-acre center contained underground living quarters for 2,000 agents or military personnel of either gender. Above the living quarters, a runway capable of handling the largest of aircraft sealed the living quarters from attack from above. The runway was 18 feet thick, reinforced with steel rebar, and 12,000 feet long and 200 feet wide. Training grounds of all types surrounded the facility, including mock buildings that depicted areas all around the world. All of these training areas were carefully camouflaged from above to avoid the satellite traffic passing hundreds of miles overhead.

The commander of the facility was preparing for the gathering of a very unusual group. His instructions were to make ready quarters for members of the Coast Guard, the DEA, the FBI, the Navy, and the Secret Service all with different levels of security...some without any security clearance. Agents and military personnel were grouped not by their agency or arm of the military, but by security clearance on different floors of the underground living quarters.

Finally, he was to prepare quarters for the President himself for a one-night stay. The executive floor was rarely used and had not been used since the early 1960s. All total, his staff was preparing quarters for 35 personnel on four floors.

This kind of advance preparation only could mean that world-shaking events were at hand. The American public would probably never know the nature of the events that were unfolding.

The chief executive of the United States sat back in the presidential helicopter for the short ride to Langley. He was alone, except for his usual Secret Service team. He reflected satisfactorily to himself that for once the press had not conjured up, or speculated or made any inferences about the President's trip to Virginia. Of course the media was still milking the murder of Senator Jacobsen's aide. Security for the President was at an all-time high, which the President felt was a complete pain.

Not involving his usual advisors in this situation had given it a secrecy that was rare these days.

Even though his second term of office had been plagued by the usual political issues, and the press had not been very supportive since the Gulf War, he felt good about his presidency.

He was known as a "doer," and was only comfortable when he had his hands on the reins. This was probably a result of his military career. His second term of office was narrowly won over a young political power broker from Arkansas. He felt sure that the good governor from Arkansas would have never recognized the seriousness of this situation. He would have been too embroiled in his health care plan, or his wife would've been. He felt good that he was the one making the decisions, not for egotistical reasons, but for the good of the country.

The Presidential "Jolly Green" was on final descent for Langley. The pilot received clearance from the tower, did a clearing circle around the landing pad, began his descent and touched down lightly on the landing-pad. A waiting limousine moved closer to the aircraft as the blades stopped turning and the chopper door began to open. The Secret Service were the first out, but followed quickly by the President. His 6-foot 3-inch frame was a little too tall for the door, and he stooped as he came through the door.

He carried himself ramrod straight and walked briskly to the waiting car. Part of his success as a politician was because of his look of leadership, and he exploited that look to its fullest.

Air

His participation in this unusual briefing was to bring the importance of his leadership to the situation and instill in the "team" the life and death consequences of their mission to the United States. The President settled in the rear of the limo and the driver whisked him to his temporary quarters.

Chapter 12

J im and Sam were surprised not only by the appearance of the Director of the DEA, but also by the presence of other passengers on board the Gulfstream business-class jet. A young, attractive Hispanic man and woman sat quietly in two of the rear seats, both apparently lost in their own thoughts.

Jim and Sam found seats in the middle of the aircraft, and the director set down with them.

"I'll brief you all at the same time when we get into the air," the director said.

Jim had buckled up and was staring out the window wondering what this could all be about. He had some theories, but really had nothing to go on to substantiate any of it. His thoughts were disturbed by the sounds of someone boarding and the sounds of the engine starting sequence. The crew in the forward compartment were running the aircraft systems off an auxiliary power unit prior to starting. The sound of the air conditioning weakened slightly as the twin turbines began spinning. Jim could hear the imperceptible roar as the hot box was lit and the engine power began to come up.

The boarding noises shifted his attention to the front of the aircraft to see who was coming aboard. He couldn't believe his eyes. He reached over and hit Sam in the arm to get his attention.

Allison Stewart was walking down the aisle, slightly

bent over because of the low ceiling. By the stunned look on Sam's face, it was obvious he was as surprised as Jim.

Allison looked up right into Jim's eyes as she walked down the aisle. "What...what are you two doing here?" she stammered.

The director stood up and shook Allison's hand and said, "I'll explain everything in the air."

The start sequence was complete and the copilot was pulling the cabin door closed. Five minds were all wondering independently about the mystery shrouding the unfolding events. The presence of the Director brought an unheard of significance to the mission.

No sooner was the door pulled closed and locked, that the aircraft began to taxi. The Gulfstream taxied directly out onto the runway without stopping. The pilot brought the power up while they were still rolling, and soon they were approaching lift off speed.

The pilot rotated and brought the nose up sharply. The landing gear thumped into the gear wells and the gear doors closed behind the wheels. The takeoff flaps were raised with a whine of the electric motors. The jet seemed to leap forward without the drag of the gear and flaps. They would be landing in Langley in four hours.

The director stood up, walked to the front of the cabin and turned and faced his audience.

"Ladies and gentlemen, you'll have a chance to get to know each other over the course of the next week, since you will all be in training together. I can't go into details, but suffice it to say, you are going to be trained for a mission that is critical to the country's national security.

"The five of you, myself, a few high-up department officials and the President are the only ones who know anything of this mission. Your security clearances will be raised to accommodate your need to know for this mission. You all have special skills and backgrounds that make you ideal candidates to work together, and you are all the number-one choices for this mission.

"Once you hear the essence of the mission, you will be given the chance to withdraw. In a way, you've all been working together already without knowing it. I suspect that Lorenzo and Carmelita there in the rear have figured out by now that they have been working on the same project for the same agency. Jim and Sam, you've been partners for a short time, and I think you have met Ms. Stewart. Here is an outline of your individual training plans," he said as he handed out manila envelopes with the individual team members name stenciled on the front cover.

"Read through your plans, and if you have any questions, let me know. I may not be able to answer your questions, but you never know. There's food and a well stocked bar in the galley, you might as well enjoy the next four hours, because it may be several weeks before you do again. Get to know each other a bit during the flight, it'll make everything go smoother."

With that short speech, he sat down and pushed the back of his seat back into a reclining position. He pulled the window cover down and turned out the overhead light and was snoring a few minutes later.

The Gulfstream had completed the climb to cruise altitude and had turned to the east. All five passengers were emptying the contents of their individual envelopes and beginning to read. No one had ventured to the galley yet.

Jim's training plan included flight instruction in an ag-sprayer of all things. He had spent a lot of hours flying ag-sprayers. Piece of cake, he thought to himself, although he had a hunch that it might be something more than a regular ag-sprayer. Along with the flight training was physical training and some light weapons training. The training plan didn't really shed any light on the mission, if anything it raised more questions. He thought about asking the Director, but knew he would get non-answers. He looked over at Sam, and got a rather perplexed look in return along with a shrug of his shoulders.

He decided to walk back and sit down next to Allison and as the Director said, "Get to know each other."

Allison was reading through her training plan when he walked up. She slid her paperwork into the envelope and gave him a Hollywood smile. The smile and the blue eyes just about stopped him in his tracks.

"Well, it certainly looks as though you've recovered from your ordeal without too much problem," he said.

"I never would have made it if you and Sam hadn't come along when you did. I know I said thanks, but just saying thanks doesn't seem to be enough," she replied.

"Don't worry about it, you would have done the same for either Sam or I."

"Any idea what this is all about?" she asked

"I was hoping you'd be able to tell me," Jim replied. "Whatever it is, it's obviously something very serious to get both the director and the President involved directly."

"Usually when they send the boss to do the messenger's job it's because they want to keep a lid on whatever it is," Allison replied.

"So tell me, what were you working on that got you dumped in the desert?" Jim asked.

"I'm with the DEA," she began, "and I was working undercover in Mexico as a primary contact for an agent that infiltrated one of the larger Mexican drug conduits. I was living a life of luxury in Acapulco as an American heiress. I played tennis, shopped, and dined at the finest restaurants, and generally tossed the good ole American buck around. At the same time, I funneled information from the field agent back to the States. I also was responsible to see that he got bailed out if he got himself in a pinch. I failed miserably at that part...he's dead."

Allison had a very troubled look in her eyes as she contemplated her statement.

"It just does not make sense," she said. "He was killed at a time when he should have been meeting with a secured contact...it doesn't add up."

Jim and Allison continued to chat for a while, until both decided sleep was an imperative. Jim walked back to his seat next to Sam and kicked back for a few winks.

Jim awoke with a start. The noise of the Gulfstream's engines had changed and it felt as though they had begun a descent. A short time later, he heard the gear doors open and the landing gear thump down and lock. Within a few minutes, the Gulfstream was flaring for touchdown and landed firmly with a squeal of rubber followed by the sound of the thrust reversers.

The Gulfstream pilot slowed the business jet to taxi speed and turned off onto one of the high-speed taxiways exiting the runway. As Jim was staring out the window, the runway and taxi lights went out, as did the running lights on the aircraft. The pilot was apparently following a vehicle through the maze of taxiways to its intended hangar.

The four hours had passed quickly. Jim had slept fitfully the last two hours of the flight. He was starting to wonder what he was getting himself into...things were moving too fast.

Sam had stretched out his long legs, laid his seat back and snored the whole trip, seemingly unconcerned about the recent turn of events.

It occurred to Jim that he was now deeply involved with a number of people he knew little about. During the first half of the trip he had unsuccessfully tried to get the

Director to shed some light about the upcoming briefing. The Director politely declined comment regarding all of his questions, but promised to fill him in soon.

The jet rolled though a hangar door and came to a stop. As the engines spooled down, the cabin completed its depressurization, and the main cabin door was opened by one of the flight crew.

The Director stood at the front of the cabin and blocked the door while he began to speak.

"Ladies and gentlemen, all of you as of this moment have the highest security clearance in the country. The information you will receive in the next few days, along with your training, will place your lives at very high risk, but with the potential to virtually save your country.

"We have a high degree of confidence in each of you, and you have been selected very carefully based on your training, background, and experience. You will be meeting more of your team over the next few days, and before the week is over you will be melded into a true team.

"Over the past few hours, each of you have been alone with your thoughts. I'm sure questions have arisen that neither I or you or your companions have been able to answer, but I assure you all of your questions will be answered to the best of our ability.

"I won't sugarcoat the danger of this mission...it will be quite remarkable if all of you return alive. However, I will also tell you that each of you will have all the tools and information you will need to complete your mission. At this time, I must ask each of you to take a moment and make a final decision about whether or not you want to continue with the mission...when you deplane and walk into this hangar you will be committed and your briefing will start immediately."

For a full 30 seconds, no one spoke. All that could be heard was the unwinding of the Pratt & Whitney engines.

"Very well then, follow me," the Director said.

Not knowing what to expect, the newly forged team stepped off the aircraft and were somewhat surprised by the diversity of what they saw.

Chapter 13

As the hangar doors closed, ceiling lights came on and illuminated the large spotless hangar. The reflection of the lights bounced off the gleaming floor. At the far end of the hangar, a classroom area with a small stage was set up. To the far left of the building, two "Ag-Cats" sat gleaming. Instead of a sprayer tank under the belly of the two aircraft, a rectangular metal box eight feet long and the width of the fuselage, with 30 or so tennis ball size holes down the side of the box, was attached with metal strapping. Each Ag-Cat was set up with two tandem cockpits under one canopy. Other than that, each appeared to be a completely normal Ag-Cat. Next to the Ag-Cats stood two Quicksilver ultralights, also fairly normal looking. On the opposite wall sat a squat hovercraft. The hovercraft had not only the skirted hull, but also a short wing on each side of the boat, and turbine engine on a pylon at the rear. The boat was at least 30 feet long and 12 feet across the beam. Although squat looking, it also looked as it would take on a whole different look on the water.

On the floor next to the main cabin door of the Gulf-stream sat five nylon duffel bags, each labeled with the team member's name. "Grab your gear and have a seat in the briefing area," the Director barked.

"This will be brief," the Director started. The Director

picked up a remote control, pressed a couple of buttons that lowered the lights and turned on a slide projector. The first slide was an aerial view of Florida Keys looking southwest from Miami.

"The NSC has evidence to show that a group of elitists have been involved in not only the sale of narcotics around the world, but in the control of the entire industry from the growing and harvesting of the illegal crops, as well as the processing of the final product and the distribution.

"This group of American citizens we believe is made up of not only members of our government, but also influential families in industry. We believe the group never formally meets as a whole, but rather in small committees that overlap into other committees. The structure of the organization and the membership probably has its roots in history from 12th century England. This group believes that the legalization of drugs will ultimately be the answer to the drug problem, and they are positioning themselves for the investment potential when that day comes.

"While it is not our goal at this time to dismantle the organization, it is our mission to accomplish two goals. One, to disrupt the drug processing and distribution part of the operation, and secondly to trace the flow of capital from the operation. By disrupting the distribution and ultimate sale of the final product, we will be able to initiate a trace on the capital flow. Based on the information we have today, we believe we know of how approximately 20 percent of the capital is distributed. The other 80 percent or so, though, is still a complete mystery. The disruption of the operation should cause a money ripple that will give us some leads on the trail of the 80 percent, of which we don't know the whereabouts. We believe one of the major processing and distribution points for entry of the final product into the U.S.is in the Keys.

"This second slide is an aerial view of the plant and

warehouse of Global Exports on Key West. Aerial infrared photography has provided us with the necessary evidence for interdiction. It is our plan to visit and tour the facility at our leisure. The size of such an operation takes too long to organize and there will be leaks. This slide is an enhanced infrared view of the entire plant showing the tunnels and underground processing and packaging facilities that cover over 300 acres underground. Our operation will start a ripple that will give us a chink in their armor.

"Tomorrow at 07:00 we will resume the briefing. Even though I said you were committed when you stepped off the airplane, you have one last opportunity to back out. If after you have considered what I have told you thus far, you do not want to go further, tell me in the morning. Each duffel bag has all you will need for your stay here at Langley. Good night ladies and gentlemen."

With that final comment, the Director pressed another button on the remote and a section of the floor the width and height of a door opened to reveal a flight of stairs leading down under the hangar. On the stairs was a detail of Marines with side-arms. "America's finest will show you to your rooms," the Director announced.

Chapter 14

Senator Jacobsen was well aware of the plans to re-con and possibly attack one of his facilities in the Florida Keys. In fact, he had been part of the oversight committee that put final approval on the plans. He would also provide information about his partners in South America that would lead to raids and destruction of that infrastructure. It would seem that he was planning the demise of the very organization that he had worked so hard to build and develop to a profitable level.

The facilities in the Florida Keys that were the targets of the task force would be stocked with enough illegal drugs to provide for a good bust. The task force would also arrest a significant group of employees. From all perspectives, it would seem like a very big bust that would allow the President to crow about the success of his war on drugs. In reality, this was a carefully planned scheme for the Senator and his true partners to dispose of the drug connection.

The briefing began at 07:00 sharp. The Director took the podium and switched on the microphone.

"Ladies and gentlemen, you have been selected for a very unique mission. All of you have been field personnel engaged in various facets of surveillance and have shown creativity, resilience and tenacity in the way you have done your jobs. We are dealing today with a drug smuggling operation that has technology that matches ours, intel that matches ours, and in some instances firepower that matches ours. If it weren't for political fallout, we could conduct an all out war at the root of smuggling operations, but simply stated we could start WWIII as a result.

"Consequently, we need to learn how these operations work from the inside. We have identified an operation in the Keys that appears to be a processing and distribution point for a much larger organization in Central America. This facility is owned by a company known as Global Exports Inc. We know for certain that Global Exports is a front for drug smuggling. We also know for certain that it is tied to the bigger organization I talked about last night."

Behind a partition, the President listened to the briefing and watched through a two-way mirror undetected. The Director knew he was there, but beyond his security detail, his presence was Top Secret. His involvement and knowledge was very necessary, but if his staff and cabinet knew, then the press would know, and if the press knew, then all would know, and that would endanger the operation. As he watched and listened, he reflected that the drug operation was only the surface. His real concern went much deeper, to the root of the covert organizations intent. No one had uncovered the real use for all of the capital generated by the drug trade. All of his sources though indicated that the use for the money would threaten the stability of the world and certainly national security. Hopefully, this mission would provide some clues.

With a flip of a switch, the screen reappeared and the briefing became visual. The same aerial views from last night's presentation of Global Exports appeared on the screen. "Approximately 75 people work in the warehouses, offices and on the grounds of the facility. A good number of these people are innocent workers who have no idea what is in the boxes and crates they are moving around.

For that reason, we want to avoid harming anyone on the grounds, and we want all to have no idea we are there.

"To accomplish this, we are going to put everyone in the facility asleep for a few hours." Another flip of the switch, and the view changed direction, showing the facility from the northeast looking southwest. The southwestern end of the grounds was shielded from the ocean view and breezes by palm trees, saw grass, and Palmetto. The northeastern end of the grounds was by comparison open and facilitated the entrance to the main gate.

"The only way we can assure that everyone goes to sleep at the same time is to bomb the entire grounds with nitrous oxide. The N.O. will knock everyone out for at least two to three hours. They should wake up with a little bit of a headache, but none the wiser. Integrated with the N.O. is a compound that will make recollection of our presence very foggy. Each day that goes by will make their memory fade completely.

"We will spin a tale in the local paper of a harmless gas spill just off the coast of the Key. The employees will assume their unexpected nap was a result of the drift from that spill.

"OK, so how do we get the gas dispersed accurately and at the time we want? Jim and Sam this is your part of the job. You will be flying the two Ag-Cats over a neighboring swamp spraying for mosquitoes. The pod on the belly of your Cats holds the bomblets that will disperse the gas. On your return to your landing site, you will make a single pass over the grounds at 20 feet or so and eject the bomblets. It's necessary that you maintain spacing from each other of 50 feet or less and you don't exceed 50 feet of altitude to keep the pattern overlap correct and the altitude will concentrate the effects of the gas at ground level. The gas will be pulled into all buildings and under-ground tunnels through the ventilation system. Within two minutes of the gas dispersion, all personnel will be asleep. From that point, you will fly directly to your landing site, which we will talk about later.

"If any of the local townspeople see you flying, they will think nothing of spray planes spraying mosquitoes. Yes Jim, you have a question?"

"Sir, the grounds are within a mile of the town, what about the noise of the bomblets?"

"The bomblets have very little explosive value. You would have trouble hearing any type of explosion 100 yards away, and then all you would hear is some slight popping... nothing significant noise-wise at all. Any other questions at this point?

"Ok, five minutes after Agents Brooks and Mitchell have departed the area, two ultralights will begin to orbit the grounds. The ultralight pilots will maintain aerial surveillance of the operation, and provide back up in the event something goes wrong. These are not standard ultralights though. While they look like production Quicksilver's from a distance, each one is carrying a load of smoke and impact grenades that can be used to cover a hasty departure. We do not want to use this weaponry unless it is needed to make a clean escape and avoid detection. Agent Stewart and an additional member of your team yet to be named will fill this role in the operation.

"Simultaneously, as the ultralights appear on the scene, Lorenzo and Carmelita will lead a small detail through the front gate. Two members of the detail will replace the unconscious guards at the front gate, and you two will handle the onsite surveillance. All ground personnel will have security tag copies of Global's tags. If something goes wrong, those of you onsite on the ground will blend in with the rest of the plant personnel and make your departure later.

"The ultralights and ground transportation equipment

will all be carried ashore aboard the hovercraft. You will be returning to your point of departure following the mission.

"Your training coordinators for each phase of the mission are outside this room waiting for my signal to come it. These specialists DO NOT know the big picture on this mission. They have only been briefed on the portion that they are going to train you on. They do not know each other nor will they have an opportunity to discuss each phase with each other.

"Following the training of each group, these agents will be assigned to separate locations and each of the team leaders in each section will carry forth the training to the final overall coordination of the mission. I tell you this to underscore the importance of the security of this mission. Any questions?"

No one stirred, much less asked a question. As several seconds of silence followed the Director's question, he pressed a button on his podium and a door to the side of the stage swung open. Through that door walked a young man dressed in Marine Corp. aviation gear. The door closed behind him.

"Mitchell and Brooks, this gentleman will begin your training." Jim and Sam stood and followed the Marine over to the two Ag-Cats parked in the hangar. Similarly, training specialists were ushered in and took their students to various points on the grounds of the facility to begin their preparation for one of the most difficult missions they would ever face.

Chapter 15

For two twelve-hour days, Jim and Sam participated in a thorough training program that included weapons training as well as many hours of flight time. The flight time focused on the basics of crop dusting approaches and reversing turns, close formation flying and low altitude nap of the earth terrain following flight.

The training site for the flight training was over a set of fields 20 miles to the west of Langley that just happened to have a group of buildings laid out in a similar pattern to the target.

Their training coordinator was not talkative, patient, or accepting of less than perfection. He reviewed their flying from a Blackhawk helicopter and filled their headsets with a constant set of directions and criticisms.

On day three, assuming it would be more of the same, the Marine met them on the flight line and told them to saddle up and follow him. With that order, the Marine climbed aboard his helicopter and began the start sequence. Jim and Sam ran to their aircraft and did the same.

Before either Sam or Jim could radio for clearance to taxi, they were given clearance from the tower to takeoff and fly an eastward heading behind the Blackhawk now lifting off.

They flew for 20 minutes out over the Atlantic towards and empty ocean. Their trainer maintained radio silence until a ship came into sight on the horizon. As Jim and

Sam closed on the ship, they could see that it was one of the Navy's super carriers cruising in an easterly direction.

Before questions about their trainer's plans could even arise in their minds, he broke radio silence.

"OK gentlemen, here is where we find out about your flying skills and your guts...this is your final exam. I want you to start out with two touch and gos with right closed traffic. You'll get landing instructions on this frequency in a minute or so. Get a feel for the approach, and remember, the approach end of the runway is 90 feet off the water, and it's moving up and down. You need to keep your touch down point as close to the approach end as possible."

Jim and Sam double clicked their mics to signal that they heard and understood, then just looked at each other through their canopies with their mouths hanging open.

"Ag Cat November niner niner three Quebec Hotel, Flight boss Richardson."

"Flight boss, three Quebec Hotel, Roger. Fly a three mile left base, we'll call your final turn," came the command from the carrier.

"Roger, three mile left base, flight boss will call the final."

"Ag Cat seven three five yankee India, set up on a two-mile trail behind Quebec Hotel, and I'll call your final turn."

The Ag Cat is an incredible performer for short field landings and take offs but this appeared to be ridiculous. As Jim in QH made his turn to final the postage stamp sized landing strip on top of the heaving steel deck looked even smaller. There was very little wind, but just enough to make one worry about drift from the centerline. It's one thing to drift a little on a wide earthbound runway, but the carrier left no room for error. Jim put his foot into the rudder to hold a 10 degree crab angle to maintain alignment, and kept his airspeed up.

Air

His first approach was high and fast and he was halfway down the carrier runway before he touched down. He hit his flap lever and fire-walled the throttle just as he touched down and lifted off the carrier near the departure end. As soon as he lifted off, he began to fly a right traffic pattern as instructed. He was just turning from cross wind to his downwind leg in time to see Sam touch down near the arrival end of the carrier runway, power back up and lift off cleanly for the touch and go. "Show off," Jim muttered over the radio. All he heard in reply was two quick clicks.

After several tries, both Sam and Jim were executing touch and goes that had them touching down on the centerline at the second or third wire. The second and third catch wires were the target spots for arriving carrier bound military aircraft. Either wire would catch the tail hook and bring a military aircraft to a full stop. The Ag Cats were not using tail hooks. They had to execute a full stall landing on the carrier and brake to a full stop. The airframes of the Ag Cats could not withstand the violent force of using an arresting hook in the cables.

The Marine trainer in the helicopter hovering a half a mile off the carrier broke the silence he had maintained throughout the touch and goes." OK gentlemen, full stop this time."

Jim set his aircraft down first, followed by Sam five minutes later. As Jim touched down and shut his engine down, a crew of Naval crewmen ran out to push his aircraft over to the main hangar elevator. Jim stayed in the cockpit as instructed for the ride down into the bowels of the carrier. Sam arrived on the hangar deck the same way Jim did, followed by their Marine trainer shortly afterward.

Both Ag Cats were refueled and all of their critical systems checked while Jim and Sam received instruction on the deployment of the nitrous oxide bomblets.

Chapter 16

Allison and her new partner, Sergio Trujillo, had a Marine aviation trainer that mirrored Jim and Sam's. Trujillo was a last minute add to the team. Originally, the plan called for one orbiting Quicksilver. One of the planners insisted on adding a second and had recommended Trujillo as perfect for the job. He had a military background in the US Army and had flown ultralight aircraft before. After his security clearance was approved, he was added to the team.

Training on the ultralights was grueling for the two pilots. While the training syllabus was different, the discipline and quest for perfection was the same. The pilots had to learn to quickly unload the Quicksilvers from the hovercraft and do some quick assembly to prepare them for flying. They also worked on takeoff and landings from the beach, and silent approaches into an area similar in size and configuration to the landing zone in Key West. The ultralights were both fun and easy to fly and highly maneuverable, unless the winds were greater than 15 mph. A 15 mph wind was manageable as long as it was not a cross wind.

The ultralights had to be ready for a quick approach into the LZ in the event of trouble. Both aircraft were equipped with smoke rocket launchers and 16 rockets. These rockets would create a lot of noise, a lot of smoke and time for the infiltrators to escape.

Allison and Sergio practiced flying a two-mile circle

with the possible landing site in the center of the circle. Then, from various points of the circle, they were instructed to land immediately or to launch their rockets and land upwind of the where the rockets hit.

Carmelita and Lorenzo, spent 12 hours a day split between reviewing the aerial photographs of the plant and running practice missions on a mock plant. Marine personnel made up the balance of their recon team. As the two DEA agents and the Marines formed a team and began to execute the practice plan, they began to anticipate their individual moves and function like a well-oiled machine.

The key to their part of the mission was to enter the compound within seconds of the nitrous oxide doing its job, and to thoroughly examine all parts of the Key West operation center of Global Exports.

Armed with the map of the tunnels and buildings of the compound, the team had been able to cover the entire mock compound in less than two hours. During their examination, they were video taping all that their eyes were seeing with video cameras attached to their helmets. They also carried digital still cameras for close-up work. While they did carry side arms, their primary defensive weapon was a pressurized canister of more nitrous oxide. In the event that one of the Global employees awoke early, they could simply put them back into their slumber. Like the bomblets, the compound in the canister also had the amnesia drug mixed with the N.O.

Senator Jacobsen and Stewart Holmsby shared concerns about allowing and using the U.S. government to sever the relationship with the drug cartel.

First, they did not know for sure when the recon raid was going to take place, and secondly, while they had confidence the recon team would find nothing but drug-related operations, they were also concerned that this raid might lead to others. And other raids might uncover the other parts of the operation.

Chapter 17

E venings following training and meals were free time to the team - at least as free as one can be in a compound. There were entertainment facilities available, including movies, television, games, and a variety of cuisines for meals. The free time was also available for social time between the team members. They began to enjoy each other's company and were becoming like old friends over the three days of training, and in a couple of cases the friendships were becoming a bit more. They all spent considerable time talking about the mission, and all had suggestions to their superiors to improve upon the mission.

Allison and Jim ate most of their meals together and lingered over coffee. They talked about their backgrounds, favorite foods, music, and, of course, the mission. On the third night, as they finished their coffee, Jim suggested a walk around the compound.

Generally speaking, the compound at Langley was constructed for the covert side of government work. There were training facilities, dormitories, transportation operations, and a full support infrastructure. But between the buildings and facilities, there was also quite a bit of open landscaped area, including walkways lined with shrubbery, and lawn areas with mature hardwood trees. If one looked past the purpose of the facility, the beauty of the area came through.

The evening was cool but pleasant, with a gentle breeze and a clear star-filled sky.

"It's quite a coincidence how we met when you think about it," Jim said. "I mean, what are the odds that I would be covering that particular airstrip on that day? Furthermore, what are the odds that Sam would actually spot you from the air? Really an amazing coincidence."

Allison was quiet for a moment before she replied. Then she said, "It kind of makes you think about the possibility of fate, doesn't it?"

"You mean we are just playing roles in some sort of supreme plan?" Jim queried.

"No," she replied, "I think we have choices and we are free to make decisions, but perhaps it's not entirely accidental that we are here together at this moment."

"Well, in that case, what's our next move?" Jim asked.

With an arched eyebrow, Allison looked him right in the eye and said, "How about going back to my room? You know, eat drink and be merry, for tomorrow we die and all of that stuff."

With a guiding hand on her arm, Jim quietly steered her in a 180 degree turn towards the dorms. They talked quietly on the way back about nothing, the weather, the job, and other members of the team. As they approached Allison's door, a silence fell over both of them. The corridor was quiet and deserted. Allison was fishing in her purse for her key when Jim turned her around and lifted her face to his and gently kissed her full soft lips. Allison accepted his kiss with parted lips. He felt her sweet tongue playfully flirting with his as the kiss became more passionate.

"I think we need to get out of the corridor and into the room," Allison said. She turned back to the door and opened the door, stepped across the doorway into her dark room and didn't bother to turn the lights on.

Jim followed and put his arms around her from behind. He nuzzled the back of her neck and ears. Allison turned in his arms and began unbuttoning his shirt. She slid her hands up under his shirt onto his chest. Jim began unbuttoning her blouse and loosening her skirt. Suddenly, she broke free of him and stepped back a couple of steps and quickly finished removing her blouse and skirt.

"Your turn," she said, while unabashedly standing in the moonlight in nothing but panties and a bra. Jim quickly undressed and picked her up, and they both fell on the small dorm bed in a passionate tumble. Their lovemaking was tentative at first, then quickly filled with a heat and passion that surprised them both. At 2 a.m., Jim slipped out to return to his own room. Training resumed at 7 a.m. and he needed the sleep. Five hours would have to do it tonight, he said to himself. As Jim quietly shut Allison's door, he was startled to look up and see Lorenzo exiting the door across the hallway. They both gave each other a look and nod, and went quietly in opposite directions to their rooms.

On the walk to his room, Jim reflected on how his growing feelings for Allison changed his perspective on her continued participation in the mission. He knew he would never talk her out of continuing, but knew also that his mind would not be quite as focused on the mission now. Remembering her touch and still carrying her scent created an enormous desire to turn around and go back to her room for the rest of the night. Stoically, he continued on to his quarters.

Jim entered his dark room and flipped on the light switch. He headed straight to the bathroom for a quick shower. The dorm room was a studio-type room with a separate bathroom and closet. The room was small but ef-ficiently arranged with a single bed, nightstand and one upholstered chair. His clothes were stowed in the closet and drawers built into the closet. Everything seemed as he had left it, but something in the back of his mind told him that something was different. He had the feeling that someone had been in his room, and had professionally searched his belongings - nothing he could prove or even see, just a feeling. He showered and fell into bed exhausted. His fitful sleep was highlighted with strange dreams about mission scenarios.

Chapter 18

The Director started the morning briefing with some startling news.

"Ladies and gentlemen, there has been a change of plans. We have changed the target, and we leave this morning for the mission. All of your gear has been packed and all equipment you will need is on board a Hercules C-130, including the aircraft and the hovercraft. You will depart in one hour. To brief you on the new site is your mission commander Sam Brooks."

As the startled looks of surprise appeared on everyone's faces, Sam stood up and started making his way up to the stage.

"Sam is a Major in the Marine Corp. and has had extensive experience in covert operations. To facilitate a smooth training program and a chance for him to evaluate the mission capability, we have withheld this announcement until now. Without going into details, his resume makes him the best choice for this mission to lead all of you in and back out safely. Sam, it's now your program."

"Thank you Mr. Director. Ok, folks, we have reason to believe that our mission has been compromised," Sam began. "For the sake of the success of the mission and the safety of all of you, we are moving the mission site from Key West to this location."

He hit a button on the podium and the lights darkened and a slide image appeared on the lowering screen. The screen was filled with an aerial map of a compound not dissimilar to the one in Key West in a tropical region.

"This is facility 319 on Barbados. It is a known packaging and shipping location for drug shipments coming out of South America. It is believed that many of the shipments are loaded aboard cruise ships that are in and out of the port on a daily basis. This facility is much larger, with approximately twice the personnel as Key West."

Sam hit the podium button again and a second slide appeared. "Here is our staging area. This is an abandoned airstrip on the east side of the island. As you can see, the facility we are going to visit is approximately 10 miles southwest of the airstrip. The aircraft carrier Eisenhower will be cruising a racetrack pattern 25 miles off the coast to the south. They are in position now for your recovery and will be receiving your coordinates by way of GPS transmissions. The carrier will direct you by radio for your intercept following the mission. Any questions? You will be given detailed briefing packets on board the aircraft. Let's saddle up."

On the way out to the Hercules, Jim caught up with Sam on the tarmac.

"So, a Major in the Marine Corp. eh?" Jim asked.

"Sorry for the façade over the past week," Sam said.

"No problem," Jim replied, "glad to know we have an experienced leader."

Senator Jacobsen called Steward Holmsby on a secured digital telephone. He had mounting anxieties about the recon mission he knew was going to take place on the Key West facility.

"Holmsby, are you sure the Key West operation has been cleansed?" "Absolutely," replied Holmsby. "All evidence of our other manufacturing efforts have been removed to another site. All they will find is a drug distribution site, just what we want them to find. As soon as they find it, they will close it down and we will be rid of our Columbian connection. They have served their purpose by capitalizing our operation, but it is now time to move on to our ultimate intent."

"Where did you have the manufacturing operation moved to?" Senator Jacobsen asked.

"The one place that is large enough to handle, Barbados," Holmsby replied.

"Good, with the extra space and increased security of the island, we should be able to move on to the next phase without interference."

The Ag Cats had their wings removed and were tied down in the forward portion of the cargo hold of the Hercules. The two Quicksilvers were anchored in place with cables bolted to the C-130's deck. The hovercraft was stowed between the aircraft and the rear ramp.

The team made themselves as comfortable as possible on and around the equipment as best as they could. In the noisy and vibrating cargo hold it was difficult if not nearly impossible to talk. The crew slept and ate during the two-hour flight. Everyone was alone with their thoughts and their briefing packets.

Jim marveled to himself about the miracle of flight and the technology that surrounded him. The more he thought it about it, the more confidence he had about the mission succeeding. He reviewed the pictures of the mission site and noted that the approaches he and Sam would have to fly were virtually the same as they had trained for in Key West.

His mind wandered about many things, including Allison. He thought about their brief encounter, and how quickly things had moved between the two of them.

His mind also jumped to the unsettling feeling he had when we returned to his room that night. He was still convinced that someone had searched his room. Yet, it didn't make sense that someone could get into a highly secured facility and into a secured building to poke around in his personal effects, unless it was someone who had regular access and was part of the base staff. That just seemed too far-fetched though. The more he thought about it, the more sure he was that he was just experiencing pre-mission anxiety.

Still, he couldn't shake a growing feeling of unease. He had come to rely on his instincts, and right now they were screaming at him. Was it coincidental that his room had been tossed at the same time he was with Allison? Her behavior had not changed a bit since then. They seemed to share a growing closeness since that night. She seemed to say and do things that meant nothing but increased interest. But how much did he know about her? Really nothing. The more he thought about it, the crazier it made him. All he could do was go forward with the mission and stay alert. He closed his eyes for a quick nap. The noise and vibration of the Hercules lulled him to sleep.

Chapter 19

The whine of the landing gear motors and the thump as the landing gear locked into a down position woke Jim up with a start. Obviously the aircraft was on final approach for the abandoned airstrip that would serve as their staging area. The two-hour flight had gone by quickly.

Sam stood up and plugged a head-set into a communications jack in the bulkhead. He pressed a "push to talk" button and spoke into the boom mic. Within a couple of seconds of his conversation, the landing gear motors were activated and the gear was retracted into their wells. At the same time, the power on the Hercules came up to full. For some reason, they were aborting their approach.

Sam motioned for everyone to put on a headset so he could talk to all. Headsets in place, Sam said, "I've asked the flight crew to make at least two low passes over the airstrip before we land. We are reasonably sure that our mission has not been compromised for this site, but we are not absolutely positive. A quick look first won't hurt."

Sam's precaution seemed to establish him as the experienced commander and leader that the team needed.

The Hercules pilot raked the big cargo aircraft over in a 30 degree banked turn to the left. An experienced flight crew could make the big bird do amazing things. The first pass was done at high speed to make them difficult to hit in case there was any ground fire. The second pass was at approach speed and gave everyone a closer look at the surrounding terrain.

The airstrip, hangars, and support buildings were cut out of heavy brush and rain forest. Weeds and small trees were beginning to pop through the concrete joints in the runway and taxiways. A small river flowed along the perimeter of the facility from the interior mountains to the Caribbean. The facility looked abandoned and as though it had not had any use for several years. There was no sign of life of any kind in and around the field. On the third approach the pilot set the Hercules down softly and taxied to the largest hangar. He shut down the engines and activated the rear ramp at the same time. The heat and humidity hit them all like a wet warm blanket. The temperature must have been well into the 90s and the humidity at the same level.

The Marine contingent accompanying the team wasted no time unloading the hovercraft and the aircraft. Within an hour of landing, all of the equipment was unloaded and the Ag Cat wings were being reconnected to the fuselages. Jim and Sam supervised and inspected the reassembly. Once the flight controls were reconnected, they checked both aircraft to make sure they were connected correctly. It just would not do to discover the controls were cross-connected in flight. Both of the Ag Cat engines started with ease. The balance of the team busied themselves with checking and rechecking their equipment.

The Quicksilvers were assembled and engines started. The hovercraft was started and hovered into place near the river. Gear was stowed in the hangar and sleep quarters were set up in the far end of the largest hangar. Food provisions were simple sea-rations for the team, so no cooking facilities were needed.

Shortly after the unloading had been completed, the Hercules taxied to the runway and took off with a roar of noise and dust. Suddenly, the enormity of the task at hand seemed to settle on the team. They were in position to start and complete the mission. They were committed at this point.

The accompanying Marine Corp. guards set up a perimeter, and maintained patrol units through the night. The ground mission group had to move out at first light to be in position to recon arriving workers at the site. The Ag Cats and the Ultralights would both depart two hours after the ground group.

Breakfast was at 05:00, and it consisted of powdered eggs, cereal with powdered milk, and energy bars. All personnel carried energy bars, protein bars, and water in their web gear as well. The modern military had learned over the years the need for energy-producing food to keep personnel operating at optimum levels. Flavoring in these foods had even been improved to encourage personnel to eat while in the field.

All of the mission group spent time before and after breakfast checking equipment one last time. At 06:30 the ground personnel set off down the river in the hovercraft. The river passed within a couple of miles of the target. Lorenzo and Carmelita reviewed maps and the plant layout on their way to the target. Despite good intel, the actual site is always different than the maps and diagrams indicate, and one can never over prepare for the actual infiltration.

The river was actually a rather idyllic slow moving river. When the hovercraft was not running, the surrounding tropical forest was quiet except for an occasional bird singing. The hovercraft moved a mile at a time under power, then drifted for five to 10 minutes.

This tactic served two purposes. First any surrounding people in the area would not have enough time to pick up the sound of the running of constant engine noise. Secondly it gave the mission group an opportunity to listen for any unwanted observers.

The slow progress gave Lorenzo an opportunity to use an infrared scanner on the surrounding tropical vegetation. The scanner picked up the body heat of birds and small animals as they drifted down the river. He scanned the lower brush and the trees looking for lookouts and any unwanted personnel in the area. Any that were found would have to be investigated. Anyone found in the area would have to be temporarily neutralized. They had 10 miles to move down the river, and at this pace it would take them well over an hour and a half. The last half mile would be by river current alone, with the help of battery powered thruster motors for maneuvering that were absolutely silent.

Three miles into the trip the scanner picked up three human forms 20 yards or so from the river bank. The hovercraft was drifting at the time. The Marine operating the thrusters was directed to engage the thrusters and maneuver to the river bank. As the craft beached, two Marines slipped ashore and moved silently through the brush, taking guidance from Lorenzo as he watched them and the targets on the scanner. The Marines were equipped with radio headsets to communicate with Lorenzo as he directed them towards the three infrared forms.

The two Marines worked their way closer and closer until they were easily in sight of their targets. They were so close that the three target forms and the two Marines merged into one infrared blob on the screen. The Marines were carrying dart guns loaded with a harmless sleep drug. The effects were essentially the same as that of the nitrous oxide that would be used at the site.

The leader of the two Marines radioed back that the three individuals were armed and appeared to be a patrol group from the target plant. They were wearing uniform coveralls and carrying side-arms. The two Marines silently aimed their dart guns and put two of the three to sleep.

Air

The third stood for a moment staring at his two comrades on the ground before he reacted reaching for his side arm. Before he could even clear the gun from his holster, he was hit with a dart as well, putting him to sleep instantly. The three were all carrying walkie-talkies. It was presumed that they would be required to check in periodically, or at least respond to radio calls from the plant. The infiltration plan called for one of the Marines to stay behind and answer any such queries to prevent any early warning of the invasion. The Marine would be picked up as they egressed from the area.

Back under way, the hovercraft moved at even a slower speed. The time table had allowed for this contingency, so they were still well within the timing of the plan. Apparently this was the only patrol out as Lorenzo, Carmelita and the ground contingent made it to the rendezvous point without any further human encounters.

At the airstrip, Allison and Trujillo finished suiting up for their ultralight flights. The wind was calm, and the air was relatively cool for the area. The conditions were as good as one could expect for flying. By afternoon, everyone knew that the tropics would generate lots of cumulus buildup and perhaps a rain storm. By the time those were to occur, all flights should be completed.

Allison and Trujillo strapped themselves into their light aircraft and started their engines. They needed a 15 minute head start over the Ag Cats to get into position before they arrived on the scene. Not only did they have to get into the general area of the plant, but they had to climb to 5,000 feet, which took a bit of time in these powered gliders.

Both of the ultralight pilots taxied in tandem out to the runway. They waited for a green light signal from a light gun back at the hangar. Sam made a quick call to the hovercraft to get the all clear before signaling to the ultralights the go signal. A few seconds after the green signal, the ultra-lights powered up and began their short run down the runway. Both were in the air in less than a hundred feet. The Quicksilvers looked like innocent pleasure craft with brightly colored wings on a silver framework. The rocket and grenade pods were not even visible from the ground. The engineers had done a great job hiding the pods to look like part of the airframes. The two aircraft slowly disappeared over the tree line and continued their climb.

Once in the air, the two ultralight pilots began to monitor their progress towards their target with their GPS displays. Allison was in the lead, with Trujillo flying the wing position, slightly behind her and off her starboard wing.

They had trained utilizing spacing of no more than 25 feet from each other. Despite the still air, Allison noticed that Trujillo kept drifting within 20 feet.

Allison keyed her push to talk switch on the ultralight stick and suggested a correction. "Trujillo, maintain spacing, you are drifting in too close."

He seemed to not hear her. He kept drifting in until he was well within 10 to 12 feet of Allison's Quicksilver. Allison looked over her right shoulder and notice how close he was and that he now had his side-arm in his free hand. "Trujillo what are you doing? Talk to me, why have you drawn your weapon?"

Horrified, Sam and Jim listened to radio exchange on the ground back at the airstrip.

Allison knew something was very wrong. Trujillo had not responded and now seemed to be taking aim with his gun at Allison or her Quicksilver. Fortunately, the Quicksilvers are extremely maneuverable and they had gained 3,000 feet of altitude AGL. She heeled the aircraft over in a tight left turn, and began diving towards the tree canopy. She heard two .45 caliber shots behind her just as she turned. She keyed her mic as she made the turn and spoke into her boom mic, "Attention all personnel, Trujillo is trying to shoot me down. I am taking evasive action and need assistance. Mayday, mayday, mayday!"

Allison looked over her right shoulder in time to see that the other ultralight was still on her 6 o'clock position, but she had gained some distance because of her quick reactions. She was now at 1,500 feet AGL, with an airspeed of over a 100 knots indicated airspeed. Maintaining her airspeed, she leveled off with an idea in mind. Trujillo followed suit and leveled off as well, trying to close the gap of the chase. Allison continued in a very slight descent which helped her maintain the 100+ knots. At the same time, she was using her rudder to zigzag to make a difficult target to hit. She heard shots being fired behind her, but did not see or hear any airframe shots. She kept up a running play by play through the radio of her position and what was happening. Just as he had closed the gap and was within 50 feet or so, Allison saw her chance to make her move. She was now under a thousand feet and needed to try to gain the advantage. She was not exactly checked out to fly these things aerobatically, but she had little choice at this point. She hauled back on the stick to its full range of movement, and made sure the throttle was open full. The Quicksilver climbed like a scalded cat. It felt to Allison like she was headed straight up. She held back on the stick until the climb turned into a loop. She was inverted and well above Trujillo when she rolled the wings level, and began a hard diving turn to port. Trujillo was searching over his head, and behind his aircraft looking for Allison, just as she rolled out of her dive on his 6 o'clock position. She quickly closed the gap to a couple hundred feet. While her armament was designed for air-ground application, she thought a rocket fired into the rear of his ultralight might just do the trick if she could line up a shot. She flipped down the aiming eyepiece attached to her helmet and hit the arm switch on the rocked pods. When she was within 200 feet, she hit the fire button on her stick and watched the laser-guided rocket fly with incredible speed into the Quicksilver's engine.

The small rockets were more for ground effect if needed, so they would not create a large explosion. The rocket hit the top of the engine just below the fuel tank and exploded with about the same power as a very large firecracker or cherry bomb. The force of the explosion and the resulting flame were enough to penetrate the fuel tank. The fuel spilling into the explosion created an even bigger explosion, turning the fabric-covered craft into a ball of flame. The burning aircraft dropped a wing and began a spin to the ground. Within 10 to 15 seconds, it disappeared beneath the tree canopy, leaving nothing but a smoke column to mark where it had hit the ground.

Back at the airstrip, Jim had heard the radio transmissions, and ran to the Ag Cat. He wasn't sure what he was going to do, but he knew he had to get to where Allison was to help her. Sam ran for his Cat as well. Neither of them waited for a signal, they started the Cats and immediately began to taxi to the active runway. The last transmission they heard from Allison was that she was going to try a loop to get behind Trujillo. They had heard nothing since. Jim was beside himself with worry. He tried multiple radio calls to Allison without a reply. The two Cats lifted off in tandem and headed in the direction of the ultralights. They kept their altitude at 1,000 feet to get a look at the ground as they neared the area where they thought the dog fight had occurred.

Allison decided she had to determine the final disposition of the aircraft remains and make a decision as to whether or not they should abort the mission. After all of their training and planning, she did not want to abort. She circled the column of smoke several times but could not see through the trees. She had only one choice, she had to find a place to land so she could recon the crash scene. There were no roads of any kind in the area, and no clearings in the trees. The river did have wide flat banks, though, that might work in places where they were the broadest. She found one section that was 40 or so feet wide and 300 feet long that would work just fine for a landing.

Not only did she need to survey the crash, but she was shaking uncontrollably and needed to get on the ground and regain her wits. She lined up on the broad river bank, and cut the power and glided easily down to the bank. Considering her mental and emotional state, she did a very good job setting the ultralight down on the bank. It rolled to a stop and she reached up and hit the cut-off switch. The engine sputtered to a stop. She unbelted the five position harness and climbed out of the seat and stood up on very shaky legs. The adrenaline was still coursing though her veins.

From her last look while she was in the air, she was about a quarter of a mile to the south of the crash. She headed off in that direction. Halfway there she remembered to switch her hand-held radio on to communicate with the rest of the mission group. In the heat of the short but momentous battle, she had completely forgotten about the rest of the group.

Just as she turned on the radio, she heard Jim's voice in the middle of a transmission.

"Quicksilver one, come in, I repeat, Quicksilver one come in." She quickly keyed her hand-held. "Quicksilver one; I have landed on the river bank and am on foot to survey the crash scene. I don't expect to find Trujillo alive. The aircraft was in flames when it hit the ground and there was no parachute. I'll advise when I am on the scene."

"Quicksilver one, Ag Cat two, negative, do not approach crash scene, we will abort the mission Jim said."

Allison replied, "Ag Cat two, no need to abort, if the aircraft and pilot are neutralized; ETA is three minutes."

In the meantime she heard the approaching Ag Cats. She broke through the brush and came to face to face with the remains of both the aircraft and Trujillo. The corpse was nothing but a blackened hull of a human form. Trujillo was not recognizable. The fabric on the aircraft had completely burned away, and much of the aluminum frame had deformed from the heat and impact. The scene simply looked like a crash scene of a pleasure flier. Even the rocket pods had melted and were not identifiable as weaponry. The fire was still burning as she turned her back and started to walk back to her landing site.

The sight of Trujillo's death caused a lump in her throat. She had not known him long and did not really even know him at all. He had been very quiet throughout their training. There was never any indication that he might be under suspicion in any way. The recollection of him shooting at her helped her get a grip on her emotions though and regain her professionalism. She radioed the results of her findings to Jim and Sam, who were now circling the smoke column.

"No need to abort, pilot and aircraft completely destroyed. I am on my way back to my aircraft and will be in the air in a few minutes."

Jim and Sam continued circling over the smoke column. They had spotted Allison's Quicksilver sitting on the river bank and were watching for her to emerge from the tree line onto the river bank. The tropical tree canopy was so thick it was virtually impenetrable from above. The thick green foliage looked like a green carpet from 1,000 feet above. Suddenly, Jim spotted Allison burst out of the foliage onto the river bank and breathed a sigh of relief as she looked up and waved to the two circling Ag Cats. While the mission was a little delayed, they were still within an acceptable time frame to complete it.

Allison strapped herself back into the Quicksilver and fired up the Rotax engine. She was airborne within 50 feet and climbing out above the river.

Jim and Sam continued circling the area to give Allison plenty of time to get in position before they made their "bomb" run. Jim pondered how Trujillo could have possibly been granted the level of clearance he had to have had to meet the mission criteria. It made him wonder who else could have been bought by the other side. He wondered who the other side might be as well. The depth of penetration that was required to get a mole this deep into a covert operation made everyone a suspect in Jim's mind. He would be on his guard at a much higher level than ever before. He knew also that everyone else would feel the same, even about him - all very disconcerting thoughts.

How could they function as a team without trust? But, they had no choice at this point. They had to go forward and test their collective mettle and integrity. He also thought that there must be much more to this operation than it appeared on the surface. He turned his attention back to his flying. He watched Allison continue to climb out and become a distant speck. She was to radio when she was at altitude and in position. She was also going to use her binoculars to recon the plant from her lofty seat to see if operations appeared to be normal at the plant.

Chapter 20

L orenzo, Carmelita and the ground team had reached their rendezvous spot and were waiting for the go signal to move into the plant. Allison would observe the dropping of the bomblets and watch for an indication that the plant personnel were asleep before giving the go code word, "Sweep".

The ground team were 400 yards outside the perimeter of the plant, well camouflaged in undergrowth. Lorenzo and Carmalita kept up a continual visual observation of the area with coated optic binoculars. The coating kept the lenses from reflecting sunlight and giving away their position. They were also enhanced with optics that had zoom and wide angle capabilities. They could either focus on an individual or take in the whole grounds with the wide angle option. The zoom capability would give them enough detail to see facial blemishes and scars.

Their observations could not detect any particular anxiety on the plant workers faces, and it appeared that all people and equipment and traffic were moving in what would appear to be a normal pace. From all appearances, the operation was going about their day to day business. Still, they knew with the discovery of Trujillo's role that the plant may know about the coming visit. Depending on what they observed, they could either abort or go ahead with the operation. Nothing would indicate an abort choice. Tensions were high though, nerves were on edge given their knowledge that they might be expected by plant security.

Equipped with the same optic tools, Allison was also looking for any indication of heightened security. A true tip off of enhanced security would be any sign of breathing apparatus, gas masks or protective clothing that would nullify the effects of the nitrous oxide. "Sweep" was heard over the radio net from the ground unit. Likewise Allison keyed her mic and said, "Sweep." With those two go signals, both Jim and Sam formed up for their run.

Fortunately, the layout of the plant grounds were quite similar to the original site in Key West. The flight parameters called for one aircraft to trail the other, with each dropping half of their load in one pass. They would then climb out and allow Allison and the ground contingent to confirm that the chemical was giving the desired effects. If it appeared that not all personnel had received an adequate dose, they would repeat their run. So, while the observations were taking place following the bomb run, the Ag Cats would fly a wide pattern to line up for a second run over the plant.

Jim was leading and Sam flying in a wing position one mile out from the plant. As they got closer, Sam would throttle back and drop back in a trail position ¼ mile behind Jim. Both were utilizing an oxygen system, in the event the gas was blown up near their altitude. They both were no more than 25 feet above the tree canopy flying at 110 KIAS (knots indicated air speed). As they approached the plant ground's perimeter, they would drop to 50 feet AGL and slow to 60 KIAS or just above stall speed.

Five miles out to the way-point was the readout on Jim's GPS. He flipped up the cover to the arming switch for the release mechanism and toggled the switch to the armed position. "Release armed," was his quick radio call. Sam replied with two mic clicks to acknowledge and then armed his release mechanism.

Jim reduced power and increased his nose-up attitude slightly to bleed off airspeed, then dropped one notch of flaps to slow to the approach speed. The aircraft controls began to get a little mushy as the airspeed bled off, but these aircraft were made for this kind of flying. The perimeter of the plant grounds was coming up quickly.

Allison was watching for any early warning of the approaching aircraft. She had an eagle's perspective of the grounds and the two approaching Ag Cats.

The picture unfolded fame by frame. Plant personnel walked from building to building, forklifts and trucks were being loaded and unloaded, guards appeared to be at ease but vigilant at their posts. Everything appeared very normal. The one road into and out of the plant was completely vacant. No sign of any traffic headed out or in, the timing looked perfect. "Still all clear," radioed Allison.

Jim was at 60 KIAS and at the perimeter of the grounds. Suddenly, the guards at the gate became aware of the approaching aircraft. They looked just time to see the first Ag Cat flash over their heads. As they were looking up, the strange looking box-like devices under the aircraft began spitting out tennis size balls and hitting the ground all around them. Little puffs of smoke exploded with very little noise as they hit the ground. It all happened so quickly they had no time to react. The smoke hung in the air as thick as fog as the bomblets "walked" across the center of the plant grounds. Just as the effects of the fog was beginning to be felt, they heard and barely saw a second aircraft overhead. As it passed, they noticed the fog getting thicker. While still conscious, they felt themselves drifting off into a trance like state. They felt a little giddy, very sleepy and very comfortable sitting down on the ground, laying their weapons next to them and closing their eyes. As conflicted as they felt about their actions, they had no choice and therefore slept peacefully.

Jim powered up his aircraft and lifted the flaps as he began a climbing turn to the right to make a wide closed pattern flight, as if he would be returning for a landing and was "in the pattern." Just as he turned cross-wind, he looked back over his right shoulder to see Sam performing the same maneuver. The grounds behind him were completely covered in a fog much like a ground fog seen on an ocean coast. The tops of the buildings were visible, but nothing else could be seen though the fog of N.O. Presumably, the HVAC systems for the buildings were pulling in the gas into all areas inside. Within a matter of a few minutes, everyone in the plant and on the grounds should be asleep. Typical of early mornings, the wind was still, and the fog just hung in place. It looked like a perfect execution of the mission up to this point. Jim and Sam continued their wide pattern on their downwind leg and headed back out to a position 10 miles from the grounds.

Chapter 21

L orenzo, Carmalita and their team fired up the hovercraft and headed towards the main gate to complete
their inspection. On their way through the gate, two
Marines were left at the gate to assume the role of plant
guards in case there were unexpected visitors. The team
was inside the plant within minutes of the N.O. dispersal.
All of the plant employees inside and out were sleeping
peacefully. It was a little surreal to be stepping over and
around all of the prone bodies.

Inside the plant, the ground floor looked like any usual
import-export warehouse type operation. Lots of high
shelves loaded with crates, forklifts, a set of loading docks
and a supervisor's office at the back of the building. They
knew that what they were after was below ground, finding the access point was the tricky part. As the team spread
through the building, they got a break. One of the employees from downstairs was coming up and through the access
point just as the N.O. was doing its job, and he fell asleep
partially in and out of the access door to the basement. The
door was disguised as a shelf unit, which was hinged and
hid an elevator in the wall behind it. Being able to find the
access point this quickly had saved them precious minutes.

Lorenzo and Carmelita headed to the basement with
one Marine, while the rest of the team stayed above to keep
an eye on the nappers. The elevator controls had only two
buttons, one for the ground floor and one of a single base-

ment stop. The one stop to the basement was a good 40 or feet down, probably for security purposes.

As the door opened on the basement floor, they were prepared to be greeted by guards that may have not been affected by the N.O. yet. All three of them had on gas masks and carried N.O. dispersal units to neutralize anyone that was still awake. As the door opened, though, it was clear that there was no one waiting for them and that the gas had been pulled in through the HVAC system and had done its job. Employees in lab coats were sleeping peacefully all around them. At least 15 people were snoozing on the floor. Surprisingly, no guards were to be seen.

The real surprise though was that there was no evidence of drug processing or handling. Instead, what they found baffled them all.

There were a number of perimeter labs surrounding a large open area that also functioned as a lab. The perimeter labs had computers, electronic measuring gear, and laser equipment. The large open arena measured roughly 100 feet long and 50 to 60 feet wide, and had three large projectors aimed at the same point in the middle of the arena. It was obvious that they were projectors since they were still on and focusing projected light to the center of the arena. The three projected lights all illuminated a large parabolic shape that resembled an umbrella hovering five or six feet above the floor.

Lorenzo and Carmelita were continuously videotaping what they were seeing and voicing a narrative description that was captured by the recorder. After doing a video sweep from a distance, they cautiously moved towards the object to get a closer look.

They walked to the center of the room right up the hovering shape and ducked under it to take a look at what was holding it up. To their surprise, there was nothing keeping it off the floor - no legs or support of any kind. They ducked back out from under the cover to take a closer look at the top to see if there were cables holding it up. Again, nothing appeared to be supporting this giant umbrella. Lorenzo ducked back under and stood up and reached up to touch it only to find that his hand passed right through the shield. The giant umbrella was a holographic image so real looking that it defied close examination until one tried to touch it. Even though it was a hologram, it cast a shadow on the floor and was impenetrable optically.

They video recorded and gave a narration of the hologram as completely as they could and examined each perimeter lab to capture the images of the equipment in each, then made their way back to the surface floor of the building. Using large capacity memory sticks, they downloaded as much data as they could from the computers. Not expecting to find a data repository this size, they were not prepared for the mass of data. They focused their downloads on the larger .exe files. They were all baffled to find the electronics lab in the basement instead of drug processing, but it was what it was.

Lorenzo gave the all clear to the rest of the team over the radio net, and they reassembled at the front gate. As they headed away in the hover-craft for their rendezvous with the carrier, Jim and Sam lined up to make one more pass to make sure everyone slept for another hour or so.

The second pass with the Ag-Cats went without a problem, and the two, along with the ultralight, headed out to sea for the carrier. About halfway out, they could see the hovercraft below them making good headway across the swells towards the carrier. The Ag-Cats and the ultralight would be recovered and stowed below on the hangar deck by the time the hovercraft arrived and was hoisted up on deck. If everything went as it should, they would all be in a briefing room within an hour.

Despite the practice and knowing they could land on

the carrier, doing it again was enough to start the sweats. It is amazing how tiny that giant carrier deck looked from a few miles out and 2,000 feet of altitude. Jim flew a downwind leg and got the solid green light gun signal that he was cleared to land. He flew a left base and onto final about ¾ of a mile astern of the carrier. Thankfully, the seas were relatively calm and the carrier was not pitching up and down to any degree. Jim had descended to 1,000 feet and had throttled back to 1700 rpm with one notch of flaps. That gave him an approach speed of 75 knots and a three degree glide-slope. He was nicely set up for a short field landing, which he needed to do since he didn't have a tail hook to catch a wire. As he descended through 500 feet, he felt a bit of cross wind from right to left lift up his starboard wing. He corrected with a little bit of left rudder and right aileron into the wind to hold his path for the landing zone. This correction had him crabbed into the crosswind by about three to five degrees. He could hold the crab angle and then kick it around at the last instant to avoid putting any kind of side load on the gear. He kept up a running narrative to let Sam know what he was dealing with. As he passed over the end of the flight deck, he was a scant 15 feet above the deck. In rough seas, that 15 foot margin could disappear in an instant. It made him realize what heroes U.S. Naval aviators were that did this day in and day out with very few incidents. Mixing rough seas with a night landing made Jim shudder to think about what that must be like, especially in a Tomcat or some other high performance jet.

The carrier was quickly filling the view out the front of his windshield. His training took over and he calmly executed what he had learned in the prior days during the training sessions. He now had full flaps and had slowed to just under 60 knots when he settled on the deck firmly. He stood on the brakes and came up well short of the end of the landing area. The Ag Cat has a tough airframe and can withstand a lot more abuse than either aircraft received on that day. Sam was in trail by about five minutes, which gave Jim ample time to taxi over to the hangar elevator and get out of the way. Sam also landed without incident, an experience that neither of them would ever forget.

The carrier commander and the on board commander of the carrier air group (CAG) both monitored the strange little parade as each component came aboard. Neither had any idea of the mission that this group had been on but knew that their assignment had come from the highest authority and were to give the infiltration team any and all support. The first on the agenda for the team was a secure briefing room with transmitting and receiving capabilities.

The team gathered in the briefing room and opened a secure connection to Langley, where the President, the head of the DEA, and the head of the CIA were waiting for their report.

Jim opened up with a description of the mission overview and Lorenzo then began describing what they had discovered in the electronics laboratory. At the same time the briefing was taking place, the memory sticks were being downloaded and sent to Langley via a separate secure connection. Once the download was complete, the memory sticks were destroyed.

As Lorenzo was describing what they had seen, a technician in Langley took the data they had sent and projected it on a screen for the President to see. They also had Lorenzo's video feed to review while he was speaking. The President and the Director of the DEA were nearly speechless as they viewed the data and the video feed.

The Director of the CIA, Howard Nixon, seemed to recognize what he was seeing on the screens. Finally, he commented that he had some additional data on the technology that was being displayed on the screen. After a few

Air

routine questions, the secure briefing ended and the mission crew were thanked and ordered to report back to Langley the next morning.

Chapter 22

In the role of President of the United States, there are few issues that arise that he must face that are beyond the capabilities of the people and the government. In this case, though, it would appear that by the serious look on the President's face that perhaps what he had just learned may fall into the beyond category.

"You mean to tell me that after all of these years of science fiction about controlling the weather, that this device may be capable of actually making it happen?" the President asked.

"This working prototype proves that this device, utilizing laser based holographic technology, can block the sunlight from reaching certain areas of the earth in a large enough scale to change temperatures in the atmosphere as well as surface temperatures enough to affect the weather," the head of the CIA explains.

"Evaporative rates will be reduced, causing less moisture in the atmosphere, and therefore less rain, less convective activity or less rain, and potentially cause temperatures to fall dramatically in other areas. We know that weather is a chaotic science and that changing minor variables can have a dramatic impact on the course of a hurricane. We also know we can create a storm front by seeding clouds that may block the progress of other weather and actually divert destructive weather from coming ashore in a particular area."

Air

The head of the CIA went on to say, "This device, handled properly, can be a tremendous asset to the world and potentially lengthen growing seasons, turn areas of the world that today are uninhabitable into productive agricultural areas, slow global warming, and manage global temperatures into the future."

"Explain the technology for us one more time, Mr. Nixon," the President asked.

"Laser generators are put into orbit around the earth in pre-programmed locations and held in place by miniature thrusters. Those laser generators fire their beams into refractor lenses mounted in the laser generator housings. The refracted beams bouncing from the prisms create a network of micro beams that in turn create an interlocking mesh of light beams that are so tightly spaced they become a reflective shield.

"The beams are passed through a chemical bath of sulfur and ammonia that is contained in a vacuum sealed vial. The sulfur and ammonia bath causes the micro beams to become even more reflective. These tiny sub-microscopic particles concentrated together in the interlocking beam make a shield or a reflective parabola as effective as a solid mirror.

"By locating the laser generators in the right spot, the ensuing shadow on the Earth cools significantly very quickly without the sun hitting it every day for hours at a time. This is the same principle as the effect the super volcanic eruptions had on the earth thousands of years ago that covered the earth in gasses, smoke and dust that blocked out the sunlight and caused wide-spread cooling around the earth.

"Since the laser generators are solar powered for both their thrusters as well as the laser power, they can be permanently held in place for the long term or moved around the earth to new locations. The shield can be built to any scale and can be located anywhere around the earth in a matter of hours."

"Here is a quick example of the impact it could have," Nixon continued. "The shield could be moved over the Sahara desert and more than half of the sunlight could be blocked for weeks. Within that time span, the average temperatures will cool from 112 degrees Fahrenheit to in the 80s. With that temperature change, evaporation at the water sources will decline immediately by 30 percent. The resulting decrease in evaporation will allow water sources to increase, and plant material will begin to spread exponentially from the water sources outward, turning the great desert into an agricultural area over time.

"By the same token, if the shield is held in place over one of the poles, melting will slow and ultimately stop and the polar ice caps will begin to grow. As they grow, global temperatures will fall, having catastrophic effects on climate.

"In addition, the sky shield can be broken into two or three reflective parabolas and used to focus sunlight on a specific area to increase temperature."

The President asked, "Why would we want to increase temperatures?"

"Simple, if there is an area of cool moist air in an area that needs rain, but the temperatures are too low to cause the water vapor to condense and turn into rain, we can focus the parabolas on that area and increase the temperature and create rain where we need it, thus droughts could be eliminated or at least minimized. Conversely, as you can imagine, in the wrong hands this can be incredibly destructive. We live in a very delicate balance with all of the ecosystems. Without careful management of a tool like this, severe damage can be caused to Earth. But as I said, used properly it can have dramatic positive effects."

"So, gentlemen," the President began, "there you

have it, the good and the bad. I cannot stress enough the importance of gaining control of this technology and not allowing it to be used as a weapon. This technology has the capability of bringing great benefits to Earth that will ease the suffering of millions of people. This technology can be a great gift to the people of today and to posterity that will help to bring peace, prosperity and expansion of free society throughout the world. Our first imperative is to find and secure all of the source material, as well as the scientific team that developed the technology. I have a hunch that the scientific team was forced to develop this against their will."

"Mr. President, as we speak, I have several intel teams looking for traces of the components of this technology and the root sources. The individual teams are not aware of the big picture and the end use technology," the Director of the CIA said.

"I will advise the NSA, Homeland Security, the FBI the Joint Chiefs, the Secretary of State, and the Congressional leadership of what we know today in a meeting at Camp David tomorrow. Have an update and an outline of a plan to locate and secure the technology for us to present by 1 p.m. tomorrow," the President said. "It is absolutely critical that this be kept out of the press until we have control of the situation. Word of this could cause worldwide panic."

Chapter 23

Jim, Sam, Allison, Lorenzo and Carmelita had become fast friends after their little adventure in the Caribbean. Not only had they faced adversity as a team and persevered, but the five of them had a certain chemistry that they all enjoyed.

At the moment, they were enjoying a well-earned vacation at the Atlantis Resort Hotel in the Bahamas Islands. The 5-star resort was just the tonic that the five of them needed to recuperate from the stress of the training and the mission. The Atlantis had fabulous beaches, spas, food, drink and all sorts of recreational opportunities that quickly diverted their minds from the mission and allowed them to relax.

Jim and Allison's friendly relationship had expanded well beyond friendship to mutual professional respect and to fully enjoying their personal time together as well. They both tried to resist the pull towards a permanent relationship, but it seemed inevitable, as they continually found ways to expand their knowledge of each other on an intimate basis.

Carmelita and Lorenzo were following a similar path, and were feeling the enigmatic pull of personal relationships along with career path conflict. Both were wary of the implications of forming a long-lasting relationship in their business, but some how they just couldn't help themselves. They both felt that it would all work out in ways

Air

neither could understand.

Sam was sometimes the fifth wheel with the two couples, and at other times he was the commensurate player having the time of his life. He liked being footloose and free, and enjoyed bringing a different woman to various gatherings that they all had together. Hugh Hefner would have been proud.

The five of them were on the beach enjoying day 11 of their vacation when a waiter delivered a sealed document to each of them. The envelopes' flaps were each sealed with wax, and on the cover was the Homeland Security emblem.

The contents of each envelope was the same - a very simple document signed by the Director of Homeland Security, stating that they had been reassigned to that department from their various posts, and that they were to report to Langley at CIA headquarters in three days.

They had time to still relax a bit, as Langley was a relatively short flight by government Gulfstream from Atlantis. They thought they could relax for the next two days while they pondered this newest development.

Unlike their previous assignment, this time around they all knew that they were on the same team and that they were most likely working together. This led to some interesting discussions amongst the group.

What they didn't know was that plans can change with startling abruptness.

Chapter 24

J im woke up at 3:12 a.m. with a funny feeling. He was not sure what woke him, but something was not right. Without moving his head or his body, he looked right and left to see what he could. There was not any obvious presence he could see, but he knew either someone was in the room or had been there recently. He could feel the warmth of Allison next to him and could feel her steady breathing. What he did not know was that Allison was wide awake with the same feelings that Jim was having. Very subtly, she let him know that she was awake and on alert. Both of them had hand guns stashed close to the bed that could be in their hand with the safety off in a matter of seconds.

Very quietly, Allison moved her hand onto Jim's back, and with her fingers signaled a count to three. At the count of three they both rolled off the bed and grabbed their guns. Just as they hit the floor, they heard the balcony door being flung open and looked up just in time to see a dark figure leap out. They both ran for the balcony to see where the burglar may have gone since they were on the 10th floor. There was no sign of anyone, until they looked directly over the edge of the balcony and saw a black nylon rope streaming down to the ground. They could just make out a shadowy figure on the rope rappelling down to the ground level. By the time they could bring guns to bear on the figure, it was out of sight.

Air

It all happened so quickly and it was now deadly silent. It was almost as though they had imagined it all, but they both knew it had really happened because they could feel the aftereffects of the adrenaline.

The next morning, Jim and Allison told the other three what had happened. There was not any evidence that the other rooms had been penetrated. None of them knew whether or not to think this had anything to do with their new or previous assignments, or if it was a coincidental burglary attempt. The Bahamas are known for a sophisticated crime element that preys on the wealthy guests in the hotels. More than likely, though, this was a case of attempted intelligence infiltration. Jim also reported the incident to their facilitator at Langley. He took it much more seriously and ordered them to cut their vacation short. His directions were to rent, commandeer or steal an aircraft capable of getting the five of them up to Langley, and leave as soon as possible.

Within 30 minutes of the phone conversation with the facilitator, the five met in the hotel lobby and headed to the airport in a cab.

The nearest airport was Nassau, which was the airport that served Paradise Island. Even though there was concern that they were being followed and watched, and that there might be an assassin or team of assassins at the airport, expediency was of utmost importance. To avoid leaving a trace, they all agreed that their best bet for a quick clean departure was to steal an aircraft. The U.S. government would either return it, or compensate the owners if it was damaged or destroyed.

What they needed was a relatively quick turbo-prop or light jet that would get them off the Bahamas quickly and back into U.S. airspace.

The cabby dropped them off a few blocks short of the general aviation side of the airport. An approach on foot would be stealthier than pulling up to the curb in a taxi and piling out in front of the general aviation terminal.

They split up and approached the airport property on foot separately. Jim and Sam entered the airport grounds at different locations with the same goal - to find an aircraft up to their needs. Almost immediately, Sam spotted several aircraft that would meet their needs. A Cessna Citation X, a light jet capable of carrying up to eight people at 400 knots per hour, was the closest and appeared to be the easiest to acquire.

Sam stashed his duffle next to a building and put on his best aircraft maintenance man act. He ambled over to the Citation and began to poke around the engines as though he was doing a routine pre-flight inspection. He checked the fuel tanks, looked inside the engine cowlings, and took a quick look inside the aircraft. The cockpit was wide open, as was the cabin door. It was fully fueled and it was hooked up to a auxiliary power unit (APU), which was running the cabin air conditioning as well as providing power for start-up.

As he stepped out of the cabin door, he spotted Jim, Lorenzo, Allison and Carmelita. One by one, they spotted him and discreetly headed over to where he was. Making sure they were not spotted, one by one everyone but Jim boarded the aircraft. Jim stayed out on the tarmac until Sam could get the primary engine started so he could unhook the APU.

With the primary engine started, the aircraft could provide adequate power to start the second engine and run the necessary systems on the aircraft. With one engine started, Sam eased the aircraft toward the taxi way and began the start up process for the second engine. Jim jumped through the main door and pulled it closed behind him. Just as the door closed, he heard the second engine start, and Sam powered up enough to roll the jet at about 10 knots toward the taxiway.

A quick glance told Jim that the other three were in the cabin belted in for a quick take-off. He made his way into the cockpit and settled in the right seat. He quickly picked up the headset and tuned in the radio frequency for ground clearance to taxi to the active runway. Immediately, ground clearance cleared them to the active runway. Jim then radioed the air traffic control unit for that area of the world and asked for a clear flight plan to the East Coast of Florida. ATC asked his final destination, but before he could reply, he was on a frequency to ADIZ to advise of their clearance, status and a Langley contact to confirm their need for a direct flight plan to Virginia.

Aircraft theft is amazingly easy if you can get the aircraft unlocked and started, as Air Traffic personnel rarely know if an aircraft is stolen or being flown by its owner. In this case, however, the owner saw his jet rolling away from its parking spot under power and called the tower and the police to have the thieves stopped.

"Citation November niner three three two Lima please hold short at taxiway Bravo," was the call from the tower.

Both Jim and Sam looked for any other traffic to try and figure out why they had the hold short call. With no other traffic in sight, it was obvious that the authorities were en-route. Without a response back to ATC, they kept rolling past Bravo, headed for the active runway. At the end of the runway, with no traffic in sight and nothing on the radio, Sam turned onto the active runway and opened the throttles to the take-off setting. The Citation leaped forward and was up to rotation speed in no time.

At 120 knots, Sam eased back on the yoke and the jet floated off the runway and into a five degree nose up attitude like magic. He eased back a smidge more and they were climbing at 2,500 feet a minute. At 500 feet, Jim leaned over and pushed the gear up lever and the landing gear motors whined while they lifted the landing gear into their wells. The gear doors closed solidly behind the landing gear, and the jet felt like a racing machine without the gear hanging out in the slipstream. Sam lifted the take-off flaps and the jet leaped forward again. The Citation X is capable of mach .85 or over 500 mph, and he planned on using every ounce of speed he could.

The Bahamas island chain is less than 100 miles off the coast of Florida at the chain's southern most point. Rather than head straight west towards Florida, Sam turned northwest on a heading off the east coast towards Virginia. At 10,000 feet, he leveled off to a climb cruise attitude and watched the mach meter climb as they rocketed up through the broken to scattered layer. His intent was to level off at 25,000 feet.

Out of the corner of his eye, Jim noticed some movement. Pilots learn early to keep their eyes moving for traffic and to look for movement, so it was no surprise when he picked up the F-5 Talon slightly below and in trail of their path.

"Sam we're being shadowed by an F-5."

"What kind of markings?" Sam asked.

"Plain wrap," Jim replied.

The F-5 was sold in several versions around the world, from complex trainer to fighter. It was not difficult to acquire the aircraft in any form, complete with weapons systems in either a one-seat or two-seat version.

Without hesitation, Sam keyed the intercom system to the other three in the cabin and told everyone to buckle up. Then, without warning, he laid the Citation over in a 90 degree bank to the left and started a turning dive back through the cloud layer they had just come up through. Jim watched out the starboard windows to see if the F-5 followed. The F-5 is faster and more maneuverable, and if it was armed and had intentions to shoot them down, they would have little chance. It was clear that they were being followed. The F-5 matched their maneuver and stayed on them like glue.

Just as Sam started to make a move back into the clouds, ATC called. "Citation 32 Lima Coast control, how do you read?" Before Sam or Jim could reply, the ATC controller continued, "I have a patch communication for you from Langley."

Sam picked up the mic. "Go ahead."

"Citation 32 Lima, Langley control, how do you read?"

"5 X 5," Sam replied. "Go ahead."

"The plain wrap F-5 is your escort," the ATC controller said.

"How can we be sure?" Sam asked.

"Well, he can out accelerate you, out maneuver you and out climb you. He could have smoked you several minutes ago, and he didn't. Guess you will have to trust me."

Jim looked back out the window, and sure enough the F-5 was just hanging in that same spot without making any threatening moves. Then as if it was being coordinated, the F-5 pilot maneuvered up along side the Citation and the pilot looked over and gave them the thumbs up and a big toothy grin. Then, just as smoothly as he had move up along side, he dropped back in to the wingman's slot. Obviously this was a pro handling the highly maneuverable fighter.

The balance of the flight to Langley went without incident. The F-5 flew the wingman's position all the way through the approach and touch down for the Citation. The F-5 pilot then did a climbing overhead break, turned downwind and flew an abbreviated pattern to final. He touched down with the grace of a dancer and taxied to the ramp where the Citation was parked. The engine spooled down as the pilot climbed down out of the cockpit.

He pulled off his helmet as he walked over towards the Citation. "Major MacDougal," he said as he stuck his hand out to Jim and Sam. "Everybody calls me Mac."

"So," Sam said, "great bit of flying. I'm guessing you've flown some combat flying at some point in your career?"

"Well yes, and also with the Thunderbirds," Mac replied. "Performance formation flying is what I do, but I have combat experience in Bosnia and in Iraq."
"Well, thanks for not locking up on us with your guns," Sam said as he chuckled.

"My pleasure," Mac replied. "By the way, I am joining your little team."

Chapter 25

The team, now made up of Jim, Sam, Lorenzo, Carmelita, Allison, and Mac, assembled in the same hangar where they originally met for their initial briefing.

This time, however, the briefing was led by the Director of Homeland Security.

"Ladies and gentlemen, as I think most of you know, I am Tom Phillips, Director of Homeland Security. First, let me congratulate you on an outstanding job completing a very difficult mission and uncovering evidence that represents the greatest threat to the American way of life today. The country that acquires the technology you have discovered and puts it to use will have control over natural resources that can change the world we live in. In short, significant controls over the temperature of the earth will be in the control of the country with this technology.

"Now, all of you have the highest security clearance this nation can allow. The briefing you will receive today will not be declassified in our lifetime. Any breaking of the clearance will result in trial by military tribunal and if convicted will carry a death sentence. It will be a direct violation of the Patriot Act. Having said that and having heard it, you will be asked to sign a document that states the exact same information I have just told you. For now, though, let's retire to a secure briefing room. Any questions?"

There were no replies, but before anyone could move,

the floor under them began to move vertically downward like an elevator platform - in fact, it was an aircraft carrier elevator platform that descended into a hidden underground hangar. The joint around the platform was absolutely invisible, so it was quite a surprise to all that were on the platform when it began to move under them. The platform descended 50 feet before it came to a silent, smooth stop.

Jim looked above as they descended, only in time to see a section of floor slide into place above them that sealed the hangar floor behind them. Once in the underground hangar/bunker, the group was in a bomb- and surveillance-proof chamber that was used for highly secret projects. The underground chamber was large enough to hold as many as a dozen C-130 Hercules aircraft. In the event that the President had to be evacuated, along with staff and equipment, this underground hangar would be used to stage the equipment and supplies needed to support his needs that were not otherwise provided for on Air Force One or in other secret locations.

Today, though, it was being used to assemble a team and put together a plan that would keep the United States in their leadership position.

Joining the Director of Homeland Security for the briefing were representatives from NASA, CIA, FBI, and the Joint Chiefs of Staff. Tom Phillips introduced the team to the various resource managers from the various departments in the room. Each component was brought in on the project in a support role to the team assembled.

"You may wonder why we are continuing to use all of you instead of one of our military or intel teams already assembled. Simple answer. By continuing to use you we have even less exposure to security leaks, and your team has demonstrated abilities that align with our needs to take this mission to the next level. Will you need support? Yes, which is why we have these resources in the room. I want to start by briefing you on the capabilities of the technology we are going to recover with this mission."

With a motion of his hand, one of the NASA people came to the front of the room and turned on a projector. As he began speaking, the slides on the PowerPoint presentation began advancing.

"This first slide shows us the technology in action. What you see here is a light-blocking laser prism generated array - essentially these individual laser arrays are bounced through prisms to create interlocking fingers of light that creates a parabolic hologram that reflects sunlight. The laser generators are held in a geo-synchronomous orbit in a specific distance and pattern to create a light-reflecting parabola needed to meet the specific need. This parabola can take on a variety of shapes and sizes, creating a shade shadow that blocks all or a portion of the sun. So this parabola can block out the sun to the point it is almost night-like or just to the point where there is still light, but the intensity of it is significantly reduced. This next slide illustrates how the array is put into orbit."

The image indicated a rocket launched with a payload bay in the nose cone. The nose cone opened the bay, and dozens of soccer ball-sized orbs floated into orbit, and with tiny thrusters propelled themselves into a pre-programmed orbital pattern. The orbs were fully self contained, providing their own power from batteries that were continuously recharged by solar arrays.

"With the laser generators and the continuous recharging, the arrays can stay on station for months if not years, with their array fully functioning. Let's consider what might happen if the array was stationed over the Sahara Desert for a year."

The slides graphically illustrated interlocking circles

of green spreading out from known water sources in the desert. Over the course of the year, nearly half of the desert had turned green with new growth.

"Let's consider cooling the equator right before hurricane season. In essence, we are slowing the evaporative process by keeping the equatorial zone 10 degrees cooler. By cooling it this much, we have lessened the intensity of the tropical storms that typically turn into destructive hurricanes. Storm activity will still occur, but not with the same ferocity that we see today. These are both positive uses of this technology, but let's consider other uses. For example let's position it over the polar ice cap in the north-pole and reduce the temperature by that same 10 degrees."

Graphically the ice cap on the slide moved progressively south until it had completely covered Canada and was beginning to cover the upper part of the United States.

"The parabola can also be turned upside down and bounce magnified sun rays into a zone. For example, let's bounce the magnified rays into the Great Lakes area."

The illustration showed the water receding from the Great Lakes until they were no longer connected and the water continuing to recede.

"In short, this can be an extremely productive or destructive tool depending on how it is used. One last quick illustration. If we focus the magnified rays into an area of known low pressure where moisture is present, we can actually make it rain by heating up the area of moisture and low barometric pressure. Think what this means to drought areas - we can literally erase the effects of drought and keep human kind warmer or cooler, or wetter or drier, depending on the needs of the area. The arrays can be moved around the globe in a matter of hours with impact as needed almost immediate. In short, we must have this technology and we need it now before it falls into the hands of someone who will misuse it for their personal gain. Any questions?"

A stunned silence followed. The presentation was extremely effective in underscoring the need to recover the technology. Allison raised her hand and was called on to voice her question. "Has the technology been developed beyond the prototype stage- do we know for sure it works?" she queried.

"Very good question," Tom Phillips replied. "What we do know is that on a smaller scale it works and that it is scalable to the size we have described in the presentation. What we also know is the array can be deployed as illustrated with current technology and we are very sure of the effects that were modeled here today. So, again, you can see why we must gain control of these systems."

With another motion of his hand the next briefer, a young lady who had been introduced from the CIA, came to the front of the room. She was conservatively dressed in slacks and business jacket. Despite the conservative dress, two things were apparent. She was in top condition, which was obvious just by the way she moved, and she was very attractive, with dark auburn hair cut in a no-nonsense short style, large brown eyes, high cheek bones and the statuesque body of a model.

The projector came back to life as she began her intelligence briefing.

"Since your raid, the site in Barbados has been abandoned. We are fairly sure that they know something occurred, but they are not sure what, but to be on the safe side, they have moved their operations. This organization has very deep pockets and have created new quarters that are state of the art when it comes to developmental technology as well as security. We also know that the brilliant mind behind this is an engineering professor from MIT who innocently developed the prototype, but has since decided that his current employers have less than scrupulous motives and would like to legitimize the development of the

technology and be assured it is not misused. However, he
and his family are being held hostage in quarters on the site
where he is doing the developmental work. The professor's
name is David Holmsby, and he is the brother of Stewart
Holmsby, who is, as you know, the Secretary of the Interior.
We are very confident Stewart is connected to the organization that is behind the development of the technology
and is probably the money manager for them. We are also
very sure that much of the billions in funding thus far have
come from the organization working with South and Central American drug cartels to import and distribute cocaine,
marijuana, and meth. We believe the organization now has
enough funding to complete development and deployment.
Our currency tracking resources developed since 9/11
have been tracing money from all over the world and have
uncovered a pattern that would support funding flowing
into a few common organizations. Those organizations are
various types of companies, associations and not-for-profits
that have one thing in common - none of them exist beyond
accounts filled with money, no employees, no products, no
services. The one thing they do have in common is that
money flows between all of them and regular expenditures
coming from the accounts have two commas in them.

"We believe the primary organization, which is ru-
mored to be known by it's members as the Founders, is a
group of American industrialists and wealthy families that
operate media empires, manufacturing, construction companies, chemical companies, and even some that hold very
high positions in our countries government. This organization has been in existence for many centuries and has been
responsible for some of the countries highest achievements.
It is not our intent to bring down this organization, in fact
we don't believe we could bring it down without severely
hurting important economical and political resources within
the U.S.

"This group is usually very low key and very effective at working behind the scenes to support the efforts of important American strategies. We do not know why they apparently have changed their ways and are involved in this in the manner in which we think they are today. We believe that a smaller group within the larger organization is operating independently of the knowledge of the larger group. We are pretty sure that once key members of the larger organization understand what is going on, they will help us separate the few renegades from the rest of the group and support our effort to pull this technology into legitimate U.S. hands for development and use.

"In the meantime, we have to gain control of the plans, materials, programs, prototypes and human resources. While your team is working on the acquisition of the technology, other resources will be working on determining who is who within this organization and separating the well-intentioned from the splinter group. I will be your liaison to CIA resources to help you do your job and to keep you briefed on our part of this. By the way, my name is Sara Steele, and I will be participating at a team level with you as the mission is executed." On that final note, Sara sat down as the FBI agent took front stage.

The FBI agent charged with the briefing responsibilities was in his early 50s, judging by the lines in his face and his graying temples. Despite his age, he appeared to be in great shape and capable of physical activity equal to someone much younger.

"Ian Smithson, Special Projects," he said by way of introduction. "Fortunately, we have successfully tracked the developmental site and it's located within the U.S. The bad news is that they are located in a part of the West that is wide open desert that cannot be approached without being detected visually or on most forms of radar."

At that point, an image of an aerial photograph appeared on the screen. The image was an enhanced satellite photo that showed roads and activity in the desert but no buildings or vehicles. The convergence of the roads and activities came to a common spot and ended.

The next image was the same area photographed with thermal sensitive film. A huge rectangular area stood out in the film that apparently was subterranean.

"We are at least 80 percent sure this is the new site of the developmental laboratories for this group," he continued. "We also believe that this is the site from which they plan on launching a rocket or rockets into orbit to deploy the array of laser generators. As you can see in this photograph, there is an area approximately two miles from the main facility that appears to be an underground launch silo. We are sure that it contains a fully fueled and launch-capable missile that can attain orbital altitudes. The launch vehicle will simply burn up on re-entry, leaving no trace after it has deployed its payload. This type of launch vehicle can easily be purchased and smuggled into the U.S., particularly with resources like we are dealing with. These missiles do not have any warheads on them and can be disguised as other items, drain pipes transported on flatbed truck trailers is the most likely way to cloak the components - very simple but very effective. Ah yes, a question?"

Smithson nodded towards Sam. "What led you to this remote location? Wherever it is, must be very hard to find."

"Good question and good point...We started from the premise that it would be located on land owned by some part of the organization. Secondly, we determined that it had to be reasonably close to power and water sources already in place so they could quickly and easily tap into those resources. Using that criteria, we created a short list of likely sites. This was the only one with development activity."

"Another question," again Smithson nodded towards

Sam. "So, where exactly is this site?"

Before Smithson could reply, Jim said, "That site is about 20 miles north of Bagdad, Arizona, where the Bagdad open pit mine is. Those two mountains in the background of the low level photo are Mohon Peak on the left at 7,499 feet and the one on the right is Mt. Hope at 7,263 feet. The flat mesa and valley area to the south of these two peaks is perfect for a hidden facility. There is nothing in this area but wild burros and other desert animals. I know this terrain like my own backyard."

"Thank you, Mr. Mitchell, you are, of course, exactly correct, which is no surprise considering the number of hours you have logged flying through this area. Which is one of the very strong assets you bring to the mission."

The rest of the group had turned and stared at Jim with amazed looks on their faces. Sam was chuckling to himself and shaking his head.

Smithson continued, "With the mine close by, the few residents and ranchers of the area are used to seeing excavation equipment and trucks in and out of the area, so as this facility was built nothing out of the ordinary was noticed. Also, the water and power sources are there to tap into. If there are no other questions or comments, I will turn the next stage of the briefing over to Major MacDougall."

Major MacDougall opened his briefing with a photo display of the area from an elevated perspective probably taken atop one of the area mountains.

"This area is as primitive and unforgiving an area as you will find anywhere in the world. At any point within the sphere of this operation, you will be at least 30 to 40 miles from any kind of civilization. No water, no shelter, no medical facilities, no food sources other than wild game, and temperatures during the day over one hundred degrees and nighttime temperatures in the 40s. An unprepared person can die from exposure in this area within one to three days."

While he spoke, the slides displayed terrain that was rock strewn dry washes, cactus, hills covered with thorny brush. "Rattle snakes, coyotes, mountain lions, bobcats, lizards, wild burros, deer, antelope, black bears and jave-lina's all inhabit the area and are plentiful. Of course we have to include scorpions, and spiders in our list, as they can make you very very ill if you happen to be bitten or stung by any of them. This mission will be no picnic from a survival viewpoint. Fortunately, all of you have had training for this type of environment.

"We have developed a multi-part plan that will be-gin with a recon mission. You will fly into a remote strip about five miles from the area and hike from there to a site where you can familiarize yourselves with the terrain and the activity. You will carry in some of the supplies you will leave there for the next phase, which will be the secure and rescue phase. You will obtain and make secure the technol-ogy, as well as rescue Dr. Holmsby and his family. Our goal here is to finish this technology and develop it into a useful tool. So we want to make sure we secure the exist-ing technology and Dr. Holmsby intact, and without harm or injury.

"To get the personnel out of the facilities and acces-sible to us so we can rescue them, we are going to stage a wildfire in the area. As the personnel come out of the facil-ity to escape the dangers of being trapped by the wildfire, we will guide them aboard our vehicles and aircraft and simply separate Dr. Holmsby and his family from the rest of the crowd and fly them to safe haven.

"At the same time, your team will advance on the fa-cility and secure the prototypes, computers, and all parts of the technology. Your team will be divided into two parts. Team A will go into the facility and bring out the technology. Team B will bring in two aircraft to airlift the team and the technology to safety."

At that moment, Jim and Sam both raised their hands.

"Go ahead, Jim," Major MacDougall said.

"Since there is not an airstrip within five miles, what kind of aircraft can we get in there to accommodate these kinds of loads?"

"Good question Jim. As part of the equipment contingent onsite to fight the wildfire, which will be more smoke than anything, we will have two D-9 Cats grading out an airstrip next to the facility. Our D-9s can carve out a pretty good strip in a couple of hours that will allow our C-130 and Cessna Caravan to get in and out without a problem. You can see this area just south of where the underground facility is; this area is about three miles long and plenty wide enough to be bladed out into a useable strip, we just have to clear the brush which is not very heavy. We will tell the evacuating personnel that we are simply building a fire break to contain the fire. To make the fire as real as possible, we will have an area about a mile away set up with chemicals to make a lot of smoke, so it looks like the fire is going to hit the facility area at any time. Our rescue C-130 and Cessna Caravan will be fire bombing and forward spotting, or at least appearing to do so. I will be flying the C-130, and Jim and Sam, you will be flying the Caravan. Carmelita and Allison, you will be responsible for finding Dr. Holmsby and his family and getting them onto the correct transport. Lorenzo, you will lead a contingent of Marines into the facility and secure the technology. If there are not vehicles available at the facility that we can use at the time, I will have a 6 X 6 truck on the C-130 that I will drop off at the newly-built airstrip, which you can use to transport all of the equipment up to the aircraft. That is the essence of the plan. Any questions or concerns?"

Jim stood up and walked to the perimeter of the group

and then turned and faced everyone. "The only concern I have is that we are able to carry this off without any serious problems, because we don't really have any backup people or resources. I understand how important this is, and my only concern is that we think about unknown problems and make sure we have a backup plan for the serious ones."

"Good point, Jim," Mac replied. "And to that point, there is a team of Marines being trained as we speak on the whole plan. They have no idea where they might have to execute their plan and the exercises they are going through, and they don't understand the technology we are after or any of the details, but if something happens to any role in team A or B, we can replace them in a matter of minutes. This team will be standing by in the C-130 if we need them. We also have equipment and plans if the weather becomes an issue, or if there are other contingencies. While it seems you are going in alone, you really aren't, so don't hesitate to let us know if you need help. We want to keep the team as small as possible, but we can fill in gaps if we need to do so."

Jim sat back down, stating, "Good, that makes me feel better!"

Mac continued, "Good. We are scheduled for Phase 1 of the recon mission tomorrow. Both Team A and B will recon the area together and we will stage a reporting area at the Kingman airport for a debrief the following Saturday. During the recon, I am in command. We all leave for Arizona in two hours on a government Gulfstream. We will land in Prescott and pick up the Cessna Caravan there for our short hop into the Bagdad area the next morning."

Chapter 26

The trip from Langley to Prescott was another uneventful trip by government transport. As they
landed, Jim could see a Cessna Caravan with a belly
pod and a C-130 with U.S. Forest Service markings for
a fire bomber sitting at one of the field. He correctly surmised that those were the mission aircraft. He was looking
forward to flying the Caravan, which is well known for its
sturdiness and ability to get big loads in and out of rugged
short strips with ease. It's powered by a 675 HP turbo prop
that will lift itself and an additional 4,000 lbs of people,
fuel and gear out of the wilderness and carry them at nearly
200 mph at 25,000 feet- truly a remarkable aircraft for this
type of assignment.

They taxied over to the hanger next to where the
C-130 and the Caravan were parked and quickly disem-
barked from their government transport. It fueled and was
gone back to D.C. within a matter of minutes.

In the hanger, they found stacks of gear for their mission. The Caravan was configured for two at flight crew
stations in the cockpit, four passengers with a massive
cargo area behind the seats, and the cargo belly pod available for their gear. Their gear included desert camouflage
clothing, desert boots, slouch hats, hunting knives, portable
GPS units, walkie-talkies with head sets, packs of rations
and water, two Yamaha motorcycles set up like motocross
bikes, and two camouflage tents. They also had first aid

and medical supplies, sleeping bags, ground pads, and all of the essentials for survival in the inhospitable terrain.

Although they did not have plans to use them, they also were equipped with Glock 9 MM automatics with extra clips and the web gear to carry them.

The Yamahas were already loaded in and strapped in place. The rest of the gear was stacked for inventory and ready to be loaded after it was checked. Jim had the Caravan pulled into the hanger for loading, and the group quickly had the gear checked and stowed into the belly pod and the cargo area behind the seats. Even with all of the gear and supplies, they were well within the loading limits of the Caravan. With the aircraft loaded and locked, they jumped in a forest service SUV and headed to town for the night. They would leave for their wilderness recon mission at first light the next morning. The Caravan was parked in the hangar, with the hangar locked and the alarm set for the night.

Prescott, Arizona, is one of the last remaining Old West towns, with the original old downtown still functioning pretty much as it did in the 1800s. The streets are paved and the wooden boardwalks are gone, but the same cafés and saloons are still there, dispensing old west grub and cold beer like they did 150 years ago.

They parked in front of the Palace Saloon on the original "Whisky Row" on Montezuma Street in downtown and walked in for dinner. The Palace still has the old wooded swinging doors, the 30s oak bar, and wooden tables and chairs for dining and card playing. Working cowboys from the surrounding ranches still come in on the weekends to "kick up their heels" a bit. Most of them are just good ole boys having some fun, but in every group there is always a bad apple or two.

Air

To protect their mission cover, they all had changed into U.S. Forest Service uniforms that the rangers and fire fighters wore. Any kind of government official, even a ranger, was not the most welcome kind of person in many parts of the Old West. Most of the ranchers viewed them with suspicion and did not really welcome their presence.

So, despite the fact that the uniforms were a good cover they might also create some sparks. The group of six clomped across the old wooden floor to a table along the wall and sat down. A small western band was tuning up in the corner, and the bar was full of cowboy hat and boot wearing men and women, with plenty of "hooten and hollerin" going on. Most of the people at the bar had obviously already had a couple of beers - after all, it was Friday evening and what else was there to do in Prescott?

The waitress brought menus and took the table's drink order - cold beers all around. The waitress was a local girl dressed in a short tight skirt, cowboy boots, a tight western shirt with the buttons almost popping open revealing cleavage, and, of course, the requisite cowboy hat and Colt six shooter slung low on her hip. She was very attractive, well built, and knew it by the way she walked and flirted with the local cowboys. She seemed to gravitate to Sam and Mac, and made a point of flashing a big smile and a couple of winks their way. Without hesitation, Mac and Sam returned the attention. It was pretty obvious that one of the cowboys at the bar did not like what was going on, as he kept turning around and glaring at Mac and Sam.

Everyone ordered a round of big steaks with onion rings, baked potatoes and beans. The dinners came with fresh-baked biscuits, and it was one of the best meals any of them had for quite a while.

After they all polished off dinner and a more beers, they all decided on coffee and apple pie, since they wouldn't see civilized food for a few days. By now, the cowboy at the bar was well into his fifth or sixth beer and was getting louder and making more and more comments about the forest service group.

Everyone finished off their pie and coffee and headed for the cashier to pay for dinner. They had to walk by the bar on the way out, and the as they approached, the loud cowboy turned and blocked their way.

"Well, well now, just who do we have here?" he blustered. "Looks like a group of monkeys headed back to their trees!"

"Look buddy," said Mac, "we don't want any trouble, just let us pass and everything will be cool."

"Nothing the Forest Service does is cool. You guys are nothing but trouble for us ranchers! You want to walk out that door in one piece, you are going to have to walk over me first!"

A couple of the cowboy's buddies were trying to pull him back to the bar, but he shrugged out of their efforts without much trouble. He was a good sized, younger athletic looking cowboy stading approximately 6' 2" and clocking in at well over 210 pounds, none of which looked like extra weight. Since he was facing three men his size, it was obvious the beer was doing the talking.

Mac stepped up and confronted the cowboy nose to nose. "Listen, you half witted shit kicker, either you back off, or I'm going to open the front door with your nose." Mac said it to him with a snarl in his voice, and for a second or two it looked like the cowboy was wisely going to give way.

One of his pals at the bar said, "You better listen to him Bob, I think he can do it!"

Everyone at the bar started laughing, which was all Bob had to hear to make him lose his temper.

"Oh yeah! We'll see about that!" he slurred.

All of a sudden, in more of a lurch than a swing, Bob

took a big roundhouse swing at Mac. Mac saw it coming in time and simply sidestepped him, came up behind the cowboy and grabbed his belt and collar, and started running him towards the front door. Just like Mac said, he opened the front door with the cowboy's nose, as it splattered on the door and flung it open. As the cowboy's nose hit the door, Mac let him go, and he stumbled out onto the sidewalk. Mac followed him out the door to see if there was any fight left in him.

By now, the crowd at the bar had moved to the door and front windows to watch, and a crowd had gathered on the sidewalk. The cowboy staggered to his feet, raised his hands in surrender and seemed to suddenly get control of himself. He apologized and grimaced as he rubbed his nose. He stuck out his hand as he apologized, and Mac quickly reached out and shook it and chuckled, "You OK, Bob?"

"Shit, man, you didn't have to make it look that realistic, I think you broke my nose!" Bob whispered as they both pretended to shrug it off like it was just a big broo-ha-ha over nothing.

The crowd, not finding any further entertainment value in the skirmish, broke up and moved on down the sidewalk or back to the bar.

By now the rest of the team had worked their way out to the sidewalk.

Jim and Sam walked up to Mac and said, "What's going on here?"

"Let's walk," Mac said, "by the way, did anyone pay for dinner?"

"Got it," Sam replied.

"Let me buy you a cup of coffee, cowboy!" Mac said this loud enough for everyone in the vicinity to hear. He slapped Bob on he back, and they all ambled down the sidewalk.

To most of the bystanders, the whole fray looked like a drunk cowboy biting off more than he could chew, which happened all the time in Prescott on Friday and Saturday nights.

After they had moved half a block away, Mac announced, "Everyone, this is Robert Pinkerton. Bob this is Jim, Sam, Allison, Lorenzo, and Carmelita. Bob is part of the famous Pinkerton family that founded both the Secret Service and the Pinkerton Detective Agency. He is our liaison here in the local area, has retained his top secret clearance from his military days and is still a reserve officer in the Marine Corp. He will be our contact for any local issues, and we will be staging some of our plans from his property. In fact the chemical burn that will create all of the wildfire smoke is on his land. Bob is also a helicopter pilot and has a couple of little speedsters on his ranch he normally uses for cattle counting and herding. He has volunteered to let us use them, as well as offered to fly one of them himself if we need it. Jim, when you asked about having backup you were right, and Bob is part of our backup, along with the extra Marine team. We've got quarters set up at the airport, and I would suggest we head back and turn in for the night. Robert, we happily accept your invitation for breakfast in the morning. Bob has an airstrip on his ranch and it is on the way to our wilderness strip. I've got the longitude and latitude coordinates for the GPS to the ranch. We'll be there by 09:00 at the latest. On that note, we will see you in the morning."

They dispersed and headed to the airport for the night.

"Why the unplanned stop to his ranch?" Sam asked.

"Bob knows this area so well that he has agreed to do a briefing on the terrain for us. He knows game trails, springs, old mines and other things about the terrain that could be invaluable for us. He also has a fairly complete first aid station at the ranch if we need it. And by the way,

Air

it was not unplanned; we just didn't mention it in the first briefing."

Chapter 27

The overnight stay in the hangar at Prescott airport was as comfortable as sleeping on a cot could be. Everyone got a quick cup of coffee at the local airport café and quickly loaded up for the hop to Bob's ranch for their breakfast briefing.

Jim and Sam had the coordinates to the ranch airstrip, and following a quick clearance, they were wheels up and on their way with all of their cargo and the whole crew aboard the Caravan. "Tally ho!" Sam called over the intercom. "Pinkerton Ranch ahead."

They had only been in the air for about 20 minutes, but with a 200 mph cruise speed the big Caravan ate up the miles quickly. "Quite a ranch," Jim noted.

Along with a massive log lodge, the ranch comprised a 4,000-foot paved and lit runway, a 10,000—square-foot hangar, a large horse barn, an enclosed riding area, numerous corrals, and two other outdoor riding arenas that were set up for grand prix and hunter jumper training. There were also various outbuildings, including what looked like a dormitory that turned out to be a well-equipped bunk house for the onsite help.

The Caravan is designed for handling big loads and still able to make stable approaches and smooth landings. It may be a backwoods airplane, but it is a very forgiving flyer that makes every pilot feel like a pro. Jim taxied up to the hangar and shut down the Pratt and Whitney turbine.

Air

Bob met them on the tarmac."Good morning, welcome to the Pegasus Ranch!" he said as everyone deplaned. "Breakfast is ready in the house, right this way. The Pegasus is a horse ranch built to raise and train horses of all kinds for all kinds of riding and use, from rodeo, to English hunter jumpers, to working cowboy cutting horses - you name it, we raise and train them. We have accommodations for over 300 horses in our barns, and several hundred others in paddocks and corrals. We have a little over 50,000 acres of fenced grazing lands that are also prime hunting lands for deer, antelope, javelina, black bear, mountain lion and quite a variety of birds, including wild turkey."

The Pegasus Ranch was clearly a very successful operation, judging by the quality of the buildings and the almost sterile cleanliness of the stalls and barns. The grounds were immaculately manicured, and everything was extremely well organized.

The group walked up a wide path to the main porch and massive double doors. Mouth-watering smells of breakfast drifted from the front door as they entered. Bob led them to the dining room, where the table was set and several easel boards with maps were ready for the briefing.

Bob's briefing was thorough and gave the team a much higher chance of success. He knew the terrain so well that he was able to mark game trails, unknown springs and streams, caves, and even large hollow trees that could be used for evasion. He was able to mark high points that would give the team a clear but hidden view of their quarry. All of this data was loaded into their individual handheld GPS units. In short, his briefing was invaluable to the success of the team.

Bob also posed the question that no one had thought of. "What are you going to do if the group in the building decide to not come up and be evacuated?"

After he asked the question, there was dead silence. It seemed like such a simple issue, everyone wondered how they had overlooked it.

When no one really had an answer to his question, Bob said humbly, "May I make a suggestion?"

"Absolutely!" was the unanimous reply.

"First of all," he began, "I believe you will have this problem, as I believe this group has already planned for this scenario. So I think there is a very real chance that at least part of the group will remain below ground in the facility. I would suggest you plan for this and be prepared. I watched the facility being built from a distance, and I can tell you they have air filters and scrubbers as part of their systems, as well as an unending supply of water and a very large supply of food. I believe they could stay below ground for months. The one thing I don't believe they have is any kind of water filtration system beyond a very basic system. Their water purification system can clean up particulates, kill bacteria, and remove the basic heavy metals from the water. However, they do not have micro-screening that will allow them to filter out toxins. They undoubtedly have an alert system in the event the water becomes contaminated, but I don't believe they have the tertiary system requirements to filter out the toxins. Their water supply is a spring about half a mile from their underground building, and it is susceptible to contamination. We can introduce a chemical that will mirror the properties of a deadly toxin without actually causing any harm. That chemical will set off their alert system, and combined with the fire alert and evacuation order, should dislodge the whole group from their subterranean quarters."

"How do we explain the presence of the toxins without causing suspicion on their part?" Jim asked.

"Good question. There is a natural gas pipeline fairly

close to the spring, and there are anti-corrosive anodes buried in the ground that protect the pipeline near the spring. Those anodes, when heated, will produce such a toxin. So we simply say that the fire has heated the anodes to the melting temperature and the toxins are running into the water supply."

Senator Jacobsen walked into Under Secretary Holmsby's office and sat down in the comfortable leather chair across from his desk. "So, how is our little project progressing in Arizona?" the Senator asked.

"We believe we will have full deployment in the next 30 days. We need one good moonless night that will allow a launch, and we will begin to place the laser generators in orbit. Once they are in place, all of the controls are in the Arizona facility to activate the shield, as well as move the shield into new orbital coordinates. The launch team actually has a date scheduled for the launch that is completely moonless and the weather is usually pretty mild this time of year, so we should be able to move into the next phase without any problems. I am actually going to be there for the launch."

"I would as well," replied the Senator, "but my travels are watched too closely, and I can't be associated directly with the project at this point."

"When are you going to give your next report to the committee?" Holmsby asked.

"Our next planned meeting is in two weeks," Jacobsen replied.

The Senator was on the budget committee, the technology sector committee, and the current projects committee. Because of his position in Washington, he was highly placed in committee leadership.

The committee was one of many overlapping committees within the Founders. The only members who were known to each other were the ones on their respective committees. Each member was assigned to three committees that had different responsibilities, so that each committee overlapped with two other committees. The communication to the whole group was done through the committees and their overlapping members. Not exactly an efficient method of communication, but it kept the overall membership of the whole global group a secret. No one member could list all of the members, no one member could prove the existence of the whole group, and it gave the members pretty good anonymity.

The downside of this type of structure is that if your committees disavowed you, the whole group would fade into the background and you would be left twisting in the wind without any support from the overall group. Given the good Senator's family had been involved in the group since revolutionary days, it was unlikely he would be disavowed.

With the shield in place, the whole group could strengthen and expand their influence on world development. By creating agricultural opportunities where previously there were none, and by controlling catastrophic weather issues, they would be able to protect their interests worldwide.

The team began their recon expedition in an area to the northwest of the underground facility. They began by following Burro Creek up from where it flowed into the Big Sandy River towards the facility. They set up their base camp at the confluence of the two small waterways, which was only about three miles from the facility, or Target X as it was referred to in the plans.

For three days, they watched helicopter traffic in

and out of the facility, hiked game trails, staked out water supplies, planned primary and secondary escape routes, and developed an understanding for the terrain that helped prepare them for most contingencies.

The one discovery during the recon that was a bit disconcerting was that the group of armed guards at the facility seemed to be a crack unit. They were mercenaries hired to protect the facility and the people in it, and they seemed to be very capable. They were disciplined, carried automatic weapons, and maintained a military decorum that rivaled any of the U.S. military elite groups. Guards were posted regularly, and they were alert and conscientious about their patrols.

After three days, the team felt confident in their mission, understood the risks, and put together a good plan to extricate the technology and key people. In three days, they would execute their plan, nicknamed Light Shield. The plan was simple - create a false wildfire and false contamination of the water supply for the facility. The combined effect of these two issues should cause the facility management to evacuate the underground buildings temporarily. During the evacuation, the team would separate the professor and his family from the rest of the group and whisk them away to safety. In the meantime, the balance of the team would infiltrate the facility and take it over, along with all of the equipment and technology that had been developed.

Jim and Sam were charged with bringing in the Caravan on cue to fly the family to safety. Mac and a contingent of Army Rangers would take and hold the facility once it had been evacuated. Lorenzo, Allison and Carmelita would be responsible for separating the professor and his family from the rest of the evacuees and getting them aboard the Caravan. From there, they would all fly to where the C-130 was waiting to take them to Washington D.C.

It was a relatively simple plan and quite straight forward. None of the group could have any idea how far from simple it would all become before it was over.

Chapter 28

The sun rose over the Arizona desert on a bright Saturday morning. Diamonds of dew drops sparkled on the desert vegetation in the sunlight. Desert animals grazed early before the heat of the day became unbearable. Most desert animals survived and proliferated only because they had evolved with the ability to avoid the daily heat when it was at its worst.

On schedule, just four miles from the target facility, 20 55-gallon drums filled with a petroleum-based but non-toxic chemical were set afire. The burning drums put out a whitish smoke that mimicked the characteristics of a desert fire. The barrels were set apart by about 100 yards each, to make the size of the smoke field large enough to look like hundreds of acres were burning.

As the barrels burned, Sam and Jim took off in the Caravan and climbed to 7,000 feet to oversee the progress of the operation, as well as to be poised for landing at the makeshift strip near the facility.

Once they received the signal from Lorenzo, Allison, and Carmelita they would land quickly to pick up the three team members, as well as the professor and his family. Mac and the Ranger team were in full camo gear within a quarter mile of the facility, ready to move in as soon as the evacuation began. Under their camo gear, they wore uniforms that matched the facility security detail uniform. With all of the confusion, they planned to move in and take control of the facility.

Inside the underground facility, the security systems were flashing red lights, buzzing and setting off alarms throughout all parts of the buildings. The staff in the security center was monitoring the growing plume of smoke billowing to the north on close circuit television, and the water supply alarm was flashing red lights.

The head of security and head of the facility were immediately on the phone to their Washington contact.

By now, personnel throughout the facility were beginning to panic and calling into the security center asking about evacuation.

While the facility management team sought advise and counsel from their bosses 3,000 miles away, the professor and his family and a number of other staff had ideas of their own. All were very worried about being trapped in an underground oven with toxic fumes pouring in through the ventilation system and a polluted water supply. Death under those conditions would be slow and painful.

Mac and his team were scanning the facility entrance area with binoculars, preparing to move closer when pandemonium broke out. The facility door swung open and people streamed out the door at a full tilt run. The professor and his family were easily identified as they held hands and started running for the nearest ravine. The sage brush in the ravines made good cover, and when they dropped into the ravine it was like they had disappeared.

Fortunately, Mac and his team, and Jim and Sam from the Caravan orbiting above all, witnessed the hasty evacuation and could see where the professor and his family had disappeared to. Mac got radio to Carmelita and Allison as to their whereabouts, and Jim and Sam gave them updates as to where they were headed as the family headed down the ravine away from the facility. Clearly they were trying to escape altogether and not just get away from the fire.

Allison and Carmelita circled around from their position and approached the family from the uphill flank of their path. Their intent was to intercept the family before they got too far away and escort them quickly to the waiting Caravan. But the best laid plans always have a way of changing.

The facility security team turned out to be a little more heads up than anyone had planned. Very quickly, the security team had spread out and was using infrared detectors to find the fleeing family. The security team was quick to get inbetween the family and the intended pick up spot, so plans had to be scrubbed almost immediately.

Allison and Carmelita heard the professor and his family before they saw them. They stealthily moved towards the voices and the crashing brush and intercepted them about a quarter mile away from the facility entrance.

Jim and Sam were tracking their progress and were constantly updating Allison and Carmelita as to their position changes. As a result, they were able to get in front of the family and wait for them as they rounded a bend in the ravine.

As the family came around a big sweeping turn in the channel, they were very surprised to see two lovely young ladies in camo gear waiting for them. Both Allison and Carmelita were standing in the middle of the ravine with their hands up, indicating that they were no threat to the family and that they were there to help. Quickly, they explained who they were and pointed to the circling Caravan and explained what the plan was and how it had now changed with the pursuing security detail.

"What we have to do is find a secondary landing site that we can meet the Caravan at, and work our way to it and evade the security detail," Allison explained.

"Our two partners in the sky are looking for a landing site right now and will radio us when they find one. In the meantime, we need to keep you moving. We have water for you and food and we can sustain a pursuit for several days. We have supplies cached all around the area, and our first objective after evading the security team is to work our way to the closest cache and get everyone re-supplied," Carmelita explained. "We will get you out of here."

The professor and his family were visibly relieved as they realized that these two women were on their side and were very capable of getting them to safety.

"OK," said the professor, "what do you want us to do?"

"First, let's get everyone to put on a bucket hat and get a big drink of water. I also want to take a look at what everyone is wearing for footwear. I have hiking boots in everyone's size with soft uppers, so they shouldn't cause blisters like most new boots or shoes."

Within five minutes, everyone had been hydrated, had a hat on and had changed their shoes. Allison made sure they repacked their old footwear to leave no trace of their path. Now moving with some purpose and help from their eyes in the sky, the group of six made good time on a new course away from the security detail.

"Eagle One to Girl Scouts," crackled in Allison and Carmelita's earpieces.

"Roger," Allison replied.

"Some good news and some bad news, I'm afraid," Jim radioed.

"Good news first," Allison replied.

"Well you are increasing your distance from the security detail. You are now about half a mile away from them and getting further away with each step. The bad news is they are blocking all of the routes to our secondary landing strips. The closest one is going to probably take you at least two days hiking. Can the family handle it?" Jim asked.

Allison replied immediately," Well it's not like we have any choice, but to answer your question, if we can get re-supplied along the way with drops from you, I think we will make it OK."

"Roger that, in the meantime enter these coordinates in your GPS" Jim replied. "The first set is the landing zone you are headed for and the other two are sites ahead where we can make drops of supplies and may make good stopping points. You won't be able to have a fire, so we are dropping survival blankets, k-rations and a couple of single burner stoves with propane. Those will get you through the night, and you can pack them with you when you leave the next morning. We have infrared tracking and can keep you apprised of the security team's position through the night. The first stopping place is a cave about three miles to the southeast of your present position. At you current pace, you should be there comfortably before night fall and get your camp set up."

"Roger and out," Allison replied.

They were going to try and keep radio communication to a minimum to avoid detection.

None of this was part of the plan, and they were improvising as they went, but even with the changes, they had a workable plan and all were optimistic.

Chapter 29

T he head of the facility had hired a crack merce-
nary team to act as the security group. Part of their
preparation for the assignment at the facility was
not only to protect the buildings and people, but also to be
ready to pursue anyone attempting to leave. Consequently,
the facility security group knew the terrain and was always
prepared for pursuit. They too had GPS, infrared targeting
and seeking equipment, two-way radio communication, and
they were armed with automatic weapons and stun grenades. All members of the team were hardened war vet-
erans trained by the U.S. military. Evading them was not
going to be easy.

The big advantage that Allison and Carmelita had was
their eyes in the sky. They knew that Jim and Sam would
be keeping close tabs on them as well as their pursuers. If
necessary, Jim and Sam could even provide some close
air support with one of them flying and the other firing a
weapon from the open cargo door. This of course would be
a last resort, but no one would hesitate if necessary.

Allison, Carmelita and their charges reached the cave
well before dark and hunkered down for the night.

True to their word, Jim and Sam had dropped supplies
nearby, and the professor and his family had hiked like
troopers. So far, things were going well.

Before everyone went to sleep, though, Carmelita had
a slightly unpleasant task to attend to. Along with the sup-

plies dropped by Eagle 1 was an inoculator for each member of the professor's family and him. In each inoculator was a pre-loaded GPS locator capsule about the size of the tip of a pencil. With a quick burst of propellant, the inoculator injected the capsule under the skin in a discreet spot. This would allow the family to be tracked anywhere in the world. It was a relatively painless procedure, but nonetheless somewhat invasive and not something anyone would want unless they understood the potential danger they were in without it. The process went without much protest and no tears, and Carmelita activated the system with a small handheld signaling device. Eagle 1 was able to verify that the system was up and running.

The desert cools off quickly after the sun goes down, and the little group of escapees huddled close together under their survival blankets to stay warm. They couldn't risk having a fire that could easily be detected. They had cold k-ration meals, a cave that helped keep them warm, and relatively soft ground to sleep on.

Mac and his team had to deal with the remaining elements of the facility security team before they could move in and secure the technology and equipment. The facility security team was not expecting Mac and his team, since most of the team was in pursuit of the professor and his family. The remaining members, though, were formidable and quick to throw up a good defense.

Mac's group was able to get fairly close to the facility with their faux uniforms and catch the security team by surprise. Two of the security team members evaded capture and had to be tracked and caught before they could proceed.

The Caravan landed nearby and took the captives to the waiting C-130 Hercules to be flown to a federal detention center.

As it turned out, the facility was so filled with equipment, prototypes, computers etc. that Mac had to call in a pair of Blackhawk helicopters to haul it all out. The caravan could not haul it all without making three or four trips.

Mac also had the remaining facility staff rounded up and under a temporary shelter, to be transported to the detention center as well. Some of the staff were key members of the development team and would be utilized to finish their work on the Sky Shield technology.

So far, the operation had been a success - if they could safely get the professor and his family out of the desert.

Chapter 30

The NASA laboratory had been remodeled hastily to accommodate the sky shield technology and its further development. Located in Oakridge, Tennessee, near Knoxville, it originally was a nuclear lab for weapons development during the cold war. The lab had the good fortune of having the most sophisticated equipment, computers, and staff in the space technology industry. The lab was directly connected to vast resources throughout the U.S., including the JPL labs in Pasadena, the Livermore labs near San Francisco, and the White Sands facility in New Mexico. The staff had access to data and virtual staff members at MIT, all of the Ivy League schools, Stanford, and many of the larger state schools around the country.

The staff, now in place at the new lab, had been briefed on the Sky Shield technology and was there to support the professor's work when he arrived. The lab staff consisted of experts in laser technology, holographic experts from Pixar studios, high level members of the software development industry, electrical engineers, NASA engineers, and a broad assortment of engineers and experts from many fields.

Once the equipment, the prototypes and the professor arrived, the team assembled would quickly take the project to the next level. The President had issued a memo directly from his desk outlining the strategic importance of this project and the need to finish the development as quickly as possible. As he said in the memo, "The finalization of this technology is more important than the mission to the moon. The technology must be handled responsibly and used for the sake of advancing the quality of life for mankind and never as a weapon in the hands of evil leadership."

The crack security team in pursuit of the professor and his family were able to pick up the trail shortly after they disappeared. The members of the team were all members of various special forces groups around the world and were well trained in survival skills and tracking, and were well equipped and armed.

Fortunately, the team was not as well briefed on the area as Allison and Carmelita, and consequently they had been successful thus far in evading the security team. Jim and Sam were faithfully orbiting above during the day to keep an eye on both the security team and Allison and Carmelita, which was another huge advantage for the escapees. They had to keep moving to get to a spot where Jim could land the Caravan and get back into the air with the increased load.

The Caravan is a very large single-engine aircraft powered by a Pratt and Whitney 675 hp turbo-prop capable of lifting 10 to 15 people and gear off a relatively short landing strip.

They also needed to time the departure during a cooler time of the day to avoid having to deal with air density issues. At 100 degrees Fahrenheit at the elevation of the area, the air density is equal to the air density at 15,000 feet. The Caravan would barely make it off the ground in those conditions with the kind of load it was going to have to carry. So the pickup needed to be early evening or early morning. The pick up was difficult enough with the pursuers closing in, but now it was going to be even more challenging.

Allison and Carmelita had about 10 to 12 miles of tough terrain to go to get to a dirt strip that would accommodate the Caravan. The canyons and ravines were so brushy and rocky that even a helicopter would not be able to land and pick up passengers. They had no choice but to hike out to the air strip.

The canyon terrain of northern Arizona was as rocky, treacherous, and hostile as any on earth. Temperatures during the day were in the 100s and in the 50s at night. The area was filled with rattlesnakes, scorpions, spiders of all kinds, and many larger predators that could be a problem if threatened. These conditions all led to a pretty slow pace of about half a mile an hour at best, which meant that it would take 20 + hours for them to hike out. Given the heat of the day, they usually hiked for about three to four hours in the early morning and about the same in the evening. At that pace, it was going to take a good three days to make it to the landing strip.

The next morning before sunrise, Allison and Carmelita roused the group and made sure everyone had something to eat and drink before starting off.

Thank God for GPS, Allison thought to herself. Both she and Carmelita could certainly navigate with a compass and a map, but using a GPS made the trek so much easier and quicker, as they did not have to stop and consult the map and take compass readings to be sure they were on the right course. As long as they followed the dotted line on the screen, they were on course for their objective.

The professor and his family were troopers, but after one partial day of hiking and sleeping on the ground, they were beginning to fade fast. The children had to be carried, so the adults traded off and kept moving as quickly as they could with their loads.

The security team pursuing them had sent an advance

scout to recon the area and had moved to within three quarters of a mile from where the family was hiding. The scout had not spotted the family at first, but suddenly caught a glimpse of movement that attracted his attention. He lifted his binoculars to his eyes and scanned the area to try and identify what he had seen. Fortunately, the family had moved out of sight behind some rocks and the scout was not able to spot them. However, being a solid soldier, he knew in his gut he had seen something of significance.

Using infrared scopes, Sam spotted the scout and identified the image as a person. Only one thing that could be, he thought as he peered into the scope, has to be one of the bad guys.

He lifted the scrambled radio to warn Allison. "Eagle One to Girl Scouts," he called.

"Girl Scouts to Eagle One," Allison replied.

"You have a single pursuer about three quarters of a mile north of your position. He appears to be an advance scout working your trail. He may have seen you, as he has stopped and seems to be scanning your area intensely with binocs. Stay down for a few minutes until we see what he is going to do.

Further north about one to two miles Sam could see the balance of the pursuing security team of five men moving quickly up a ravine towards their advance scout. Unless Allison and Carmelita could pick up the pace, the security team would overrun them in just a few hours. Finally, the advance scout dropped the binoculars and used his radio to advise of his position and what he thought he had seen.

Sam knew that they needed to do something to slow down the pursuing team. He racked his brain trying to come up with an idea. They were orbiting the area at 4,000 feet AGL and he was staring out the window trying to come up with a plan when he saw a cloud of dust stirring in a ravine. He used his binoculars to see what was going on in that ravine only to find a small herd of wild horses trotting through the small canyon. Something had probably spooked them, and they all took off down the canyon at a gallop.

All of a sudden it came to him! The wild horses were in an adjacent canyon to the security team and separated by about one to two miles. He could see the canyons at their convergence, and it appeared as though the horses could traverse the entire canyon dry river bottom on the run. If they could stir those horses up and some how drive them down the canyon, they would overrun the security team and slow them up. It was certainly worth a try. He told Jim his idea and Jim just got a wide grin on his face as he anticipated the low and slow flight through the canyon. If they were lucky and timed it right, they might get the horses to catch the security team completely by surprise and actually injure some of them, and perhaps even damage some of their equipment.

They waited for a while until the horses and the security team were on a converging path. The security team stopped in the dry creek bed and took off their packs and laid down their weapons to take a break. They were all laying on the ground with their feet up on their packs, and probably most of them had their eyes closed to catch a quick catnap.

The canyon the wild horses were in was off to the west of the team's position and angled into the security team's canyon in a v - a winding scraggily v, but a v nonetheless. The winding canyon was about a 10 mile canyon with many blind curves and sheer canyon walls.

Jim descended in the Caravan to 500 feet AGL and slowed the big Cessna to 80 knots. They entered the canyon at the far west end to evade detection by the security team, and began their winding wild ride down through the canyon clearing the canyon walls by less than 200 to 300 feet, which sounds like a lot of room, but at even slow speeds of 80 knots there is very little reaction time to avoid a canyon wall.

Jim handled the big bird like a fighter jet, jinking and turning and banking steeply to make the tight canyon turns.

The distance from the canyon entrance to where the horses were did not take long. They could see the horses up ahead a couple of miles, and as they neared the herd they could see the horses begin to mill around nervously at the sound of the aircraft.

At about half a mile from the herd Jim throttled up to increase the engine noise and that was all it took. The horses took off on a dead run down the canyon right towards the security team. Just before the canyon intersection, Jim pulled the Caravan up in a steep banked turn and with the shadow of the airplane and the increased noise the horse herd ran even harder right into the napping security team. The team was caught completely off guard and barely had time to react before the horses were upon them. The members of the security team were knocked off their feet, equipment and packs were trampled and it appeared as though at least a couple of the team were seriously injured.

Jim and Sam climbed back to a safe altitude to recon the havoc they had wreaked. The stunt could not have worked out better. Given the injuries and the damaged equipment, they had just bought Allison and Carmelita a few hours at least.

The security team forward scout was unaware of the little diversion Sam and Jim had created with the horses, and he was still on point like a hunting dog. He had a scent of the professor and his family and he was not letting up.

"Eagle One to Girl Scouts," Sam called.

"Girl Scouts here," Carmelita replied.

"We just bought you some time with a little diversion.

Air

Your pursuers won't be moving for a while. If you are able to get moving you can widen the gap a bit"

"Roger," Carmelita replied, "but we still have the little problem of the scout less than a mile behind us. He has not spotted us yet, but with where the trail has to lead us it is just a matter of time. Once he spots us he will be on us in a matter of minutes. Are you still able to spot him from the air?"

"Negative, have not seen him for a while, but let me take a closer look and I will get back to you."

Jim began a wide lazy spiraling descent to 1,500 feet to get a better look. With the engine at idle and the prop wind-milling, they made very little noise. With the Caravan in a steep right bank, Sam was able to look down at the ground in a fairly wide area and scan the ground with his binoculars.

After several minutes, Sam caught sight of some movement and focused his scanning on the area where he sensed the movement. Slowly closing the gap between the escapees was the lone member of the security detail. Sam couldn't tell if he had actually seen his quarry or if the scout was acting on instinct, but he was making steady progress in their direction

"Eagle One to Girls Scouts," Sam called.

"Roger Eagle One, Girl Scouts here," Allison replied.

"The forward scout is still about three quarters of a mile to the north northwest moving in your direction. I don't think he has spotted you yet, as he is moving slow and deliberate. Keep your heads down for a bit and let Jim and I think about what we can do to slow him up. To continue your progress without being seen, you could move down that ravine to your west. It curves back to the southeast after about half mile to the west. That way, you won't have to climb up on the trail where he can spot you. That canyon essentially circumnavigates the hill you were going to have to climb and may actually be easier going. I would imagine your little troupe is getting a bit weary, eh?" Sam asked.

"You got that right. The canyon idea is a good one - looks like a nice soft sandy floor on the ravine as well. Everyone is getting tired of the rocky terrain, and this will be a welcome break. How far around does the canyon take us out of the way and how much extra time do you think it will cost us?"

"Given the faster speed you can probably make on flat sandy terrain, it probably won't really take you any longer," Sam replied.

"Roger, we're moving out now, keep us informed of our tail."

"Will do, out for now."

Sam had kept his binoculars on the scout the whole time so he would not lose sight of him. Sam knew that if he got to the spot where the escaping family headed off down the canyon, he would pick up their trail very quickly. Even if they brushed out their tracks, he was enough of a professional that he would spot the anomalies on the trail and be in quick pursuit. They still had to do something to remove him as a threat.

"Eagle One to Home Plate," Sam radioed.

"Home Plate here," Mac replied.

"We've got a bit of a problem here."

Sam outlined the situation with the advance scout and what they had done to slow up the whole team. "The only thing I can think to do to divert this scout is to set a brush fire out in front of him in the canyon he is in with a couple of our marker rockets. I'm sure if we hit that dry brush with a hot rocket or two it should get things burning pretty quickly. At least it will create a lot of smoke and should slow him up. Do you approve, or do you have any other suggestions as to what we might be able to do?" Sam queried.

Mac pondered the problem for a few minutes and then called back with his approval. "Give me about five to 10 minutes and I will make sure we have a water tanker in the air to put out the fire if it gets out of hand. If you don't hear back from me in seven minutes, proceed to set the fire ahead of him as you have suggested."

Sam looked at his watch and noted the time. "Roger," he replied, "and thanks."

Jim and Sam immediately began looking for the best concentration of brush out ahead of the scout to set the fire. The marker rockets they had hanging on the hard points under their wings were designed to create smoke to show water tankers where to drop their load. Generally, it did not matter if they generated sparks and heat, as they were being fired into forest fires any way. In this case, they would be used to start a fire in the tinder dry brush. The smoke and fire would block the scout's way and force him up the canyon wall or to back track the way he came, giving the escaping family, Allison, and Carmelita a fighting chance to get further out of reach.

Seven minutes passed pretty quickly, and Jim and Sam had their target zone all picked out. The scout was in an area of the canyon that had sheer walls for about half a mile. Out in front of that area was a widening in the canyon that was heavy brush. With a fire burning in that brush, the scout would have no choice but to back track at least half a mile to an area where he could possibly climb out of the canyon. By then, he would have a hard time flanking the canyon and picking up the trail again. This should give the escapee's at least a three-hour advantage. That amount of time should be enough to improve their chances to even odds. They certainly weren't out of trouble, but they were gaining on the situation.

The brushy area was a good half to three-quarters mile ahead of the scout, and Jim and Sam were going to target their rockets to hit on the southeast end of the brush to create a big enough fire to deter the scout.

Jim descended to 1,000 feet and lined up on his target zone a mile to the east and slowed the Caravan to landing approach speed. With flaps deployed and the throttle back to about half, the Caravan plowed through the sky at about 80 knots.

Sam thought to himself, we are a sitting duck up here. I just hope there is not someone else from their team anywhere near. He knew Jim was probably thinking the same thing, and didn't even bother to verbalize his thoughts to his partner.

Sam lined up the rocket targeting sights on their planned target zone. Jim called off distance to where they need to fire the rockets. Sam hit the fire button just as Jim called off the distance. Two marker rockets streaked for the target zone and hit right in the middle of the brush.

"Bulls-eye!" Jim yelled. "Great shooting Sam!"

Just as planned, after firing the rockets, Jim raked the Caravan into a hard left turn with a 60 degree bank and 20 degrees of nose up and full throttle, while he retracted the flaps. The result of the maneuver was for the Caravan to turn tail out of the area as quickly as possible and to try and climb out of small arms range as quickly as possible. The Caravan was lightly loaded so it had no trouble putting a big gap between the foe and the aircraft very quickly and with a very skinny rear profile as well. Jim climbed to 3,000 feet and began a slow turn back towards the target zone to see if the fire was underway. Meanwhile, Sam was using his binoculars to try and spot the scout and determine his intended path and actions.

The fire was catching very quickly and was creating

a lot of smoke blowing right up the canyon towards the scout. Sam spotted the scout standing on top of a small outcropping of boulders in the middle of the canyon scanning the canyon ahead of him looking at the smoke. He was obviously trying to work out a plan as he scanned the canyon walls around him and then turned to look behind and calculate his odds for each possible route.

So far so good, Sam thought to himself. The scout was behaving as they guessed he would. Just as they were starting to feel pretty smug about how well their plan and worked out, Jim and Sam watched in fascination as the scout walked over to the sheer canyon wall and began to free climb out of the canyon instead of back tracking. If he made it to the top of the canyon he would lose very little time getting back on the escapee's trail, maybe only 30 to 40 minutes, as he could quickly traverse around the fire and pick up the trail of the escapees.

The scout was obviously an expert climber, as he moved with very little hesitation up the canyon wall. From the orbiting aircraft, he looked like spider man picking his way up a seemingly impossible smooth granite face.

"Jim, there's only one other alternative," Sam said. "You need to drop me on top of that canyon so I can be there to meet this clown and put a stop to his pursuit. I can catch up to our group and help Allison and Carmelita. I'll run it by Mac and see if he concurs."

Sam outlined his plan to Mac and got approval. Within a few minutes, Sam had strapped on his parachute and was ready for the drop. He slipped into a shoulder holster with a 9 mm Glock and several magazines of ammo; slung a Browning twelve gauge shotgun with a shortened barrel over his shoulder, and strapped on a 10" all purpose military knife.

Jim watched him prepare for the jump and realized that Sam had obviously done this sort of thing before.

166

"Someday, you will have to tell me more about your past experience that makes this sort of thing seem routine to you,"

Jim said over the intercom to Sam. Sam nodded and said, "It's never routine, but getting ready for each mission is about the same."

He also strapped on a chest pack that had basic survival gear in it to sustain him until he could catch up with their other party. Jim was orbiting the drop zone at 1,500 feet beyond the canyon wall out of sight of the climbing scout. When Sam was ready, they would head into the wind and Sam would jump a half mile from the intended landing zone; he would use the wind to help guide him with some precision as he spiraled and "s'd" his way to the ground.

Sam nodded to Jim and opened the side door at the same time. As agreed, Jim would hold up his hand with all five fingers extended and count down one at a time, when Jim had a closed fist, Sam would step out into the slipstream and pull his ripcord three seconds later.

Chapter 31

The technology, equipment, computers and staff were all en route to Oakridge to the new lab. However, for the project to be fully realized, Professor Holmsby had to be a part of the final development.

The technology was proven in a small scale, and now they were ready to deploy a small shield in low orbit and test it in a space environment. The professor was the key to the geometry and physics of transferring the small prototype into a working model. Laser generators had to have enough power, photovoltaic cells had to be created that would sustain the required power level, navigation and orientation equipment had to be very precise, and the thruster bursts had to be controlled within a thousandth of a second.

Each sky shield sphere oriented itself in accordance with the adjacent sphere, which all led back to the commands emanating from a single sphere and radiating out to the whole array via radio telemetry. Each sphere could be designated as the lead sphere depending, on how the array was to be configured or in what direction it was to move. If the array was to have multiple configurations, then there would be multiple lead spheres communicating not only with their assigned community of spheres, but also with each other to reconfigure according to the computer commands. The code development for the navigation and orientation of the spheres was exclusively the design of the professor. Before being falsely lured into the project, he had been working under a federal grant to build an entirely new language that would control future weapon and navigation systems. The code would be so new and so different, that hopefully the enemies of the free world would not be able to break it down and use it for many years. Hence the professor's key to transferring the project from prototype status to a large-scale working model. He had to be recovered and returned to the project at all costs.

Stewart Holmsby called Senator Jacobsen and arranged for a lunch meeting in Washington D.C. They met in a small neighborhood restaurant in Baltimore to avoid curious eyes.

"We have a major problem," Holmsby began. "Because of a local brush fire near our production and development facility in Arizona, our staff has had to be evacuated. I just got a report from our security team that they are in pursuit of the professor, his family, and possibly an unknown helper or helpers that may or may not be a part of the evacuation team. Something tells me that all is not right in this picture. It is not like my brother to strike out on his own and endanger his family. The reports coming from the forest service on the fire in the area are very sketchy, as in no detail of any kind, and we have not heard from any of the facility administrative staff for several hours. There is some unknown force at work here. I don't believe it's the Columbians, because this is much too organized and strategic in nature. In short, I am very worried that the CIA, the FBI and or other federal agencies are on to what we are doing.

"The other part of this that comes into play here is what happened on Barbados about a month ago. As you recall, we believe someone successfully infiltrated our facility and was able to get a look at our plans. We don't know to what degree we were compromised, but we are fairly sure something's going on that could destroy our plans."

"Besides what you have said, what do you have as proof that we need to be worried? All I have heard is conjecture without proof. I admire your intuition and judgment, but we have hundreds of millions of dollars on the line, and the many families in our group that head up technology and manufacturing behemoths are prepared to use this newly-developed technological breakthrough to trigger the next industrial/agricultural, and development revolution. Neither they nor I are prepared to quit or change direction without a clear sign of infiltration or threat," Senator Jacobsen replied.

It appeared that the two were at a standstill in terms of what to do next. The caution Holmsby urged was not enough to squelch the growing greed Senator Jacobsen displayed. Obviously, all associated with this technology would stand to profit in a huge manner if it was successfully deployed. Every day that passed, they were closer and closer to full deployment.

"Fly down to Arizona and charter an airplane up to the facility and see what is going on, then let's talk again as soon as you return. I'm sure you will find things back to normal as soon as the fire is out and the staff is allowed to return to work. Our security team will recover the professor and his family, and we will be back on schedule soon. Call me as soon as you get there and assess the situation," the Senator said.

Stewart Holmsby certainly had the authority and reason to travel to the site of a wildfire to review and assess the situation, but it would be somewhat strange for him to do so for something that appeared to be inconsequential. In his position of Secretary of the Interior, he would have to come up with a reason and float it out into the press as a cover story.

The next day, a small story hit the press regarding the danger to the wild burros in the area of the fire. The story listed the positive attributes of the burro and how wildfires such as the one in Arizona threatened their continued existence. The story went on to say that the Secretary of the Interior would himself undertake an aerial review of the damaged area and the impact to the wild burro herds.

The director of the FBI was the first to pick up on the story and suggest that this was very strange and warranted further investigation. The President and the balance of the group agreed. A select agent from the FBI was chosen to trail the good secretary and inform the director of Stewart Holmsby's movements. Obviously, the agent did not know anything of why he was shadowing Stewart Holmsby, but knew it was highly significant and could either make or break his career.

Stewart Holmsby boarded a federal Gulfstream G-5 the next morning bound for Prescott. Immediately afterwards, the FBI agent was in a government Citation in trail of the Secretary's aircraft. The only major difference in the aircraft, besides make and model, was that the Citation had the markings of a standard corporate aircraft, while the G-5 was obviously a government aircraft on a government mission

Senator Jacobsen had a meeting with one of the interlocking committees of the shadow group. He reported that the project being developed was nearing completion and would be ready for full-scale deployment very soon. He made no mention of the problems asserted by Stewart Holmsby.

Within the Founders that had influenced historic events in America for centuries was the highest committee, known simply as the Seniors and made up of the eldest and most powerful members of the Founders. The other of the interlocking lower committees did not know of their significance, nor did they know of the Seniors. The structure was suspected, but no one but the highest committee members themselves knew that it really existed.

The Seniors had already caught wind of the problems threatening the project. They all knew that the project could potentially be traced back to some of the members in their group, which could not be allowed to happen. There was only one thing they could do - if the FBI or someone else got too close, they would have to sacrifice one or two of their members as the fall guys and erase any trace of evidence back to anyone in the Founders.

There were many cases like this throughout history, where an individual who had been highly thought of had a sudden and precipitous fall from status. Either the presumption of guilt, along with manufactured and planted evidence, allowed the system to dispose of them, or in some cases they just disappeared.

In any case, the life and perpetuation of the Founders had to be protected at all costs, if for no other reason than the United States needed a group that could get things done as society became more and more complex. Getting things done frequently meant operating outside of legal complications, and the Founders certainly had the resources to do exactly that, be it money, manpower, special skills, or virtually anything else, if the Founders needed it , they commanded it in one form or another.

Chapter 32

D espite doing over 300 jumps, Sam was always a bit surprised by the violence of the jolt of the parachute opening, but equally grateful that it opened, as on low altitude jumps, there was barely enough time to cut lose a bad chute and open the reserve. The canyon winds were a little tricky, but Sam steered his chute to the LZ on top of the canyon rim and managed to land without breaking or twisting anything or injuring himself. He was about a quarter of a mile from where the advance scout was scaling the canyon wall.

Jim was giving him a progress report from above as he gathered his chute. "The scout is directly east of your position, about 400 yards. He is still about 50 feet below the rim and should be on top in about 10 minutes. You may want to work your way over there and extend your finest greeting before he actually gets on top of the rim!"

"Roger," Sam answered. "Best idea you've had all day!"

Sam jogged over to the top of the canyon rim edge in about two minutes, despite the rocky terrain. He bellied crawled the last 10 yards so he could carefully see over the edge to observe his quarry.

Immediately below the rim of the canyon was a ledge about three feet below the edge. The ledge sloped down from the top of the rim and led into some shallow erosion caves in the side of the canyon wall. Just as Sam stuck his head over the edge of the canyon, he came face to face with the largest diamondback rattlesnake he had ever seen. The serpent was coiled and was looking right at the canyon edge where Sam was crawling. He had obviously heard his approach and was in a defensive posture ready to strike.

"Holy Shit!" Sam yelled involuntarily. Just as he said it he realized what he had done - his quarry now alerted, Sam had lost his element of surprise.

Sam rolled back away from the canyon edge to avoid the snake and scrambled to his feet, drawing his Glock from his shoulder holster. Warily, he approached the canyon edge and peered over. As he expected, the forward scout was nowhere in sight. He had been warned off and had quickly hidden from view.

Sam retreated a few steps and called quickly on the radio," Eagle One, Eagle One, how do you read?"

"Loud and clear," Jim answered.

Sam relayed the situation and asked if Jim could spot the scout.

It took Jim a couple of minutes to get in position in the air to get a good view of where the scout should be.

"Eagle One to Eagle Two, don't see him. Either he retreated down the cliff, or traversed over to one side or the other, or he is behind a rock or in a cave on the cliff side."

"Roger Eagle One," Sam replied. Damn, he swore to himself.

The pursuing security team had sustained a serious setback when the wild horses stampeded through their resting spot. The herd of 50 horses or so had galloped through their spot in the canyon and trampled equipment, as well as injured a number of the mercenaries. A few weapons had been damaged beyond repair. Despite the injuries and delays, the group commander had quickly assessed their

situation and was preparing to link up with their forward
scout.

The scout had not reported in for some time now and
the commander was beginning to get worried. He simply
could not raise him on the radio, which was unlike this particular soldier, usually very resourceful and very responsive
to command and control, which is why he was selected as
scout. The lack of response indicated some serious problems.

All the commander could do at this point was to
start out in the last direction they were headed before the
encounter with the horses and wait for contact from his
forward scout. No sooner had they set out at a slow pace
when the commander got a series of mic clicks over his radio. His scout was signaling him via Morse code, using the
mic button on his transceiver as the code key. The decoded
clicks gave the commander the scout's position in latitude
and longitude, which the commander immediately put into
his Garmin portable GPS unit.

The scouts signal also indicated that for some reason
he could not speak over the radio. The location on the GPS
showed that the scout was about three miles south southeast
from the main party's position. The commander immediately had his team moving off towards the scout. Given the
rough terrain, it would take the team at least three hours to
cover the three miles.

As the commander suspected, there was more information forthcoming in code on the radio from his scout.

"Have lost sight of the escapees…at least one unknown pursuer near my position…not sure who they are
pursuing, me or the escapees…am pinned down waiting for
pursuer to make their move."

Sam's scanner picked up all of the scout's transmissions, so although he did not know where exactly he was,
Sam knew he was sitting tight and had lost sight of the

professor and his family - all good news. However, the bad news was that the security team was moving again and quickly closing in on his position. There was only one thing Sam could do at this point - find the scout, overpower him, and try to then steer the security team in another direction.

Sam started moving across the rim in a flanking move relative to where he had last seen the scout. He was making a big assumption that the scout had not moved much from where he last saw him, but he really had nothing else to go one. He had intercepted the GPS coordinates tapped out over the radio mic by the scout, but that was only good within 10 meters or so, which could make a big difference right now.

Sam moved up the rim about 200 yards, before he lowered himself carefully over the edge and began to traverse back from a lower position to where he believed the scout was hiding. The going was extremely slow, as he was trying to move silently. The cliff side was covered with loose rock and brush growing out of the cracks in the rocks, and every noise seemed to echo through the canyon.

Sam had moved about 50 yards back the direction he had come from and had stopped to look for some movement above him. He was sitting completely still in the shadow of a rock, not even moving his head, just shifting his eyes back and forth across the terrain, when he finally spotted the scout.

A flash of sunlight caught Sam's eye, and when he looked in the direction of the flash he saw a hand and a wrist next to a large rock outcropping. The scout was sitting on the other side of the outcropping, leaning on his hand and his watch lens was reflecting the sunlight from the West.

Somehow Sam needed to flush the scout out of his hiding spot and distract him to move in the wrong direction so he could make an approach from behind and catch the scout unsuspected.

The terrain on the cliffside was steep and covered with loose granite and gravel, all very unstable. Even climbing carefully would send rocks skittering down the slope and clattering over boulders. A stealthy approach was impossible, which is why he needed to make the scout think he was ahead and above him so the scout would be focused in that direction as Sam approached him from behind.

If Sam could throw a large rock up onto the cliffside high enough and beyond where the scout was sitting, the scout would have to assume that he was trying to come down the cliff in that direction. In the meantime, Sam would be approaching him from behind. Sam scoped out his options and decided to move another 20 yards closer before he tried his distraction attempt. He gingerly traversed the cliffside to within 30 yards of the scout. The hand and wrist were still visible next to the rock - apparently the scout was resting quietly just listening for movement.

If Sam was going to take this guy, now was the time, as it would not get any better. He had not been in hand to hand combat for many years, but with the importance of this mission weighing heavily on his mind, he knew he had to succeed. His plan was to throw the rock high on the cliffside and let it roll noisily down the hill well over on the other side of the scout. This would make the scout think he was in that area, and while the rock was clattering down the hill, Sam would move quickly up behind the scout.

With the old phrase "it's now or never" flashing through his brain, Sam heaved a rock high up on the cliff, well out in front of the scout's position. He waited for the rock to hit and for the noise of it tumbling down the hill. The rock must have hit one of the few mossy spots on the hillside, because he did not hear it land, and apparently neither did the scout, because he did not move, or at least his hand and wrist did not move.

Suddenly there was a clattering of rocks up near where Sam had thrown his rock. Apparently it had landed soft and then began to roll down the cliff side. Sam had just started to move towards the scout when his peripheral eyesight picked up movement to his left. He turned to look just in time to see a man dressed in camo leap off of a boulder above him and dive straight at him from about six feet above his position.

Sam's combat training took over immediately, and he ducked under the diving combatant and used his momentum to push him further past where Sam had been standing. Instead of the scout hitting Sam with full force, Sam's push propelled the scout over the cliff where he landed some 30 feet below on a large granite boulder. All Sam heard was a loud thump when the scout hit the rock - the scout did not scream or yell and apparently died upon impact. A large blood pool oozed out from under his body and the scout's body lay prone and still.

Thinking that he have must have been one of a two-party scouting team, Sam looked back to where he thought the scout was and was perplexed to see that the scout's arm and watch had not moved. Could he be asleep?

Not taking any chances, Sam covered the remaining few yards to the scout's position ahead as quietly as he could, watching for any movement the whole time. The scout ahead of him never moved, even as Sam stepped around the boulder with his gun drawn. The scout's arm remained completely still the whole time.

Sam stepped around the boulder and said, "Freeze, don't move or I will..." His voice trailed off and he felt completely the fool as he got the full view of the resting scout.

The resting scout was a camo sleeve of the scout's shirt with a large tree branch in the sleeve with his wrist

watch strapped around the branch. The scout had anticipated Sam's move and had outflanked him, using his shirt
and wristwatch as the distraction that held Sam's focus. It
almost worked too. Had Sam not seen the movement and
successfully defended himself, he would be the dead one.

Sam quickly filled in Jim over their encrypted radio
system as to what had happened. The scout had left most
of his gear at the resting spot, including his radio and GPS
unit. Sam might be able to use them to steer the security
team in the wrong direction. The scout's GPS unit had the
last position of the security team on the GPS unit, which
was about three miles away, and by now they were probably closer to two miles in trail.

Sam pulled out his USGS terrain map to consider
where to try and pick a direction to send the security team.
USGS maps had terrain and roads well marked in the area.
Directly west of his position and in the opposite direction
of the escapees was a secondary gravel road about a mile
away. He traced the road to make sure it was accessible
from a main highway before he radioed Jim with his plan.

"Eagle Two to Eagle One," Sam called.

"Eagle Two," Jim replied.

Sam quickly outlined his plan. He would use the
scout's radio to tap out false directions to the security team,
sending them towards the gravel road. In the meantime,
Jim would radio Mac and have him bring an armed contingent in by helicopter to be waiting for the security team in
the area where they would intercept the road.

If the security team fell for it, they would walk right
into a trap and the pressure would be off. Jim conferred
with Mac and all agreed it was worth a try.

Sam used the scout's radio to tap out a Morse code
message to the trailing security team. "Escapees changed
direction...headed for road," and gave the coordinates or
the road. "Suggest you intercept ahead and I will cover

rear approach." He waited for confirmation and then radioed Jim that the trap was set.

Sam would head after the escapees and help get them
to the planned LZ to meet Jim and the Caravan. If the pursuing security team fell for the diversion, they would all be
in the as clear soon as Mac met the security team and took
them into custody.

Chapter 33

The advance team in Oakridge, Tennessee, had made great strides in anticipation of Dr. Holmsby's arrival. Studying the files taken from the Barbados lab, as well as parallel studies in other areas, the scientists on the team had been able to validate the technology. Reverse engineering the prototype gave them a very high-level understanding of the genius behind the creation of the technology. By utilizing the combination of cold plasma particles blended with lasers passing through light-scattering prisms, each sphere generated a network of light and plasma beams roughly the diameter of a human hair. The array of thousands of hair-size beams being emitted from each sphere overlapped with the other beams emitting from the other spheres in a preprogrammed pattern to form a holographic geometric shape that reflected light. One of the scientists had introduced a methane compound in miniscule amounts to enhance the reflective quality. In essence, the methane mimicked the effects of smog on earth.

This technology was probably going to revolutionize agriculture, demographic distribution, erase famine, and minimize the effects of hurricanes, tornados, thunderstorms, and damaging winds. Because of temperature moderation, the impact should also include the reduction of power usage for heating and air conditioning. Potentially, arid and uninhabitable spots on Earth can be made green by reducing the evaporative rate of critical water supplies.

When needed, evaporation rates could be increased by also raising the temperature of the ocean near the equator to put more water vapor in the atmosphere. Presumably, by making life easier and creating some equality in opportunity by making life more sustainable, conflict would be reduced as well. The possible impact of this technology in a fully deployed and managed state was really only limited by one's imagination. Like harnessing the atom, the management of the solar shield would have to be done by a world coalition.

All of these thoughts rolled around almost aimlessly in the President's mind. Selfishly, he could be considered one of the most significant leaders in the world if he managed the deployment and control of this technology to the broadest benefit of mankind. The more he thought this through, the more he realized that self-serving or not, he would need to initiate contact with world leaders and industrial factions to assure the future of the technology was safe and only to be used carefully and scientifically to the benefit of mankind.

Historians would probably accuse him of having ulterior motives, but nonetheless, he must collaborate with these leadership factions while keeping the United States firmly at the center of control. Early development of this infrastructure was almost as important as the technology itself. Without the collaboration of key nations, the solar shield could be considered a threat by some nations. Indeed, the use or withholding of the solar shield could be used very effectively for leverage with uncooperative nations. Moderation of temperature in the Middle East, for example, is really more strategic than oil. Using the solar shield to assist key nations as they joined the coalition in exchange for price moderation of energy resources was more than a fair trade. The President thought to himself, this alone could get me re-elected to a second term. The public would certainly see that continuity on this issue is critical and keep him in office. With that thought, along with all of the earlier mental ramblings, the President came to a quick and important decision.

Early reports indicated that the professor and his family were making their way slowly to the pickup point and were being harassed by a security team in pursuit. The President decided he could no longer leave this to chance - he needed to get help to the resources he had in the area. He needed to send in the Marines to quickly extract the professor and his family and wrap this up quickly. Secrecy was no longer the priority.

Quick to act after making a decision, the President called the Joint Chief of Staff for an immediate briefing.

Marine Colonel Bruce assembled his team of two Blackhawk helicopter crews within an hour of being called by the Marine Commandant. His orders came straight from the President and were at the highest level of security within the armed forces. The Colonel and his two Blackhawk teams were to extract a fleeing professor and his family in central Arizona, and safely transport them to Tennessee to a secure lab.

The professor and their escorts were in an area northwest of Prescott near Bagdad, literally running for their lives. A team of mercenaries were also in the area and presumably in hot pursuit. Colonel Bruce commanded an air wing for the Marine Corps. in Yuma, Arizona, which was roughly a two-hour flight to where the quarry was located.

The escorting team had been briefed that help was on its way and they would guide the Marines in to the pickup site. The mercenaries were still a complication, as they were still in the area. They had been diverted for a while, but apparently they did not completely fall for the scheme, as they divided into two factions - one that stayed on the original trail and one that investigated the diversionary trail. The team on the original trail quickly picked up fresh sign of the escapees and the two teams rejoined in pursuit.

Colonel Bruce and his team would leave the Marine Air Station in Yuma at 04:00 and be on site by 06:00. The Blackhawks were armed with 50 caliber waist guns, and each helicopter had a team of four armed Marines that had undergone special training for extraction. These troops were much like the Seals, the Rangers, and the Green Beret, but trained specifically for hostage rescue. This team would let nothing stand in their way of successfully rescuing the professor, his family and their escorts.

The smell of jet fuel hung in the air as the Blackhawk pilots lit the hot box of the spinning turbine engines. The massive rotors were gaining speed and beginning to make the recognizable thump, thump, thump that the tip of the blades make as they pass through the air at near the speed of sound as they whir around the central axis of the rotor.

The Marine team members all had their game faces on, with grease paint covering their reflective skin, and dressed in camouflage with light packs, web gear, and M-16 Carbines. Each Blackhawk had a designated gunner who manned the 50 caliber mini gun in the door, a pilot and a copilot/radio officer for a total of six Marines in each aircraft. This still left room for the professor, his family and their escorts.

The pilots flew straight up the Colorado River to the area around Parker Dam and then cut directly east to the landing and pickup zone.

The terrain in this part of Arizona was truly beautiful in a very rugged way. The outcropping of granite and basalt, along with the hills and native brush, made for a nearly monochromatic view as it whirred by at 120 knots and at an altitude of 100 feet. The pilots were experts at nap of the earth flying and found it to be extremely satisfying and fun. Rising above 100 feet was almost a sin that neither pilot would be caught doing - the lower the better. The Black-hawks nimbly zigged and zagged their way up through canyons and over hills with a roar. These pilots knew the diameter of their rotors and how or if they would fit in the tight confines of the canyons. They knew intuitively when to increase altitude to safely clear the canyon walls, as well as when they could fly so low over the canyon floor as to create a steady dirt cloud in their wake. Machine and man were one.

"LZ 10 minutes ahead," the radio officer in the lead helicopter announced. No sooner had the radio officer released the push to talk switch than a small arms round hit the windshield. The bullet just grazed the wind screen and left a small star.

"We're under fire!" the radio officer yelled. A second round hit the side door and ricocheted harmlessly. Apparently the team in pursuit of the professor was equally determined to capture them as well.

The Marines had two choices, fly on to the LZ and hope they could land un-harassed and pick up the professor, or deal with this security team now. Close analysis of their orders would suggest that they should dispose of the pursuing mercenaries if at all possible. The Colonel had correctly read the tea leaves on this issue, and immediately ordered the two Blackhawks into a defensive posture. This would allow them to evaluate the threat, and then take the offensive after they understood what they were up against.

One of the Blackhawks climbed to an altitude of 3,000 feet to provide protective cover, while the second chopper circled looking for the ground threat.

"Blackhawk One to Blackhawk Two - looks like we have a stick of approximate 10 ground personnel dug in immediately north of our position." Blackhawk One was hovering just above a hill within view of the mercenaries but hardly within range of small arms. A lucky shot might hit them but it was not probable.

The mercenaries had obviously never witnessed the effective fire power of two Marine Blackhawks. If they had, they would have never taken them on in this kind of a fight. This is exactly what these gun-ships were designed for, not to mention the troops aboard them.

Without exchanging a word, the two Blackhawk pilots maneuvered their ships into flanking positions on either side of the mercenaries. The first Blackhawk gunner lay down a five-second burst of 50 caliber rounds immediately in front of the mercenaries. The effect was simply awesome. The cloud of dust generated from the rounds hitting was enough to choke anyone within 100 feet. The message was clear - surrender, or we will make the next shot lethal.

The mercenaries laid down their arms and walked out with their hands on their head. They obviously knew the drill as they were on their knees with their hands on their head by the time the first Blackhawk landed on the canyon floor.

Colonel Bruce ordered that the mercenaries be handcuffed, and he left two Marines to guard them until they could be picked up in about three hours. A third Blackhawk was already in the air on its way to pick up the prisoners.

Chapter 34

With the chasing security team neutralized, Carmelita, Lorenzo and Allison felt they were home free. The two rescue Blackhawks were inbound within about 10 minutes and the harassing team of security personnel from the sky shield facility had been captured.

Everyone breathed a big sigh of relief. They were all tired, trail weary and emotionally spent. With 10 to 15 minutes of stress-free respite, everyone closed their eyes for a quick rest. The last thing Allison did before she closed her eyes was to activate an electronic locator beacon for the choppers to follow directly to their site.

"Thank God for the Marines," she mumbled as she drifted off into a light sleep.

Jim was instructed to land the Caravan at the dirt strip, where he was to wait for the Marine helicopters to meet him with the precious cargo of the professor and his family, and Carmelita and Allison.

The desert landing strip was about 3,000 feet long and 40 feet wide, which really is generous compared to many primitive strips. This particular one, though, had some ruts and rocks that a weary pilot had to be ready for, as well as soft, sandy spots that would at times grab a wheel and threaten to ground loop an airplane.

Jim lined up the spinner on the center of the strip at about 700 feet altitude and eased in 10 degrees of flaps. He felt a slight right to left cross wind as he made his approach and dipped his wing into the cross breeze and held a straight line with left rudder. He would kick the aircraft out of the crab angle just before touch down and rollout. He touched down within the first 100 feet of the end of the runway and kept a bit of power on with a nose high attitude with the nose gear still off the runway. This soft field approach gave him more control as the big bird began to slow on the roll-out. As the Caravan slowed to under 30 knots, Jim applied some differential braking and swung the nose around to taxi back to the arrival end of the runway. He could be ready to quickly depart as soon as the Marines arrived. Sam had been picked up by the Marines and would help facilitate the final rescue effort and then rejoin Jim for the quick trip to Phoenix.

It seemed like just a few seconds had passed when both Allison, Lorenzo and Carmelita awoke to the thump, thump, thump of helicopter rotor blades cutting through the air.

Expecting the Blackhawk's arrival, they all began to scan the horizon. When they did not see any helicopters in the air, they surmised that the choppers must have landed just over the rise in a flatter landing zone. They expected the Marines to come double-timing over the hill at any moment.

Sure enough, within a few minutes they heard the approach of booted feet jogging across the desert floor in their direction. Allison gently awoke the professor and his family members to prepare them for extraction.

Just as they got the family to their feet and ready, a contingent of armed uniformed soldiers jogged into their campsite. They knew immediately that they were not Marines. These soldiers had on black pants and tunics and wore unmarked black berets.

The commander of the paramilitary unit barked out orders to Allison, Carmelita, Lorenzo and the family to raise their hands and follow him back to the waiting aircraft. The tired, rag-tag team was caught completely off guard, as they expected the Marines and had already laid their weapons down. They were completely unprepared.

The captors drove their captives hard for about a quarter of a mile around a small hill and into a clearing where a Pave helicopter was waiting. The Pave, built by Sikorsky, is a heavy lifter and a nimble flier for its size.

The loading ramp at the rear of the helicopter was down, and the family was forced up the ramp and into the helicopter. The three team leaders had their hands and ankles tightly bound with nylon straps and were forced to their knees as the family was loaded on the helicopter. They were sure that their lives were over and had thoughts of regret as they quickly examined their lives mentally. Just as they expected gunshots, they both felt a needle enter their arms. Within a few seconds, the world just faded to black as they toppled onto the desert floor.

The Pave lifted off quickly and easily and flew up through a canyon barely 20 feet off the ground and headed to the northeast. Professor Holmsby and his family were shown very good treatment and were immediately given water and food and relatively comfortable seating. All were safely strapped into their seats and told to prepare for a quick but perhaps bumpy flight.

Sam and the Marines arrived at the site from where the electronic homing beacon was transmitting only to find a deserted patch of ground. Hovering off to the side at about 50 feet, it was clear that someone had been there recently from all of the foot prints in the ground. But there was no evidence of any of the escapees or the three team leaders.

Air

Completely puzzled, Sam had the commander drop a rope from the door so he could rappel down to the ground.

Sam hit the ground and began looking for clues as to where the party could be. His headset crackled static an instant before the commander's voice could be heard. "Sam, we see a set of tracks leading away from the campsite around the hill to your northwest."

Sam immediately picked up the trail and began to cautiously follow it. The Blackhawks were both in a stand off position where they could visually monitor his progress and be ready for any kind of an encounter.

"Sam, the tracks lead all the way around that hill. You may want to go over the hill and approach that way rather than follow the same path."

"Great idea," Sam replied.

The hill was not steep and he easily scaled it. As Sam came over the crest of the hill, he could see that the area was heavily tracked with foot prints and an area that had been swept smooth in a giant circle.

Sam radioed to the Blackhawks what he was seeing, and the commander suggested that the giant circle was the imprint of a helicopter rotor. Sam started down the hill, and on his way down he spotted Allison, Lorenzo and Carmelita. His heart sank as he contemplated their death. He had grown close to them and had an incredible feeling of despair.

He kneeled over Allison and gently probed her carotid artery for a pulse. Just as he touched her, one of the Blackhawks landed nearby. He wasn't sure if it was the vibration of the helicopter landing or if he really felt a pulse. No, there was no doubt about it, Allison had a pulse. Quickly, he checked Carmelita and Lorezo, and again was relieved to feel life pumping through their bodies. All three were clearly unconscious and not going to awaken soon. He cut the strapping on their ankles and wrists just as the Marines brought over three litters. The Marines assigned to the mission put them on a drip of ringers to hydrate and stabilize their blood chemistry.

The two Blackhawk helicopters flew to the waiting Cessna Caravan and Jim. The Marines transferred the three litters to the Caravan and waited until the Caravan was climbing up from the primitive strip, then took off and followed the Caravan most of the way to Phoenix.

Sam immediately radioed to Mac what had occurred. Someone somehow had known where Professor Holmsby and his family were, and knew that they had a very tight window in which to make the abduction. Whoever they were up against had inside information, and they had the money and resources to pull this off right under their noses. Beyond knowing they were looking for a large military-size helicopter, they had no idea where the abductors were or even what direction they had headed. Judging by the rotor dust pattern in the desert floor, it had to be one of the heavy lifters, like a Pave or Jolly Green or even another Blackhawk. Whichever it was, it certainly indicated they type of connections this new enemy had and that they had deep pockets.

Chapter 35

The Phoenix office of Homeland Security received a call the day following the abduction of the professor. The voice was a nondescript male with a slight Middle Eastern accent. The caller was articulate and concise, and his message was straight forward and simple.

"The professor and his family are healthy and are being tended to with the utmost care. Our organization does not want money, nor do we have any intention of injuring Professor Holmsby and his family. In the interest of expediting the return of the professor and his family, have a representative from the office of the President contact our organization via the following url…www.xyz.com."

The url had a single phone number on the one and only landing page - a phone number in the U.K. as indicated by the number prefix.

The gentleman who answered the phone was very British and very polished. "My clients are all businessmen from Saudi Arabia, Kuwait, Oman, Libya, Egypt, and the United Emirates. My clients understand the concept behind the technology that the professor has developed, and further they understand the economic implications behind the use of the system. We will return the professor to whoever you designate, as soon as the President issues a document that establishes a multinational governing body that will set the rules for the use of the system. The multinational body must include representatives from all of my client's nations.

"The document must be hand delivered to an address that will be given to you when we next contact you. The document must also be sent to the United Nations, and published in every major newspaper to which you have access. The whole world must know of this technology and that it will be used responsibly by a responsible governing body."

As soon as the President was briefed on the recent events, he ordered the drafting of a document per the instructions of the kidnappers. He didn't have any plans to follow their instructions, but involving them in an editing process of the document would buy him time.

He also asked for an update in White Sands Labs on progress on finalizing the development of the device without the professor. Professor Holmsby as definitely the fastest way to complete the project, but probably not the only way. With all of the talents and skills of all of the government labs, universities and schools in the U.S., there was a good possibility that they could complete it without him.

Within a few minutes of concluding the call from the kidnappers, the NSA had traced the call and analyzed the voice print of the polished voice on the phone. The call originated in London within an office of MI 5. The voice print and the current inhabitant of that office were not a match, but at least they had a starting point.

Because of the transmitter chips injected into the family members, the NSA and the balance of the nations security force were tracking their discreet and encrypted signals and had exact coordinates on their location. The family was being held about 60 miles from where they had been kidnapped, in a remote part of the Arizona high desert. Plans were immediately implemented to launch a recon and rescue mission.

The office had been closed for re-painting and the officer who normally used it was temporarily relocated in another part of the building. The security camera recordings were quickly reviewed to find the coverage of the time when the painting crew was in the building. Within a few minutes, British Intelligence had a license plate number from the painter's van and facial images of the painters. One of the painters was positively identified and linked to an organization known as Peace Now.

Generally, Peace Now worked behind the scenes to open lines of communication where they had closed down, or help to shape peaceful perspectives within minds that ordinarily were bent on violence. Not much was known about the group, except that it was Middle Eastern in origin and multinational in its structure. Not much attention was paid to them, since they were usually quiet and generally thought of as constructive in nature.

The dossier on Peace Now was quickly opened, and any and all information about where they operated in the southwest U.S. was being compiled quickly from multiple databases around the world.

The scientists at White Sands Laboratories, New Mexico, Livermore Labs in California, and Oak Ridge, Tennessee, were all working night and day to perfect the sky shield system. They were very close to identifying the quantum physics formulas that controlled the precise location in space of each orbiting orb. Without the precision, the beams would not interact precisely enough to create the holographic effect, which in turn either created the shield or the parabolic mirror.

The navigational/GPS computer that located the hundreds of orbiting orbs was a DNA-based system that utilized very little power, was hundreds of times faster than any existing silicon based system and could survive in a much broader range of temperatures. The DNA compound was extracted from carbon based elements, and once stabilized it was injected into a wafer with sealed channels. Those channels ran parallel and intersected on each wafer in patterns that drove millions of variations of commands that in turn controlled the location of the orb. The wafer containing the DNA compound was electrically stimulated at such low levels of voltage and amperage that if traditional AAA batteries were used, they would last at least 50 years. The orbiting units had perpetual power from solar cells on each orb that stored electrical power on a unique battery that would last centuries if not longer.

The exact formula of the DNA compound was the missing element that Professor Holmsby kept on file mentally and had never put on paper. The scientific team was working very hard to reverse engineer the compound to duplicate the captured material. The measurements of the various components to create the DNA compound was at six decimal points for each compound, and with 25 elements involved, there were thousands of potential formulas but only one that worked correctly, which is why Dr. Holmsby was such an important factor in final development. Even working at the feverish level with all hands on deck, the best prospect to be able to reproduce the formula was unknown.

It was quite apparent that while Dr. Holmsby was a key factor, no one but the U.S. intelligence and scientific community knew the specifics of his value. That alone helped protect him and his family from harm. The U.S. intelligence community knew that they had to move quickly to prevent him from being moved from the country and recover he and his family as soon as possible.

Chapter 36

Jim, Sam, Allison, Lorenzo, Carmelita and Mac had been melded into an official team and were no longer reporting to their previous employers. Each team member had a cover which allowed them to function in everyday society.

The team had one point of oversight, and that was the NSA, which in turn reported to the President. Major Mac MacDougall was named the strategic commander of the team, and each other team member had specific duties. Jim was tactical command, Sam was in charge of weapons and resources, Lorenzo had authority over communications, Allison was charged with interdepartmental liaison, and Carmelita oversaw logistics. This interlocking multifunctional team gave the very small group agility and flexibility with tremendous power and resources at their fingertips. The extreme high level of secrecy without congressional oversight kept the team out of the spotlight and able to conduct missions at a completely covert level.

The new team was dubbed Security Stealth Team, or SST, as it would come to be known as over time. The skills found within this group were varied and many. To name a few, fixed wing and rotary wing aircraft piloting and mechanic skills, explosives, weaponry of all kind, interdiction tactics, technology being used for navigation and remote observation, combat command experience, hand to hand combat, underwater operations utilizing re-breathers or scuba gear survival training, and many other skills rarely found together at such a high level in a single team.

Since their last operation, when they tried unsuccessfully to extract Dr. Holmsby and his family from central Arizona, the team and gone through refinement and updating on many of their operational skills to prepare them for future missions. Having Dr. Holmsby nabbed out from under their noses was a wrong that they intended to make right. While the reason given during the debriefing was that a lack of intel created the fiasco, it nonetheless did not sit well with any of the team.

Dr. Holmsby was not without survival skills in his own right. He had spent two years in the military and was an engineer, a physicist, and a chemist. He and his family were being held on a ranch northeast of Prescott in an isolated part of the state. He knew that even if he was able to escape, he would have a hard time eluding his captors while trying to get his family to safety. Nonetheless, his mind was busy formulating a plan. In the meantime, they had more than adequate accommodations, good food, and it was clear harm was not the intent of the people holding them. After a few days, he and his wife and their children had regained their strength and had started to feel somewhat normal again.

They essentially had the run of the ranch house. Their captors stood guard outside and in the outbuildings, and had set up their command center in the ranches bunk house. The barn housed a number of vehicles, including the helicopter that brought them to the ranch.

Dr. Holmsby was a private pilot and had even received his rotary wing certification and had flown helicopters in the military. He only had to overcome his captors, get the helicopter out of the barn, disable any other vehicles to prevent pursuit by his hosts, and successfully start the helicopter up, get it in the air and figure out how to fly a large military chopper, which is quite a bit different than the Robinson R-44's he had trained in. It all seemed pretty overwhelming. But, he had nothing to do but think and plan, and a plan of sorts was starting to take shape in his mind. He knew his value to both the U.S. as well as whomever his captives were, and felt that even if his attempt was unsuccessful they would not harm him. He knew he was a valuable pawn in a very high-priced game. His wife, Lisa, was a very able-bodied partner, and he knew that she would have to be a part of the plan to make it work.

The first thing he had to do was to convince his captors to allow he and his family to spend some time out of the house. It was obvious that he wasn't going to be able to get help or run away - he didn't even have any idea where he was. If he could get outside, then he could quickly determine if his plan was really workable. He needed to see into the open barn door to see if the helicopter was on a dolly with a tractor or something with which to tow it. The plan was really very simple; concoct a chemical bomb from the household cleaners in the kitchen that would emit a knock out vapor. By successfully setting off the smoke bomb in the bunk house when they were all in eating or sleeping, he could buy enough time to pull the chopper out of the barn and get it started. In the meantime, his wife could pour enough chemicals into the fuel tanks of the vehicles to prevent pursuit. He could get the kids on board and hopefully get the chopper started and ready for take off while his wife disabled the cars and trucks. The key was to knock out his captors all at once in the bunk house. The best time was during meal time. Since they were so isolated and very sure no one knew where they were, they were not being very diligent in their guard responsibilities. Dr. Holmsby did not look or act threatening, and they did not expect that he would even be capable of concocting such a plan, much less actually pulling it off. Of course, he wasn't sure either.

He built five Molitov cocktails that would emit a ammonia and bleach mixture of smoke that would very quickly knock out, perhaps even kill, all or some of his captors. He mixed the formula in a diluted mixture to be a knock out smoke only. He wasn't sure that if someone got too much of it that they wouldn't die, but that was a risk he was willing to take. He hid the bombs and waited to develop his opportunity. They had a moonless night coming up in a few days. Darkness would really work to their advantage to pull the plan off, and he decided that moonless night would be their first attempt.

That evening, when the guard brought food in for the family, Dr. Holmsby made a plea for fresh air.

"My children need to get out and get some exercise and fresh air. They are used to a very active life, and the constant sitting around without any stimuli of any kind is starting to have a very negative impact on their behavior. My wife and I also need to stretch our legs, can we be allowed out at least in the evenings?"

The guard promised to forward their request and agreed it was a reasonable thing to ask. As Dr. Holmsby pointed out, where would they go? They were in the middle of nowhere, they might as well be on a desert island.

The leader of the guards agreed almost immediately, and that evening the professor and his wife and kids had their first breath of fresh air and exercise in days. It felt wonderful. Despite the situation they were in, the countryside was absolutely stunning, the air was fresh and cool, and at night the stars were incredible. The Arizona night sky was just amazing.

Within a day or two, they had established a routine in the evening, and the guards really didn't pay any attention to them. It was almost like they were on a dude ranch on vacation. An escape attempt by the professor and his wife probably did not even cross the guard's minds. Sometimes surprise was the best weapon.

Over the course of the first few days they had out on the grounds, the professor and his wife finalized their plans. They would make their attempt the next evening. The smoke bombs were ready, the containers with the vehicle-disabling mixture were ready, the kids had been told of the upcoming adventure, and the professor was scared out of his wits.

The evening of the new moon was like the previous 10 evenings that the family had been in captivity. The guards had become almost friendly as they got acquainted with the Holmsby family, letting them wander the grounds most of the day and even into the evening.

As the guards sat down to eat, Dr. Holmsby retrieved his smoke bombs from the hiding spot and prepared to set them off while Lisa readied herself to go into the barn and disable the various vehicles. Dr. Holmsby wedged a piece of 2 x 4 against both of the two doors in and out of the bunkhouse. Doing this trapped the guards in the bunkhouse as they sat down to eat. He then lit each of his smoke bombs and gently sat them inside the windows of the bunk-house so the smoke would fill the building. After lighting them and setting them in the building, he quietly closed the windows and watched as the smoke began to fill the build-ing. Within a matter of seconds, he heard the yelling and screaming of the guards as they try to figure out where the smoke was coming from. The chemical smoke did its job though, and within about a minute or so, all of the guards were out cold. Being a humanitarian, the professor opened the front door and allowed most of the smoke to clear out, as well as checked the pulse of each guard. He then picked up the arms of the smallest guard and pulled him out the front door. Outside the building, he tied his feet and hands, put him in a fireman's carry, and loaded him into the helicopter. Lisa and the kids also scrambled aboard, lisa having done her part to disable the captor's other vehicles.

The Sikorsky Pave helicopter is a huge machine by any standard, particularly compared to anything that Dr. Holmsby had any experience with. It was going to be interesting trying to get it into the air. Fortunately, all of the controls are the same and he quickly oriented himself in the cockpit, with one exception. The Pave is powered by a turbine engine, and the start up procedure is very different from starting a piston engine. He located the operator's guide, and as he read through the steps, it appeared as though it would not be as difficult as he thought. The first step was to start the turbine spinning from battery power, and as soon as the rpms hit optimum level, then switch on the fuel pumps, and finally hit the ignite switch to light the fuel in the hot box. At that point, the key was to monitor outlet temperatures and keep them under the redline.

The engines spun up smoothly, and as he rotated the throttle, the helicopter began to lighten on its wheels. He had his feet on the pedals, and as the chopper began to lift he was able to control any yaw with the appropriate tail rotor control. He rotated the chopper away from the barn, and as he added throttle he dipped the nose of the big machine and picked up speed as he began to climb. Surprisingly, the big helicopter was fairly easy to fly and was as nimble as anything he had flown before. It had been several years since he flew a chopper, but it all came back to him as he began to get a feel for how it handled.

The next step was to figure out where they were. The control panel had a Garmin 530 GPS built in, and he powered it up to get a read on their position. As the Garmin powered up, he reached behind him and pulled a set of headsets off the hook in the ceiling. His next step was to communicate with some authorities. He knew that the Garmin would have nearby airport frequencies, and he could call the nearest FAA station and get help.

Just as he put the headset, on he heard and felt several "pings" hit the outside of the chopper airframe. He looked out the window and saw that his captors had come to and were firing warning shots into the lower airframe and motioning him to return to the landing position. He had no choice but to comply, his efforts had failed and now he knew he would not get another chance - his captors would not trust him again. Worse yet, they may want to punish him for his effort.

Just as the professor was about to touch back down, he heard the unmistaken sound of a 50 caliber machine gun being fired in long bursts. The ground around the captors was rapidly turning into a huge dust cloud as the rounds pummeled the area as only a 50 caliber can do. It is an awesome sight, and if you are on the receiving end of that gunfire and not used to seeing or hearing it, one's immediate inclination is to either surrender or run for your life. The professor slowly pivoted the Pave around and was thrilled to see a pair of Marine helicopter gunships hovering 50 feet off the ground and steadily firing warning shots around the captors. Without hesitation, the team of captors threw down their weapons and put their hands on their heads. One of the Marine helicopters landed, and a dozen or so Marines jumped out and double-timed into position, taking the captors into captivity.

Within a few seconds, the professor heard instructions in his headset. "Professor Holmsby, it looks like you have the situation well in control. We are happy to assist you and give you escort to Prescott airport...follow us."

The Marine chopper passed him on the left, and as the

professor looked over he saw the Marine officer in charge give him a salute. Relief flooded through him and his eyes welled up with tears as he returned the salute and powered up the chopper to follow his rescuer.

Within minutes, Jim and Sam were in the traffic pattern for the Prescott airport. As they approached the downwind leg of the landing pattern, they could see the big Sikorsky and the Pave sitting on the tarmac with their rotors slowly rotating in the breeze. Several local Sheriff vehicles were parked around the helicopters with their emergency lights on, and in the distance they could see several more emergency vehicles speeding to the airport. This was probably the biggest thing to happen in Prescott since the days of the Wild West.

Out of the corner of his eye, Jim picked up movement and swiveled his head to react to the movement. A plain wrap black unmarked helicopter was bearing down on the scene from the southwest. Sam radioed a warning to the Sheriff department on the ground as the helicopter appeared to be a potential threat. "Yavapai Sherriff, be aware we have an inbound plain wrap helicopter inbound from the southwest at high speed, not sure of intentions."

No sooner had Sam released the talk button when the inbound helicopter arrived over the airport and proceeded to make a pre-landing circle. The helicopter descended in a hover to 20 feet in front of the Sikorsky and began to rake it with automatic gun fire. The gunman sprayed the Sikorsky and most of the Sheriff vehicles and had all of the officers pinned on the ground. The Marine rescue party was returning fire, but clearly the plain wrap helicopter had the advantage as they continued to pound away at the vehicles and the big choppers. The machine gun fire was devastating, as each round hit home punching half inch holes though cars, trucks and the grounded aircraft. Several vehicles were burning, and officers and bystanders were running in all directions in complete panic. Only the Marines held their position and attempted to return fire, but they too were pinned down.

Jim broke off the final approach in the big Cessna and turned out of the pattern away from the devastation. The Cessna wing on this particular airplane was built for lift and quick climb outs at steep angles, and Jim put it to the test with a high angle of attack steep bank turn away from the action.

Sam practically yelled in the intercom, "Go around and make a pass over that chopper!"

As he was talking, he was reaching behind the front seats for a Browning Automatic Rifle. With a 50 round clip of 30.06 ammo, it could rain down a lot of damage. Jim pulled the Cessna in a tight turn back towards the airport and lined up above and to the port side of the helicopters position.

Sam was already in the back seat with the rear door open with one clip in and two spare clips ready to go.

Jim was going to approach the helicopter on the left and orbit the position while Sam fired out the starboard door opening down onto the chopper. He was in a harness connected to the seat restraint system, which allowed him to sit sideways at the door, a system typically used for looking out the door not firing a weapon, but it adapted nicely in this case.

As Jim approached the chopper from above out of sight, Sam opened fire down into the chopper's engine nacelle. The steady whump, whump, whump of the BAR could be heard over the engine and through the headsets very clearly.

Almost immediately, the well-placed rounds had an effect. Smoke started pouring out of the engine, and the helicopter began to attempt a climb out. Clearly, though, the engine was not producing full power and appeared to be failing quickly.

Concerned that the chopper could turn soon enough to bring weapons to bear on them, Sam changed clips and began pouring gunfire into the tail rotor as Jim orbited the position. Officers on the ground had also recovered and were on their feet pouring gunfire from the ground into the chopper. Suddenly, the tables had turned on the helicopter and it was in serious trouble. Smoke was pouring out of the engine and the chopper was now spinning out of control. It had managed to climb to about 100 feet when it completely lost power and plunged to the ground. The impact broke the fuel tank and the entire wreckage was engulfed in flames. The threat had been eliminated, thanks to the quick action and bravery of Jim and Sam.

Jim pulled out of the orbit and went around for a landing approach. As they made their final approach, the airport fire brigade had rolled up to the burning helicopter and were attempting to get water on the flames to contain the fire. The fuel had burned so hot that the only thing left was bare frame and engine; most everything else had either been burned or was broken into tiny pieces.

Jim and Sam landed and taxied up to the parking area and were greeted by Sheriff Deputies and Marines cheering and applauding their timely arrival and quick action. Unfortunately, the heroic glow would not last long.

Chapter 37

O ne of the gunman's rounds had hit Dr. Holmsby as he sat in the Sikorsky waiting for an escort to safety. He was currently clinging to life from an injury to his lung where a bullet penetrated his chest cavity and caused his lung to deflate. He had lost a lot of blood and he was still hemmorrhaging internally. Until he stabilized, all they could do was replace the blood as quickly as it bled out. He was in and out of consciousness as he struggled to survive. That was the report given by the duty nurse at the hospital. Since the professor was in the ICU, no one was allowed in to see him.

With nothing else to do but wait, Jim and Sam found a conference room in the hospital to check in with Mac. They plugged in a portable encryption device into the hospital phone and called Mac on his secure cell phone that never left his side.

Mac listened for the first couple of minutes of briefing, then interrupted Jim and Sam. "Look, I think the local law enforcement can handle the protection of the professor at this point. I need you to both fly to White Sands, New Mexico, this afternoon, you will be briefed when you get there."

"But Mac…" they protested, but it was too late, as he had already hung up.

They caught a ride back to the airport with one of the

deputies within 30 minutes of hanging up with Mac. Both Jim and Sam traveled light and had some backup clothing in their Cessna, so they could be wheels up and on their way to White Sands as soon as they refueled. The flight in the Cessna was a little over three hours and gave them both time to speculate on their impending assignment. But with no real answers forthcoming, they concentrated on getting to White Sands as quick as possible.

The White Sands Labs in central New Mexico were one of the key facilities used to build and test the first atomic bomb produced by the United States during World War II. Since then, it had been used for many top secret projects and was one of the most secure spots in the U.S.

The flight plan essentially called for Jim and Sam to fly to Albuquerque and then turn south. The airport at the lab was more than adequate to meet their needs, as it handled military transport traffic on a regular basis.

As they approached the White Sands airfield three and a half hours later, they noticed a fair amount of activity around an Air Force Hercules C-130. The ramp was down, and a black Suburban was backed up to the edge of the ramp. A small party was being escorted down the ramp into the Suburban under heavy guard.

From their vantage point and with binoculars, Sam was getting a pretty good view of the activities.

"Holy shit!!" he exclaimed. "That Mac is a sneaky bastard."

"What's goin' on?" Jim queried.

"You aren't going to believe this," Sam replied, "but the group of people getting off the Hercules looks like Dr. Holmsby and his family!"

Jim's mind quickly deduced the answer to the seemingly impossible scenario. "You mean he wasn't really injured a few hours ago? The whole hospital scene was just a ruse?"

"It sure looks like it," Sam replied, as he continued to scan the scene while Jim flew the landing approach.

It all added up as soon as they both thought about it. There's no better way to assure someone's security than to make the world think they are dead or incapacitated. After reaching that conclusion, both men pondered what their involvement would be in this next evolution. Their questions would be answered by Mac soon.

An Air Force line crew met Jim and Sam at the parking ramp. One of the enlisted men directed them to a waiting Hum V, while the rest of the crew pushed the Cessna into one of the giant hangars on the airfield.

They jumped into the Hummer, and the driver sped off down the ramp towards the lab campus. The Hummer pulled up to a grouping of buildings that looked to be a combination of administrative and buildings that could have been found on any university campus. They were escorted into the largest building through a polished lobby and into an elevator. Their escort selected the third floor button in the elevator and whisked them into a conference room.

Already seated around the conference room table was the whole balance of the Security Stealth Team. It had been almost a month since they had all been together, and nearly that long since they had spoken as a group. The group stood up and greeted Jim and Sam like two heroes - handshakes, hugs and back patting was the business of the moment. Not only were they all glad see each other, but Jim and Sam had single-handedly managed to stop the professor and his family from being killed.

Mac called the meeting to order after a few minutes of revelry. "Ladies and gentlemen, I am pleased to call the first staff meeting of the SST to order. The first order of business is to congratulate two of our team members on a great job dealing with a potential devastating situation in

Prescott. The press nor the public will know the details of that event or even much of what will be following in the upcoming weeks.

"As you may or may not have seen or perhaps figured out, the person in the ICU in Prescott is not Dr. Holmsby, but rather one of the attack team in the helicopter that should have died after being shot down by Sam. By the way Sam, that was some fine shooting - great job! He was thrown clear just before the impact, and even though he sustained serious injuries he probably will survive. He, along with the prisoner that Dr. Holmsby brought back with him, helped us capture the balance of the team where Dr. Holmsby was being held, and they are all being inter-rogated now.

"In the meantime, we have to protect Dr. Holmsby as he travels between this lab and two other locations for the next several months. We have four separate teams working on the finalization of the system, and two other locations involved in the launch details. We are going to be carrying the system in orbit with the shuttle. The deployment of the orbs will require some system development with the shuttle arm, which will take us to Cape Canaveral as well. The scientific team, along with Dr. Holmsby, should have most of the bugs out of the system in the next couple of weeks."

Over the next several weeks, the work on the Sky Shield progressed at high speed without further events. What had started out as a rather exciting assignment had turned into a mundane bodyguarding. No one was really complaining, because everyone knew that what was bor-ing today could be dangerous and exciting very quickly, particularly with the initial deployment of the Sky Shield coming up soon. The bodyguard assignment had allowed the team to have a very close view and high level of under-standing of how the Sky Shield worked. Dr. Holmsby did not violate his clearance, but he did enjoy chatting with the

SST about his pet project.

The initial deployment consisted of several hundred of the laser generating orbs to be positioned somewhere over central California, probably near Death Valley. Once the system was in place, it would be switched on and put through a battery of tests. The test region chosen was selected due to the extremes in temperature. By varying the placement of the shield over the extremely hot desert conditions, the scientific team could very quickly see the effects of the shield. The initial deployment could shield up to 1,600 square miles, or an area roughly 40 miles square. The shield could be fully switched on or partially to cover an area as small as a square mile. The shield could be deployed as a cover, or tilted and used as a parabolic mirror to focus the effects of the sun's rays on an area. All of these variations and many more were slated to be a part of the testing.

Following the launch of the shuttle to deploy the initial orbital grouping, the team would join Dr. Holmsby and the balance of his brain trust at the test site to measure the effectiveness of the orbiting array. The test site had been kept strictly top secret at the highest level to avoid espionage at the test site. The capabilities of the system were to be kept within the confines of the use and knowledge of the United States military and security units.

Chapter 38

The launch of the shuttle with the orbiting array went off without a hitch. The news media had been advised that the shuttle mission was one of resupply and repair to the International Space Station. Shuttle missions such as this had become routine in the media's view, and while the launch did receive headline coverage, the mission itself was a side story for the most part.

The shuttle roared into space with its unique and very special cargo and a very unique shuttle crew. Two members of the crew had a strictly scientific background, with nothing more than a very rushed bit of training about the shuttle and space life. The shuttle commander and the balance of the crew, for the first time on a shuttle mission, were kept on a need to know basis regarding the mission details. The two scientists had control over the cargo bay and its contents, as well as the robotic arm in the cargo bay. They had received extensive training on the use of the arm and the opening and closing of the bay doors. During the deployment phase, the scientific team would have control over the shuttle to effectively manage the placement of the orbs.

The orbs were loaded into tubes, with each tube containing five of the laser generators. As the shuttle moved through space, the team would release the contents of a tube by gently firing an inert gas discharge, which in essence puffed out the orbs gently into their prescribed position. The shuttle would fly a plowing path back and forth along a predetermined route while the scientists fired their air gun. The system was incredibly simple and fully automated, and only required the scientists to monitor the systems to be sure the gun was firing on target.

Once free of the tube, the laser-generating orbs would turn on their individual navigation system and position themselves within a centimeter of their predetermined position and face their individual laser window correctly. Once in position, they would switch their micro thruster systems off and only turn them back on when repositioning was required. Each orb would run through a self check of the on board systems and link to a computer on the ground to fix problems or get updated data.

Because of the vacuum of space and no air pollution of any kind, the laser generating orbs could see each other and beam a laser to and from each other two miles away. This would require the placing of 20 rows of orbs with 20 orbs in each row, spaced two miles apart, or 400 orbs.

The developmental scientific team knew that the orbs could see each other and effectively bounce a strong enough beam two miles, and hypothesized that that distance could probably be expanded. One of the tests would be to slowly increase the amount of space between each to determine the final operational distance. It would take two 12-hour days to fully launch the 400 orbs, if all went well. Then the real fun would begin.

Furnace Creek in Death Valley rarely had visitors in the summer. The resort facilities were open October 1 through the end of April and closed for the summer. There were caretakers left at the resort, but otherwise it was deserted.

The resort had a golf course, an airport, hotel facilities, and food storage and preparation facilities. The usual caretakers were told that they were relieved of their responsibilities for the summer and paid to take those months off and return at the beginning of the tourist season in late September. They were replaced by a government team that descended on the area like a hoard of locusts. Aircraft of all shapes and sizes carrying scientists, security personnel, cooks, janitorial staff and housekeeping staff, equipment and supplies came and went steadily for several days. Regardless of the job or task assigned to the staff members, each had to meet a rigorous security screening to earn the assignment.

The SST was the first to arrive and served as the welcoming committee and oversight group in preparation of the arrival of the scientific team. The quiet little resort had been transformed into a scientific testing site and support community literally overnight. Luckily, when the resort was closed, all of the very meager residents in the area left for the season. In essence, there really was not a town of any kind, even during the height of the season. Once the scientific, security and support teams occupied the area, they were there alone. Area 51 in central Nevada was a very short hop away and became one of the key staging areas for much of the needed traffic in an out of the area. Nellis AFB in Las Vegas was also utilized to spread the traffic around, reducing curiosity that always follows increased activity around known military bases.

As the scientific site took shape, the personnel enjoyed the desert evenings and a few of the braver souls even tried a little golf very early in the morning. Otherwise, most everyone spent their days inside, tinkering with their equipment and completing the final set up details.

Beyond getting the site set up, Sam and Jim were charged with developing a patrol pattern around the surrounding area. Mornings and evenings were done in the

Skywagon they normally flew on their regular patrols, and during the day they operated a UAV drone with infrared sensors and high resolution cameras. They considered using helicopters, but they are noisy attract attention. The UAVs were very quiet and very difficult to spot and shoot down. If they spotted an intruder or detected a threat with the UAV, they had a very unusual weapons system to use to thwart any attack or intrusion.

In the confined air space of Death Valley, they needed something with speed, but also the ability to fly slow and seem relatively non-military in appearance. Because there were a few year-round residents, they could not have military jets and helicopters flying around, particularly if they had to bring weapons systems to bear on an intruder.

Parked in the larger hangar at the Furnace Creek airport was a P-51 retrofitted with six 50 caliber machine guns. The Mustang could make a strafing run pass at 400 knots or a slower pass at 120 knots to look over an area. It could also orbit on station for a very long time with the drop tank. While it was a WWII U.S. military aircraft, it was painted like a private pleasure aircraft, and residents of the few scattered ranches would not think much about seeing it flying around.

Jim and Sam were both checked out in the Mustang and had received some quick training at a military gunnery range, learning how to at least scare somebody away with the 50 calibers. The routine was to roll the Skywagon out in the morning and evenings and fly preplanned patrol circuits. During the heat of the day, when temperatures could hit 125 degrees, they would use the UAV to patrol from 15,000 feet with the camera and sensors operating. If intruders were spotted, the Mustang would be scrambled in preparation of a potential attack and weapons brought to bear if necessary.

* * *

The Sky Shield was fully deployed and each orb was running through a self check to verify that all of its various components were operational. The day was nearing that the scientific team would initiate the program that would begin to activate the laser generators. As the lasers were shot through the lens prism, the light would refract into the color spectrum into tiny beams that would interlock with beams from other lasers. The network of beams would form a gigantic holographic arched rectangle that would reflect 90 percent or more of the sun's rays, including the harmful UV rays. As the orbs were moved further apart, the strength or density of the shade lessened. As it lessened, more light was allowed to pass through. This allowed an almost infinite degree of change in the strength and sun blocking capability of the shield.

The need for security during this phase of testing was critical. Sam and Jim had to be absolutely sure that the hills and surrounding terrain were clear of spying eyes. The local residents scattered around would be oblivious to any changes, since the tests would be short in duration and not extremely noticeable. The size of the shield and the resulting shadow on the ground could be varied by the number of orbs used to create the size and shape of the shadow.

Jim deployed the UAV throughout the day while Sam sat in the Mustang in the air conditioned hangar. They ran drills every three or four days to make sure all was ready in the event the UAV cameras spotted unauthorized parties staked out in observation points.

The 60-year-old aircraft was in like-new condition, including the 1800 horse power Rolls Royce Merlin engine. Sam and his flight crew could have it started, the hangar doors open, and Sam taxiing to the runway in under three minutes from the time of first notice.

Sam was sitting in the cockpit about to doze off when the loud speaker blared.

Air

"UAV has unauthorized intruders on camera...coordinates on the way...suggest that Mustang 1 taxi into position for immediate take-off."

Sam sat up with a jolt and within seconds had the master switch on and was going through his pre-takeoff check list. The flight crew had pulled the chock blocks away from the main gear while Sam turned the engine over. The big eight-foot-four bladed prop swung through its arc while smoke puffed out of the exhaust stacks. With just a few turns of the prop, the Merlin engine caught and rumbled with a very satisfying sound that only that engine could deliver.

Right on target, Sam was taxiing out to the runway while he was sliding his canopy closed. While he taxied, he finished his check list, including dialing in 15 degrees of right rudder trim. The torque of the engine and the propeller was so strong even at ¾ throttle, that pilots could not hold enough right rudder to hold the big fighter on the runway. Without the trim adjustment, the aircraft engine and propeller torque would pull the airplane off the left side of the runway.

Sam turned onto the runway and ran the throttle up to ¾ and aimed the big nose into the wind. Without waiting to hear anything else from Jim, he released the brakes and accelerated down the runway. Within a few seconds, he was at takeoff speed. The tail-wheel was off the runway, and Sam eased the stick back and the Mustang was climbing out at 3,000 feet per minute. Sam toggled the lever to retract the gear and dialed the rudder trim back to zero. The WWII was as responsive as a modern jet and felt as though it was merely an extension of the pilot's being.

Sam rolled into a 60 degree turn and headed up the valley towards Scotty's Castle. The Castle was a hacienda built in the early 1900s by a wealthy family from Chicago. The family would spend a good portion of the winter months at the Castle each year. Scotty was the family's caretaker, builder and maintenance man. He had lived there year round and ultimately was deeded the house when the last member of the family died. It was ultimately given to the State of California and was now a state park and closed for the season. Jim radioed coordinates and Sam dialed those into the GPS unit built into the instrument panel. The cameras on the UAV had picked up fresh signs of activity in an around the Castle grounds. There were fresh boot prints, tire tracks and other indications of activity. Jim had not actually seen any people, but the signs of activity were clearly there.

Sam collaborated on the radio with Jim as to the best strategy. Both agreed that his first pass should be a high speed one to avoid being a target for much longer than a couple of seconds. Jim could fly the UAV in an orbit well above Sam and watch his passes through video.

He watched as the Mustang roared up the valley at 500 feet AGL and overflew the Castle grounds at 350 knots. He then pulled up into a near vertical climb and rolled over on his back to look back over where he had just been. The beauty of the maneuver was that while anyone in the buildings would think he was gone, Jim had the cameras rolling at full magnification watching for any reaction to his low pass. He was not disappointed either - the first pass caused two men to come running out of the Castle to look and see what had just roared over the top of them. The UAV caught them both clearly on camera as they looked up into the sky looking for the aircraft that had just buzzed them.

"Say cheese," Jim said as the two faces came into focus. The UAV captured all images digitally and down-linked them to a ground based computer. From there, the images were sent through a data file to compare the faces with all of the pictures in the file. Using facial feature recognition software, the computer was able to match the images with pictures in its data file and identify the people in the photos.

Sam had moved off to the south out of sight to see what Jim and the computer came up with before he made any further passes. While he was out of sight and out of hearing range, he armed his guns and fired two quick bursts to make sure the barrels were clear. The rattling of the guns shook the airframe as if a giant hand held the airplane and was gently shaking it.

The two men that had been posted on the ground were of Eastern European descent, approximately 20 to 30 years old and with average builds - very nondescript in their appearance. Surprisingly, the data file had no record of either of these men. With the UAV orbiting at 15,000 feet, it had a clear view of the whole compound at Scotty's Castle. Infrared sensors and telescopic lenses on the camera told the whole story. There was evidence that the generator had been running. Hot spots in various buildings indicated cooking as well as the use of hot water for bathing. Whoever was there had been there a while and was planning on staying.

Jim and Sam had to develop a strategy to dislodge them and force their retreat before the tests on the ground could commence at any scale.

"Sam, make one more high speed pass," Jim radioed. "Lets see how many guests Scotty has." Sam rolled the Mustang into a 60 degree bank and eased into the rudder to make a smooth coordinated turn. Viewed from the ground, the P-51 looked like it was on rails. He advanced the throttle and pointed the nose down hill and was approaching 300 knots in a matter of seconds. He leveled off at 100 feet and rocketed across the desert. As he approached the Castle, he trimmed another 50 feet off the altitude and roared over the compound at over 300 knots at 50 feet off the deck. Anyone in the compound would be stirred to come take a look. At that altitude and speed, they heard him coming for two or three seconds and were probably moving towards the door even before he arrived. Even though he was only directly overhead for a couple of seconds, the sound would have rattled the doors and windows.

Meanwhile, Jim used the joy stick control and his eye in the sky to watch the whole scene unfold. This time there were five men out in the open scanning the skies looking for Sam. All of the men were of Eastern European descent, male and appeared to be in their 20s or 30s. While none of them were wearing any kind of uniform or web gear, they all had a military bearing. Clearly, they were there with the intent of at a minimum observing the curious happenings in and around Death Valley.

Now that they knew where their quarry was, Jim and Sam could focus on keeping an eye on Scotty's Castle. They were still watching the rest of the area, but there weren't any signs of life elsewhere. Most likely, the small troop at the Castle were the only unwanted eyes in the area.

Chapter 39

The orbiting array had completed the systems checks as well as the controls that made subtle changes in the orb configuration and all was working at 100 percent effectiveness. The scientific team was ready to light up the lasers and create their first holographic shield. The plan called for the system to create a shield about a tenth the size of full capacity. The small shield would be roughly four miles by four miles in size and was located over the Furnace Creek Resort. If it worked, a 16-square-mile shadow would gradually appear over the resort and lock into position.

"Uh-oh, we've got a problem," Jim announced as he watched the intruders at Scotty's Castle. The troop had not made any move to get any closer to the resort where the scientific team was operating, so the decision was made to just keep an eye on them for now and not draw further attention to the project.

"What's up?" Sam drawled

"They have a UAV as well and it looks like they are getting ready to launch it."

Sam was running for the hangar before Jim even finished his statement. There was only one solution for this problem - shoot it down after it was out of sight of the controller. If he did it right, their eyes in the sky would disappear and they wouldn't know why. The 51 was in the air in a matter of minutes. Sam's plan was to climb to 12,000 feet and wait for the UAV to come into sight near Furnace Creek. He could approach it from behind and remain undetected, and with a quick burst of the 50 calibers, he could shred the engine causing the UAV to crash. With any luck, the scientific team could recover all or part of the UAV and perhaps learn where it came from, which may lead back to the origin of the intruders.

The UAV already in the air controlled by Jim had its camera locked onto the UAV being launched by the intruders. He would be able to guide Sam into the location of the intruding UAV. The trick would be to knock the UAV down well away from the view of the controllers so they never know what ultimately disabled it.

Sam followed Jim's coordinates for an intercept course and began straining his eyes to try and pick up the much smaller unmanned aircraft. The other issue he was working through in his mind was how to fly slow enough to get a long enough bead on the UAV to knock it down. The UAV would be motoring along at 100 knots or so and the Mustang's handling would be getting mushy around 140 knots. He had to intercept it before it reached Furnace Creek and the remote pilot could focus the cameras and sensors on the test region.

Sam's two tours in the military had given him experience in aerial combat and he did know how to fire an airborne weapons system and actually hit targets, but it had been more than just a few years. He knew he had to approach the UAV from the rear to stay out of the camera's view. Even as he eggressed after shooting it down or if he missed, he had to be careful about staying out of the camera's view.

Scotty's Castle was roughly 45 miles from Furnace Creek, and Sam needed to knock the UAV down before it was able to get inside a 10-mile perimeter. Hopefully, it would be visible soon so he had plenty of time.

Air

"UAV four miles at 1 o'clock," Jim's voice crackled over the radio.

Sam squinted into the sunlight pouring through the canopy, straining his eyes for the tiny speck of an aircraft at that distance. He had to keep his eyes moving to look for movement. He banked slightly to his right and eased in on the rudder. He did not want to make a head on pass, rather he was now maneuvering to approach the UAV on its 6 o'clock position. The UAV was now at the 10 o'clock position and down to a mile and a half distance.

Just as Sam called out the position change, Sam saw a speck of movement in the clear blue desert sky. He reached up and hit the arming switch for his guns. Now that he had the UAV in sight, he could maneuver visually. It was headed in a southerly direction and he was headed east and well beyond the perpendicular point of intersection he began a slow arcing turn to the north, which continued into a westerly swing and then finally on a southerly heading behind the UAV. It was roughly two to three miles ahead of him as he began to throttle back to 150 knots. His plan was to make as many passes as necessary from the rear and if he missed he would make a hard turn to the west and swing around in a full 360 degree turn to bring guns to bear again.

Jim was using the joystick controls for their UAV to follow the action, and the entire scientific team was huddled behind his 50-inch monitor. It truly was like watching a movie unfold. His UAV was positioned above both the Mustang and the intruder UAV by 5,000 feet, but the high resolution telescopic lens made the images appear to be much closer.

Sam lined up his visual sight on the UAV as he closed within a quarter of a mile from the rear. He just tapped the trigger to see how his aiming was and watched the tracers arc out in front of him. The Mustang shuddered as the big 50 calibers rumbled. His rounds were low and about three degrees to the right. He adjusted his aiming and tapped the trigger again. By now he was only 200 to 300 yards, and would have to make a hard turn away. The second tap of the trigger hit the mark and the UAV shredded in pieces as the rounds hit home. The UAVs were not armored in any way and were made of lightweight carbon fiber material, so it took very little to cut it to pieces. Now in multiple pieces, the intruding UAV was falling to the ground harm-lessly, well out of the perimeter of the test site. Hopefully, the intruder controlling the UAV never knew the reason why his equipment stopped functioning. Jim dispatched a couple of men to go retrieve the parts of the UAV on the ground.

Sam did a victory roll, while Jim and the entire team erupted into cheers as though he had just achieved ace sta-tus. Sam eased out of the roll and leveled out on a heading back to Furnace Creek. The Mustang was truly a joy to fly, and Sam almost regretted turning onto final for the runway. The mains chirped as he touched down and the speed bled off and the tail-wheel settled on the macadam. The han-gar door was open and he taxied straight in and swung the tail around with the long nose facing the hangar door. A crewman hopped up on the wing and helped him slide the canopy back and get out of his safety restraint.

He stepped down off the wing and was immediately greeted by the entire SST, or Monkey Wrench Gang, as they had begun to affectionately refer to themselves. They had all read Edward Abbey's book, *The Monkey Wrench Gang*, and thought the name fit them very well. Abbey's gang used creative tricks and methods to achieve their ob-jectives, not unlike Jim, Sam, Lorenzo, Allison, Carmelita, and Mac.

"Great shooting, Ace!" Jim exclaimed.

The team closed in around him and congratulated him with slaps on the back and hugs. Cold beers were in the offering, so they headed back to the main buildings.

The first test was scheduled for the next morning. The desert air would be at its coolest and the tenets of the test were to see if the Sky shield could cast a shadow strong enough to hold the cool temperature. Jim had the UAV in the air early, and Sam was also in the air with the Mustang orbiting at 12,000 feet giving high cover for the test. He was stationed about halfway between Scotty's Castle and the test site to keep a visual perspective of any intrusion path from the Castle area.

Dr. Holmsby began a five minute countdown to powering on about 25 percent of the system. The segment of the system would cast a three and a half mile square shadow, or roughly 10 square miles. The test regimen called for 10 grades of shadow varying by 5 percent intensity in each grade. At full intensity, the Sky Shield shadow should block enough light to reduce the temperature on the ground in the center of the shadow, making it a full 20 degrees cooler. The light being blocked would be similar to putting on a pair of high-quality sunglasses.

Sam was flying the UAV over the test site to be sure there weren't any local residents out wandering in the area. The actual test site was well away from any road or residence. Even if someone happened to be in the test site, they would notice a slight shadow encroaching on the area.

"Test site all clear," Jim radioed.

"Highway clear," Sam announced.

"T-minus 30 seconds and counting," the system director announced.

As the system came on line, the only indication that it was working were green lights blinking on the control panels. Then, just as though someone had turned the knob on a rheostat, the visual image on the screens showed a shadow being cast over the test area. The group in the lab erupted into cheers.

The instruments in the center of the test site were attached to radio telemetry equipment. The test section of the orbiting array came to life within a second or two of the scientific team sending the signal. The designated orbs came to life with lasers coming to life and shooting their concentrated beams through the prisms. On command, a 10 percent density shield appeared in space and blocked a portion of the sun shining on that segment of the earth. If one had been flying by in the shuttle, they would have seen a giant rectangular shield of light floating in space.

The test director strengthened the intensity by another 10 percent, and the shadow on the ground began to darken ever so slightly. The temperature read out on the ground dropped by one tenth of a degree. Comparatively, the temperature outside of the test region was continuing to climb to an expected 118 degrees for the day. The internal test region temperature was holding and even beginning to decline.

Sky Shield strength was increased by regular steady levels as the test plan was written. The shadow on the ground darkened and the temperature dropped to three degrees lower than the beginning temperature. The temperature a few feet outside of the test area had increased, and there was now a 10 degree differential between the two areas. This was absolute proof of the systems success. The scientific team, Dr. Holmsby and the Monkey Wrench Gang were ecstatic.

Throughout the day, the tests continued. At the peak temperature for the day, the test region did not go over 97 degrees, and outside the test region the temperature hit a high of 115 degrees. An 18 degree variance was incredible. This kind of variance is indicative of a different agricultural growing zone. Desert soils could be tilled and used agriculturally with this kind of difference.

A group of three men in desert camouflage huddled down behind rocks and covered their heads and gear every time the Mustang made a pass overhead. With their binoculars they watched the rectangular shadow cover the desert floor and gradually get darker as the day wore on, an amazing and extremely impressive sight to see from their lofty perch. It appeared as though a giant cloud was settled over the desert, but the sky was clear.

They use secured and encrypted sat-phones and video gear to capture the test. They were part of the team in Scotty's Castle, and were in their perch in case the team at the Castle was discovered. The backup plan paid huge dividends with their discovery. They radioed back to their coalition bosses in the Middle East what they witnessed and uplinked the video coverage as proof. The video images were stunning and undeniable in their effectiveness. While the unwanted observers could not guess at the temperature changes, it was obvious the difference would be significant.

As part of his patrol path, Sam overflew Scotty's Castle periodically to check on activity levels. It was clear that the contingent of intruders were still there but laying low. Sam reported this and asked Jim to discuss it with Mac. The scientific site director overheard the discussion and offered a solution. His idea was simple - use the Sky Shield to be configured as a giant mirror and bounce concentrated rays onto the Castle. The heat increase would be more than enough to flush out the intruders and push them out of the area. Mac concurred.

The director walked over to an input keyboard where a tech was sitting and gave him some quick instructions. Ten minutes later, the shadow over the test site disappeared and a bright beam appeared bearing down on Scotty's Castle.

Temperatures in roughly a half mile square area began to soar.

Jim's UAV was orbiting off to the side of the Castle area and he focused his cameras on the buildings and grounds. The light from the beam was so bright he had to close the aperture to improve the contrast, otherwise most everything was washed out in the natural light.

The view from Jim's UAV of the Castle was up on the monitors. Within five minutes, several of the occupants at Scotty's wandered outside and looked up into the sky. Clearly they were feeling the heat and did not realize that it could be so warm in Death Valley. The concentrated sunlight was probably driving the temperatures past 125 degrees. The masonry buildings and asphalt would soak up the heat and be like an oven through the night. Even as the sun went down and temperatures dropped, all of man's creations would hold the heat.

Within an hour, there was evidence at the Castle that the occupants were packing up to leave, and an hour later a small convoy was headed out of the state park. The test of the sky beam had been a huge success, at least in that type of application. Being able to use the technology in the battle against terrorism would be very useful. The beam could simply be focused on known terrorist bases to flush the terrorists out into the open.

Two U.S. Army Blackhawk helicopters intercepted the intruder convoy and captured the intruders. Once the intruders were in custody, a separate Blackhawk was sent to Scotty's Castle to be sure that no one was left behind.

The Blackhawk dropped a stick of troops off under cover of a nearby hill and then lifted back off to provide gun cover with its mini-gun. As the troops moved from building to building, all they found was evidence that the intruders had been there, but all personnel were gone. They had also left behind satellite radio equipment with an encryption device, which would indicate they had been able to communicate some of their findings as limited as they were, back to their sponsors.

With the area cleansed of intruders, the Sky Shield/ Beam testing could begin in earnest. The test regimen included temperature measurements, either stimulating a storm from an existing system through heat, or minimizing or stopping a storm by cooling the temperatures in the storm system.

Death Valley had been chosen as the test site for a lot of reasons, not the least of which was the presence of many small isolated storm systems over the mountains that rarely turned to rain. In many cases, the storms simply evaporated due to the high temperatures. By cooling the system off, the storm would condense its moisture into droplets and perhaps actually rain on the desert.

Meteorology is not particularly exciting unless it becomes controllable in the hands of responsible science, then it becomes one of the most exciting tools known to mankind.

Chapter 40

urricane season had hit and was beginning to
threaten the Caribbean and Gulf areas. The National Meteorological Service (NMS) satellite and
radar systems were tracking the building activity around
the equator and monitored each system closely as it either
moved towards inhabited areas or rained itself out over the
ocean. The hurricane season destroyed homes, businesses
and lives each year and cost the human infrastructure billions of dollars each year.

In the meantime, the Sky Shield system had been
moved and reconfigured over the southeastern Caribbean
area. The NMS noted with some curiosity how none of the
storm systems they were tracking were turning into either
serious tropical storms or hurricanes. By now, the region
would have experienced at least a couple of tropical storms
of some strength, if not a hurricane or two. Fairly strong
systems just seemed to lose strength as they moved close to
any land mass. The islands or inhabited areas in the path
of the storms all received the benefit of the rain from these
storms but none of the high wind. No one was complaining,
but at the same time it was an oddity not seen at any other
time in history. Meteorologists all around the world speculated that this was the effect of global warming or the loss
of the ozone layer or whatever theory could be concocted.

The scientific team operating the Sky Shield was
enjoying the great satisfaction of successfully knocking

the big storms in the Atlantic and Caribbean to their knees. As storms tracked to land, the team would simply focus the shield over them and cool the air in the storm, allowing the rain to occur but removing all of the volatility out of the convective forces of the storm. Instead of hot moist air mixing with cool fronts and creating a swirling eye, the shield cooled the hot moist air and moderately warm air met with cool air, creating a simple rain storm.

It was amazing how effective the system was with predictable results. The team was gathering data on how the system functioned and how long it took focusing the shadow on a system to get it cool enough. Their quest for data was being supplied to them unknowingly by the NMS as they continued to fly P-3 Orion aircraft into the storms and drop probes into them to record the temperature, humidity, dew points, lapse rates and wind speeds associated with each system. That data was routinely accessible by virtually anyone. It wouldn't be long until one of the meteorological scientists would notice the trend of temperature drops with regular frequency.

In the meantime, the Santa Ana winds were beginning to blow in California and the brown hillsides throughout the state were turning into dry tinder. A cigarette butt or a bolt of lightening could set one of those hillsides or canyons afire at any time. The conundrum facing the Sky Shield team was where they should be focusing their efforts and where the shield should be located. Clearly, the United States needed to quickly build and launch more Sky Shield systems.

Getting appropriations to add to the system would take months if not years, not to mention the knowledge of the system would have to emerge from a cloak of Top Secret, so Congress could understand what they were funding. The President was not yet ready to share the system publicly. He wanted more test examples of successful use of the system before he asked for money. He wanted enough data to avoid lengthy congressional debate.

What the President was considering could either earn him an impeachment hearing or leave a legacy that would be unprecedented in how much a presidential administration helped mankind. He needed to assemble the Monkey Wrench Gang.

The President met with his small circle of advisors and gave them the opportunity to resign before they willingly and knowingly became a part of a set of acts that at the very least could be construed as serious abuse of executive authority.

Without divulging his plan, he simply said that the future of the country, as well as an unprecedented advancement for mankind, hinged on acquiring massive amounts of cash and securities very quietly and very quickly. The assets needed to pay the scientific team, purchase the materials, and successfully deploy the system on a broader scale had to be done quickly and quietly. The money could not pass through normal systems, it could not be kept in a bank, it could not be electronically transferred, and it would have to be stored safely offshore.

Without exception, the President's entire team remained solidly in place and all swore to secrecy. Even though what he was doing was for the right reason, the Presdient felt odd skirting the law. Truth be known, many Presidential acts throughout history were unconstitutional and at least questionable, yet were done in the right spirit and produced the right result for mankind. Executive leadership called for tough decisions in tough times, particularly when the result of those decisions could have such an impact.

Decades earlier, not even Vice President Harry Truman nor Congress knew anything about the atomic bomb project until FDR died in office. FDR knew he had no choice and he knew it could not be a debatable issue in either the house or the Senate. He took a chance and made a decision, one that changed the world.

The assets and money would come from a variety of sources. One major source, the membership of the Founders, had been contacted through their convoluted system of overlapping committees with a request and a proposal. The proposal was pay up or face criminal prosecution for drug smuggling, money laundering and many other assorted illegal activities. While the charges may not stick for lack of evidence, many members would see their family names besmirched in the press, and the Founders organization would lose much of its strength of being able to quietly operate below the radar. The hundreds of families and companies in the Founders that represented the top one percent of the wealth in the nation all agreed to ante up, per the President's request.

The second source was a little trickier. The Federal reserve system both put newly-printed money into circulation and removed old and tattered money from circulation. As money passed through the federal reserve bank locations, the older, tattered money was set aside and destroyed and new money was put into circulation at about the same rate, keeping the currency level relatively stable. The Treasury department had the responsibility to balance the ebb and flow of money to keep the value stable. However, the auditing process of the amount in circulation at any given moment was a gargantuan undertaking, and one that would rarely if ever completely balance. The plus or minus error percentage was around 1 percent of the GNP at any given moment.

This meant that additional money could be printed and used for a temporary need without harming the credibility of the money supply. It had been done before with the balance restored after the need had been met. Usually this required Congressional approval and took time to pass through the Ways and Means Committee for final authority. The President was going to bypass this step. Even though the Ways and Means Committee could handle this without it going to the floor for debate or discussion, it would require bringing more participants into the mix than the President wanted at this time. Again, the money would have to be handled physically and not electronically, and moved offshore very quietly and quickly.

Alltogether, the President was going to pull $25 billion to take Sky Shield to the next critical phase.

Even in larger denominations, $25 billion in cash would fill several pallets stacked in 4-foot cubes. Armored trucks, forklifts and cargo aircraft would be needed to move this amount of money. Logistically, it was going to be a nightmare to accumulate it and move it offshore and out of the eyes of the federal banking system.

The President's call to the Secretary of the Treasury summoning him to the White House caught the Secretary a little off guard. He was accustomed to attending meetings there for the gathering of the cabinet, but it was somewhat rare to be summoned unexpectedly. He had a high regard for his boss the President and did not worry about the reason for the meeting, having faith in the President's wise use of his time.

The President welcomed him like the old friend he was. They both sat in the sitting area in the Oval Office and chatted for a few minutes, catching up on family and fiends. Finally, the President broached the topic at hand with a question.

"My old friend, how would you characterize the effectiveness of this administration throughout my term?"

Not too sure where this was headed, the Secretary

gave the President a fairly generic response.

"I would agree," the President replied. "Some presidents are presented with moments that require strong leadership, things like war, terrorism, economic problems, and unrest in other parts of the world that they have to grapple with and find solutions. We have been fortunate not to have been faced with any real Earth-shattering events that have required the kind of presidential notoriety that accompanies said events. However, what I am about to share with you and ask for your support on is no less important than those types of events." The President went on to outline the operation of the Sky Shield, to which the Secretary's response was that of being predictably stunned.

His mind racing over what he had just heard, the Secretary of the Treasury thought, what does he want from me? He quickly realized that the President was going to ask for emergency funding - funding that would never be a part of a appropriations bill or appear anywhere on a budget or even on a ledger. This money would be cash used to pay for the manufacturing of components, materials, and material transportation to facilitate expansion of the system before the President's second term was up.

He quickly understood the nature of the request that would be forthcoming. He also understood that the use of the money was much more than a political issue - it was an important leap forward in technology required to keep abreast of the changing world. The technology would put the United States in the driver's seat technologically for decades to come. Before the President even made his request, the Secretary of the Treasury volunteered his personal assistance to fund the project. The President's face beamed with warmth and pleasure at the support the Secretary had just offered.

In essence, the President of the United States, the Secretary of the Treasury, and a select group of personal advisors were co-conspirators in an act or series of acts that could potentially land them all in prison. However, if done carefully and quietly, the Sky Shield would be expanded quickly and the financial part of the whole story would never be heard or questioned. This type of act was not unprecedented, and the Secretary of the Treasury, the President and most of his advisors knew it. Through the decades, many similar emergencies were handled quietly and off the books for the sake of national security.

Chapter 41

Mac had done an amazing job in a very short time developing the Monkey Wrench Gang into a better equipped and more tightly organized team. They all carried PDAs that were specially encrypted but looked like normal Blackberry Curves. The highly specialized communication devices were capable of communication anywhere in the world in voice, email or text messaging or two-way voice radio, all of which was encrypted. Each PDA had 200 gigabytes of storage and operating systems that were faster and more powerful than most desktop computers. Each nondescript looking device had a titanium outer shell with a scratch-proof screen, as well as a high resolution camera that could digitally capture still or video images. Through infrared ports or through a USB connection, the operating system could read any operating system in the world and download any type of data from any computer. This was truly the most powerful spy tool in the world in terms of communication and digital storage. Via an encrypted email, Mac could blast out a simul-message to the whole team with instructions anywhere in the world. Oh, and each was equipped with GPS transmitters and receivers that allowed them to track one another, as well as find their way anywhere in the world.

Jim and Sam were back flying the deserts of Arizona for the DEA as their cover. Lorenzo and Carmelita were in Mexico setting up drug dealers, and Allison was doing liaison work for the team within the confines of the restrictions of the deep cover of the team.

Through contacts within the office of the President, she used her impressive administrative skills, along with her field training, to procure equipment, money and needed data resources.

At any moment, she could literally be anywhere in the world seeking support or resources as needed.

She and Jim had maintained their romance even though separated a good part of the time. When they did have moments together, they lost little time pickup up where they left off. If anything, their relationship was more of growing continuity than starting and stopping.

Sam was the playful brother to everyone, dating several women and not making any commitments to any of them, but not losing the interest of even one of them. He personified the concept of footloose and fancy free. Ruggedly handsome and with always a quick smile and a joke, he had a devastating effect on the ladies.

Jim and Sam were strolling across the tarmac in Lancaster, California, at Fox Field. They had stopped for fuel and a break from the hours of sitting in a cockpit scanning the desert. Both were wearing army flight jumpsuits and boots, along with a shoulder holster with 9 mm Glocks, and they could have been military or tied to a police agency or government security assets. However, Sam could not give up his Tony Lama cowboy boots. Jim opted for the more standard black lace-up military issue boots, which he found to be much more comfortable than "pointy cowboy boots".

They were headed back to their Cessna when both their Blackberries buzzed, indicating a text message had just been delivered. Simultaneously, they both put in their passwords into their PDAs to get the message. On the main message menu they saw "New Assignment" in the subject line.

Air

Mac's message was brief and to the point.

To: The MWG

From: Mac

Our special team skills are needed again in support of the project that initially brought us together. Report to Bob Pinkerton's ranch no later than tomorrow at 17:00.

It was roughly a 90-minute flight in the Cessna back to Kingman, and from there it was an easy 30-minute flight to Pinkerton's ranch.

"Well," Sam said, "duty calls. We'd better saddle up and get moving."

The DEA Cessna had been refueled and was ready to go. The pre-flight was quick as they had been flying most of the morning and the aircraft was performing flawlessly.

Jim responded, "I wonder what's going on? Mac's message makes it sound somewhat urgent, which is not really his style unless something big is happening."

"Yeah, I thought of that too," Sam replied. "I really thought our work on the Sky Shield project was finished. It seems like the scientists are quietly working their magic at this point."

"I agree," said Sam, "but with something as strategic as that system is, there is always something going on with it. Check the fuel sumps and I will un-chock the wheels."

Jim took a quick sample of fuel at each fuel sump to be sure that they did not have any water or debris surreptitiously creep in to the tanks from contaminated fuel.

"All clear," Jim called out.

He and Sam both climbed into the cockpit, strapped in and put on their headsets. It was a warm day, so they kept their doors open a couple of inches to keep some air flowing into the cabin, not only for their own comfort, but also to cool off the avionics, as radios and navigation instruments and equipment do not work well when they get overheated.

"Clear prop!" Jim yelled out the door as he visually checked the area for anyone walking in the area of the airplane, particularly near the propeller.

He thumbed on the master switch and turned the key to start the engine. Predictably, the engine turned over about one and a half times and caught with a rumble. Not only was it a good engine, but it was superbly maintained back in Kingman at their base.

Jim advanced the throttle just a touch, and they began to roll towards the taxiway.

"Fox ground, Cessna on the ramp ready to taxi to the active runway with current ATIS," Sam called on the radio.

They had their clearance, and without any delay were cleared for takeoff. Jim fire-walled the throttle, and the big Cessna was in the air within a few seconds.

The flight to Kingman was uneventful. All along the route, they both scanned the southwestern desert out their windows for activity and they both enjoyed the view. From their vantage point, they could see the wildlife and vegetation of the area and appreciate the beauty of Mother Nature.

Sam and Jim walked up the expansive front walk to the lodge-like home of Pinkerton's ranch. Not surprisingly, they found Mac and the balance of the Monkey Wrench Gang sitting in the grand hall near the fireplace. The furniture grouping of leather chairs and sofas could easily accommodate a group of 10 or so people. Bob and Mac were huddled over a laptop computer that was connected to an LCD projector. As they prepared for the briefing, the other members of the team greeted each other like old friends. Working as closely with each other as they had in the past created a special bond amongst all of them. They truly were a family in many ways.

"Ladies and gentlemen," Mac started, "The President has called upon us to handle some very special deliveries for him. These deliveries will be to facilitate the expansion of a project that is near and dear to your hearts, the Sky Shield project. The cargo we are moving around is extremely sensitive material and we will be moving it along the whole route. Aircraft, delivery vehicles, cover and decoy vehicles, and military convoys will be used when necessary to complete the mission. This series of missions is of the highest national security and each of you has had your security clearances upgraded to accommodate the necessary information access. In some cases, there will be lay up time between mission segments, in other cases, the mission will require an immediate turnaround to complete the whole segment.

"The first segment is without a doubt the most dangerous, the most important and is critical to completing the other segments."

He powered up the projector onto a screen that was descending from the ceiling before he continued. "You are going to pick up a very large load from this warehouse near Frederick, Maryland, and transport the load to the Cayman Islands. This load has a value of billions of dollars and must make it safely to the Caymans. As I said, if this load does not make it, it could jeopardize national security in many ways. While it is Top Secret, as you know, these things have a way of leaking, and I think we need to plan for an attempt by any number of nefarious groups to attack and steal the cargo.

"The main cargo will be flown in the initial leg by Jim and Sam in a C-130 Hercules. This C-130 is not a normal

Herc, it has been armored and it is armed with automatic mini-guns on both sides, the nose and the tail. All weapons can be targeted and brought to bear on any number of targets from any direction simultaneously from the cockpit by either pilot. In addition, I will be flying cover in an F-22 Raptor. The balance of the team will be in the Cayman Islands awaiting our arrival with special assignments that will facilitate the final delivery of our cargo. The U.S. military does not know of our mission and will not be available to help us on this portion, so we are completely on our own. We may get some assistance from the armed forces later in subsequent segments but not this one.

"As you know, flying to the Cayman Islands requires flying through Cuban airspace, which requires special clearance. We will be skirting Cuban airspace and not requesting clearance, as shown on this slide. This is likely to attract even more attention from the Cuban Air Force, but we can't afford to request the clearance and have even more people know of the flight or the route. If the Cuban Air Force or any other Air Force or aircraft of any kind approaches the Herc or orders you to land or detract from your route, you are authorized to shoot them down without further discussion or communication. Likewise, when the cargo is on the ground, if approached, we will destroy anyone who approaches and ask questions later. We cannot take a chance on this cargo not making its destination or of anyone finding out about it. Any questions thus far?"

Sam broke the deadening silence. "What in the world are we going to be hauling?"

"That is strictly a need to know issue, and you don't need to know to complete your mission. If the need arises, we will tell you. Until then, you are better off not knowing. I can tell you that the cargo itself is not anything that is volatile, or chemically dangerous, toxic or a threat of that nature. By itself the cargo is completely harmless. Other questions?"

"I've heard of the gun systems you described, but I haven't ever used them. I'm guessing we'll get some training?" Jim asked. "Only in a simulator," Mac replied. "We don't have time to give you any extensive actual flight training. I can tell you this though, the systems are very intuitive, and essentially you will target through a heads up display, maneuver the guns with a joy stick, and fire the guns with a button on the joy stick. There is a gun selector on the joy stick, as well and both air targets and surface targets can be selected. Surface targets are radar guided, as well as by GPS. If you can play video games, you and use this weapon system."

The stunned silence continued as the team absorbed the seriousness of the mission and their involvement.

Mac took the silence as an indicator to continue. "OK, once Jim and Sam reach the Cayman Islands, the cargo will be brought ashore by a high speed yacht piloted by Lorenzo, Carmelita, and Allison. The three of you will be lounging around on this yacht awaiting the drop from the Herc and then transport it to a warehouse, where you will turn it over to an armored car service. Question, Jim?"

"Yeah, Mac. How will the drop be done? Low pass with a drogue chute, or…?"

"No," Mac replied, "actually the packages will be in watertight containers inside a remotely guided glider that you will launch out the open tail hatch of the Herc from high altitude. You will get a code from the yacht indicating it's ok to launch. As soon as you launch though the glider deploys its wings and homes in on a radio beam broadcast from the yacht. The glider with the packages will land on the water near the yacht and float until the yacht can pick it up with their hoist. Once the cargo is aboard, the glider will be allowed to sink. The ocean is very deep in that region, so we're pretty confident it won't be recovered. As I

said earlier, our biggest threat that we can think of is an unexpected response by the Cuban Air Force. There are other
factions that would like to acquire your cargo, but none that
will be in proximity and most won't have the capability to
bring down an armed Herc. If you do get in a gun battle,
do what you have to do to complete the mission and the
State Dept. will do what it can to cover for you. Any other
questions? Additional details are on your Blackberryies.
Let's roll."

Chapter 42

The transfer of U.S. currency totaling $25 billion to the warehouse at the Frederick, Maryland, airport was completed without problem. To avoid raising suspicion, the pallets were not under obvious guard. The pallets were being watched carefully by an armed response that could be on the premises within 60 seconds.

Also in the warehouse, a very unusual craft about the size of a motorhome with a streamlined nose and folded wings sat near the pallets. One by one, the pallets were loaded into the enormous cargo hold of the strange looking vehicle, until all were loaded and the cargo hatch was closed and sealed.

Jim and Sam picked up the Herc in Phoenix, where they received training on the gun systems. After a thorough checkout on their new bird, they flew it across country to Frederick and landed and taxied up to the warehouse doors. Once in front of the massive warehouse doors, they used their engines to turn the big bird on a dime and spin it around so the rear ramp and hatch opened directly in front of the doors. The glider was on a roller and they were able to simply hook onto the roller and winch it into the Herc hold. Once on board, it was a simple task to secure it with strapping.

The whole process took less than an hour from the time Jim and Sam shut down their engines until they re-started them and began to taxi for take-off. Their course from Frederick was preloaded into their GPS system.

From Frederick, they were to fly southwest on a course that would take them over central Alabama. Upon arrival in central Alabama, they were to descend to between 50 and 100 feet AGL and remain at that altitude until clear of the ADIZ. After clearing the ADIZ, they were to climb to 30,000 feet for the remainder of the mission. The pop-up maneuver was designed to catch anyone monitoring the flight off guard as to whether it had landed or not in Alabama and then not reappear until in a completely different sector. They would not have a filed flight plan, they would not communicate with any ATC, and they would not turn on their transponder. To anyone monitoring radar, they would simply see a blip at between 10,000 and 12,000 feet, which could be any VFR aircraft. Their flight plan had them skirting all controlled airspace, all military operation areas (MOAs) and any restricted airspace. By staying clear of airways and controlled and restricted airspace, they should be able to fly their mission without raising too much suspicion.

The take-off and initial departure went without a hitch. The Hercules was a joy to fly - very stable, and with an incredible amount of lifting power and a cruise speed well over 250 kias.

Their course was southwest from Frederick to Mobile. One hundred miles northwest of Mobile, they would descend from their cruise altitude to an altitude well below 100 feet AGL.

While they knew Mac was flying high cover in the F-22 Raptor, they did not have any radio communication with him, nor could they pick him up on radar due to the stealth technology of the Raptor. They weren't even sure when or where he would intercept their route and begin flying cover. They just had to trust that he was there monitoring their flight and providing cover if necessary. Both the Raptor and the Hercules were completely unmarked and painted in a non-descript gray color.

Over the aircraft intercom, Jim announced his intentions to Sam. "Beginning our initial descent for low altitude maneuvering," he stated as they approached the intercept point northwest of Mobile. They had been cruising at 25,000 feet so the descent had to be planned for so it would not attract attention of any controllers in the area that might be picking up their unidentified blip on their screen.

At a descent rate of 2,000 feet a minute, they would need 12 to 13 minutes to get below 100 feet AGL, and at their present speed they needed to start that maneuver 85 nautical miles north of the IP. Any controller who just happened to pick them up on radar would interpret them as a normal flight making an approach for landing somewhere and ignore them.

At less than 100 feet AGL and 225 KIAS, the pilots had to be ready to maneuver quickly to avoid obstacles without gaining too much altitude. They needed to get out over the Gulf of Mexico and past the ADIZ without being seen or detected if possible. The terrain northwest of Mobile was relatively flat and uninhabited, making the flight through the area about as easy as possible. Nonetheless, the speed and the lack of altitude made it crucial that the two pilots were on their game and quick to react.

The Mississippi countryside flashed by at 100 feet. Small villages and isolated farms and settlements came and went in the blink of an eye as Jim and Sam flew the big Herc like a fighter on a strafing run. Their biggest worries were tall power line towers and broadcast towers that reach as high as 700 feet or more. The problem with the broadcast towers was many times they had guide wires that supported them from the side that were, for all intesnt and purposes, invisible.

After about 15 minutes of nap of the Earth flying,

suddenly they were over the beach and out over the Gulf, flying so low it felt as though they were taking the tops off the waves. Another five minutes or so and they would be well clear of the ADIZ and they could resume a more normal altitude, although both Jim and Sam had grins plastered across their face as they concentrated on the low high speed flying. In a lot of ways it was the same thrill as a high speed roller coaster - scary but intoxicating.

As they cleared the ADIZ they took a quick look at the GPS and knew for sure they were in international waters. Jim eased back on the control wheel and the Herc rose to about 500 feet. Sam armed the remote fire mini-guns and turned up the gain on the heads up display for aiming the guns. They both visually cleared the area and Sam aimed the forward mini-gun at the ocean surface below and hit the trigger. Instantly, a stream of fire leaped out of the nose of the aircraft and zipped across the ocean surface. One by one he tested each gun. Following the gun test, Jim eased back on the yoke and the big bird soared up to 10,000 feet. They had roughly 600 miles over the ocean before they made their drop off the Cayman Islands. Any air traffic control that might pick them up on radar would assume they were just another commercial flight, or so they planned.

Allison, Lorenzo and Carmelita were anchored 15 miles off the southwestern shore of the Cayman Islands. They were on board a 200-foot converted trawler with a 40-foot cigarette boat tied off the starboard side.

The swells were running a gentle 2 feet high and the trawler was doing just as it was designed to do, riding the swells as easy as a piece of driftwood. All three were comfortably seated on deck chairs on the aft deck enjoying the sun and incredibly beautiful sea.

The Caymans are famous for having clear waters and

represent some of the finest diving in the world, not to mention sport fishing and island hopping. Just 150 miles to the south of the Caymans is Jamaica, and many yachting parties run back and forth between the Cayman Islands and Jamaica for a change of scenery and entertainment. Today, the ocean was empty for as far as the eye could see. Nothing but deep blue water, blue sky with a few scattered clouds, and a very slight trade wind - a perfect day to be enjoying a bit of R and R on the open sea. All three of them knew that within a few hours they had a lot of work ahead of them.

When Sam and Jim released the glider from the back of the Herc. Lorenzo would pilot it to a safe landing on the water near their trawler. They had a remote control set up below decks that would allow them to control the craft with a set of instruments, a control joy stick, and a screen that gave them a view from a video camera mounted on the nose of the glider. The glider would land on the water and it was buoyant enough to float for many hours. The trawler was equipped with a small crane that would lift the glider aboard so it could be unloaded, then it would be sunk in the Caribbean. The entire load from the glider would be stored below decks until it could be taken ashore with the cigarette, making several trips.

Despite the beauty of the day and the idyllic setting, time drug on as they contemplated the enormity of the task ahead of them. They could only speculate as to what the delivery detail was of or for, only that it had been impressed upon them that the value of their cargo was such that it could determine the strength of the nation for many years to come. They sat in the sun and sipped ice tea, wishing the job would begin - all three suffered with the inactivity and the anticipation.

Lorenzo went below deck to review the chart of the area and to find the inlet on the island that they were to take into the dock where they would unload their cargo. For the most part, it was a straight shot into the island, but there were some coral reefs off the coast of the island with some shallow areas that had to be carefully navigated. The cigarette was not only fast, but it also had a shallow draft and could go where a lot of boats of similar size would not be able to go.

As time drew closer, all three began to pace the decks, check gear, look at charts and try to chase the butterflies from their stomachs. It didn't work - the harder they tried to occupy themselves, the worse it became. They all knew they were completely alone in this task, and they all knew they had to succeed.

After he checked his equipment, Lorenzo started pulling canvas tarps off of four large pieces of deck equipment, which turned out to be 50 caliber machine guns on deck stands - one on the bow, one on each side and one on the stern. They also had a mortar launcher on the bow that could be used to fend off an intruder.

Like their partners in the air, they were given instructions to not allow any boat, ship or aircraft anywhere near them and they were authorized to bring guns to bear as they saw fit. The 50 calibers were loaded with spend uranium shells that would punch a fist-sized hole in most boats or ships. A few well-place hits at or below the waterline would sink most boats. The mortar could land a mortar round on the deck of a ship half a mile away and easily set it afire.

They were prepared to defend themselves and the cargo of their country to the death if necessary. All three of them could pilot the trawler, the cigarette and could fire all of the weapons. They were only a team of three, but they were very skilled and committed to their jobs.

One by one, Lorenzo prepared the machine guns and fired a short burst through each one. The big trawler shuddered as the guns spit fire across the water. The thumping of the recoil was a visceral feeling that could be felt from the feet all the way up the back of anyone on board. Feeling the recoil and hearing the guns reminded them all of the seriousness of the job that the beautiful day belied. The mortar went untested, as they were concerned that the explosion might be a bit too loud and attract unwanted visitors.

The cigarette also had a gun mounted on the aft deck. With a top speed of well over 100 mph, they could easily outrun most craft. The pivot mount for the gun was permanent, but the gun was stored out of sight in a deck trunk close to the pivot mount, and it could be readied to fire within a few seconds.

Chapter 43

The President paced in the Oval Office, trying not to think about the consequences if his little operation failed. The success of the Sky Shield was still not known by the public. The tests continued to be highly effective, and he knew if he could take it to the next level before he went public with it, the success of the whole project would erase any future criticism, should his abuse of executive privilege ever be discovered.

Meanwhile the Shield continued to knock out tropical storms as they lined up in the southern Atlantic and marched up through the Caribbean on their way to the U.S. coast. Not one serious storm or hurricane had hit the U.S. shore, despite the formation of five serious storms. The Sky Shield had already saved the U.S. government billions of dollars in damage from the storms. Once it could be shown to be effective in desert lands and other positive ways, the U.S. would be riding a crest of prosperity not seen for decades, and his popularity would be forever instilled in the history books as the President who changed the game.

He knew there were a number of factions that were working against his success. All were still relatively cloudy, but it was starting to come into focus. One of his long-time rivals, Senator Jacobsen, seemed to have a common thread in many of the scenarios his staff had been putting together.

Air

Besides being a charter member of the Founders, his name was connected with the Columbian cartel, albeit in a way that would indicate that he was trying to break up the cartel.

Interior Secretary Holmsby had speculated that Jacobsen may have deeper involvement in many of the activities that supported the development of the Sky Shield off the federal grid. Those activities alone could be considered treason. He had assigned the FBI to investigate Senator Jacobsen's activities for the past year to see if any of the threads could be traced back to him. The FBI had put together a file on the good Senator that was extremely damning and probably in a normal court of law would be enough to convict him of a number of crimes, not to mention conspiracy against the nation. But this was not a normal situation, and a U.S. Senator was hardly a regular citizen in terms making accusations and making them stick. He would have to find other means to neutralize the Senator's game plan.

Senator Jacobsen was just landing at Ronald Reagan when he received a text message from his new assistant. It would seem that the President was summoning him to the White House the next morning.

Depending on how events unfolded, there was a good chance that the President would cancel that meeting. Tipping off the Cuban Air Force that there may be a rich target in the area of the Cayman Islands could help turn the tables in his favor and give him one more shot at getting control of the Sky Shield back.

He had to smear the President's name and prevent the development funds from reaching their destination. His internal sources had been able to piece together the plan as they reviewed intelligence data from a variety of sources. The final tip off was when the newly-organized National Oceanic Research Meteorological Agency (NORMA) went into action. Many resources had been blended, including the SST, to set up this group and they had been nothing but trouble for him. It was time to get rid of them and put a stop to the President's grip on his project.

Secretary Holmsby was in his Washington office, wearing a path in his carpet pacing back and forth. He was faced with multiple conflicts that he was having an obvious difficult time reconciling. He never contemplated that working with Senator Jacobsen would endanger the lives of his brother and his family. The work his brother was asked to initiate started as such a simple thing. Before he realized it, his brother was engaged in the development of a fully-developed system.

Then, Jacobsen started talking about the immense profit potential. The flow of the illegal funds from the drug operation was a case of the end justifying the means, but turning off that relationship had become much more difficult than anticipated.

To top everything off, he knew that Jacobsen had lied to many of the Founders and he also knew that he was escalating his plans to a level of treason. If he talked to the President, he himself would be implicated in the mess, but he thought it better to escape now before his actions became capital offenses.

He stopped in mid stride. He knew what he had to do - all of a sudden it all became crystal clear. He sat down behind his desk and placed a call to the President. Surprisingly, he was patched directly through to the President after being handled by just two gatekeepers.

"Mr. President, Stewart Holmsby here."

"Well, Stew, how are you? Good to hear from you."

"Thank you Mr. President. I need to meet with you as soon as possible. I have some very difficult topics to talk with you about. Once you hear what I have to say, I know you will agree that speed is of the utmost importance."

"In that case, I will clear my calendar for you right now Stew. How soon can you be to the Oval office?"

"I can be there in 10 minutes."

"Very well, I will be waiting."

As the President hung up the phone, he knew why Stewart Holmsby was coming, and for the most part what he would be telling him. He felt somewhat pleased that he was coming forward, but at the same time, he realized that self preservation was most of the motivation.

Holmsby would ask for a deal in exchange for the information, and most likely the President would protect him in exchange for broader cooperation, plus the fact that his brother was the key to the success of the Sky Shield project.

He had great faith in the team carrying out the final steps in securing the funding he needed to complete the project; the self-proclaimed Monkey Wrench Gang were the field team under NORMA (National Oceanic Research Meteorological Agency), which had been created to provide management structure of the Sky Shield once it was all public.

Secretary Holmsby was ushered in to the Oval Office without hesitation. For nearly an hour, he laid out his involvement with Senator Jacobsen and the Founders to develop and advance the Sky Shield project. With the recorders turned off, the President grilled Secretary Holmsby and got hard answers to the details of many pieces of the puzzle they suspected were there but had no proof of before.

Based on what he heard, the President had very strong concerns that someone tipped off by Jacobsen may have initiated an attack or intercept of the C-130 over the Caribbean or the trawler and crew that awaited the delivery. The President dispatched a message to Mac warning him of the heightened potential. Even though Mac was flying high cover, he got the message and within a few seconds had warned the balance of the team.

The President asked Secretary Holmsby if there were any other issues and if he was withholding any information that might help the mission to succeed. The Secretary assured him that he told him everything he knew.

"Very well then," the President continued, "I need you to begin taking some positive steps on behalf of your country. What you have done here today is a good start, but I need more from you.

"First, I need you to get word to the senior Founders that the U.S. Government is taking eminent domain of this project and that they should cease and desist any involvement unless it is something that I specifically ask them to do. Secondly, before you leave the White House I want you to write out a statement summarizing what you have told me and sign that document and delivering it to me and me only. Third, you are to have no further contact or communication with Senator Jacobsen. Fourth, you are not to leave the country. Any questions?"

"No sir, Mr. President!" Secretary Holmsby practically saluted as he responded emphatically.

Chapter 44

Each team member in the Monkey Wrench Gang received the same text message. Unlike a regular commercial PDA, each BlackBerry used satellite technology rather than cellular, and the messages were encrypted. Mac was able to fly one handed while he forwarded on a message he had just received from the Office of the President: "Threat of intercept or attack is eminent. Attack or intercept could occur on the water or in the air. Handle as briefed."

The last part of the message essentially gave the team license to use whatever means to accomplish their goal. The benefit of being part of a black ops team was that as long as no one knew of the mission, one could be as creative as necessary.

Sam reach overhead on the sub panel in the Hercules and turned up the gain on the long range radar, which gave them the capability to see a 360 degree arc around them up to 100 miles, as well as the basis for the targeting radar on the weapons systems.

Almost immediately, two blips appeared on the radar 75 miles to the southeast. Based on the closing speed, they were jet aircraft and they had just departed Cuba. Good chance they were Cuban Air Force fighters scrambled to investigate the Herc's presence.

"Let's head for the waves and see if we can lose them in the return clutter," Jim announced as he pushed the control wheel forward and brought the aircraft into a 10 degree descent angle. At the same time, he began a turn to the west to change course, which would negate the accuracy of the intercept angle plotted by their potential pursuers. Radar waves bounced off anything including waves, sea traffic, whales on the surface, and if an aircraft flew low enough the radar beam would not be able to discern between all of the stuff on the surface, including the aircraft.

Within a few minutes, Jim had jinked his way through several headings and descended to 50 feet above the ocean surface. By the time he reached 50 feet, he was back on his original heading and doing 200 knots.

Captain Jacinto Lopez of the Cuban Air Force tried desperately to track the blip on the radar he and his wingman had been scrambled to find and assess. The two Cuban pilots were flying Mig 21s, an aircraft manufactured in Russia in the early 60s that could perform many types of missions, including surface and air to air attack missions. Equipped with both guns and missiles, it could be a formidable threat in capable hands. Even though he had lost track of the aircraft, he had a pretty good idea of where it might be and decided to play that hunch.

He looked at the jinking pattern of the target, looked at the trend line, and mentally drew a line through the middle of it, discovering it was the original heading of the target when they initially picked it up. Without breaking radio silence, he hand signaled to his wingman that they were going to descend and change headings. Captain Lopez laid his aircraft over on its back and headed to sea level. At 2,000 feet, he rolled upright and scanned the Caribbean surface for movement. Within a few minutes, he spotted the big transport aircraft skimming the ocean surface.

His orders were to "splash" the target at any cost. He slowed up his aircraft to match the 200 knot speed of the target and swung in on its 6 o'clock position. In trail of the big transport, he began to size up the target when he noticed the mini-gun pods on the sides of the aircraft, and then his eyes focused on the rear of the airplane and saw the movement of a pair of gun barrels protruding from the rear ramp area.

Within a nanosecond, his guts turned to water, and he realized that he and his wingman might be in grave danger. A mini-gun equipped C-130 Hercules could only originate from one source - the U.S. military. With their targeting radar, they may not be able to escape.

Just as his brain processed that thought, he heard the pip of targeting threat radar go off in his headset. The hunter had just become the hunted.

Before he could lay his control stick over to evade, he saw a 10-foot flame leap out of the twin gun barrels in the Hercules. Half a second later, his wingman's Mig burst into flames. His wingman didn't even have a chance to punch out, and probably did not even realize what hit him. The 50 caliber depleted uranium slugs shredded the Mig from the nose back to the fuel tanks. The red-hot ammo hit the fuel tanks and it all vaporized in a puff of smoke.

Jim and Sam watched the whole thing evolve through a rear view camera lens presented on a small screen in their control panel. They watched the laser-like trail of fire stretch out behind them and take out the Mig. They also watched the lead aircraft go ballistic and head for the sky above before they could re-aim. Their high-fiving and celebrating was short lived as they both realized that the Mig would be back. They also realized that they needed to be rid of any threat before they could make contact with the balance of the team.

Captain Lopez knew he just barely escaped with this life. He leveled off from his climb at 15,000 feet to contemplate his next move. He had his radar on looking for any other threats, so he was not looking around or over his shoulder, as he was confident the radar would pick up any other threat.

His complacency almost cost him his life again within a couple of minutes. A bit of movement caught his peripheral vision on his starboard side. He slowly swung his head to the right and was shocked to see an unmarked Raptor F-22 Stealth fighter in his wing position. Looking directly at him was a pilot with a big toothy grin on his face waving at him. Without even thinking, his hand came up and he slowly waved back.

While he was still waving and still comprehending his fate again, the grinning pilot started pointing at him with his index finger and then giving him the thumbs up motion. He was either offering congratulations or telling him to get out. To eliminate any confusion, the grinning pilot mimicked the action he would need to take to trigger the escape seat in his aircraft - he was telling him to punch out over the Caribbean, to leave his aircraft. He knew he had no choice, he also knew that within a day or so he would be picked up by a vessel and that he would survive. But if he tried to stay and fight the most sophisticated airplane on Earth, he would die.

He had no choice. If anything, he should be grateful to the pilot for giving him a choice. He looked over at his foe, gave him a smart salute of thanks, and then punched out by blowing off the canopy and igniting the rocket under his seat. Within a few seconds he was floating lazily in his parachute headed for the sea. He looked above and watched the Raptor drop back behind his Mig and casually blow it out of the air. With no markings of any kind, he wondered who just put him on the sidelines. He had no idea what he would report to his superiors, but he had plenty of time to think about it.

Jim and Sam continued on their heading, practically breaking their necks looking around them for the Mig.

Air

They didn't have long to wait, except that it wasn't a Mig. Without the warning of the radar threat pip, they were very surprised to look out the cockpit windows and see an aircraft pull up along side them. Instantly, relief washed over them as they realized it was Mac in the Raptor. The big grin was easy to recognize as he signaled to them that the Mig was no longer an issue and they were clear to complete the mission unimpeded. He gave them a quick salute and then pulled up in a vertical climb to return to his high cover position.

Rather than becoming another target on radar somewhere, Jim and Sam agreed to stay at low altitude until they got much closer to the delivery site. With any luck, they could deploy the glider and head back to the mainland before they could be found and intercepted again.

Chapter 45

Senator Jacobsen was awaiting a message regarding events in the Caribbean. He hoped he would hear that his tip to the Cubans would have paid off, stopping progress on Sky Shield expansion. He had an appointment with the President in an hour that he was hoping would be canceled. He had been trying without luck to connect with Stewart Holmsby and could not seem to either get a response or find out where he was. It seemed all of a sudden that he was in a bit of a communication vacuum - no one would return his calls and no one seemed to have any answers for him.

He decided to have a cup of coffee, take care of some official paperwork and try to put the whole think out of his mind. He poured the coffee, stirred in some cream and walked over to his desk and plopped down in his leather executive chair.

He picked up his cup and cradled it in both hands as his mind returned to the events at hand. He just couldn't shake the feeling that there were unknown events unfolding. He sighed heavily and took a drink of his coffee and turned to the stack of paper in front of him.

The stack of correspondence in front of his was routine and required a quick review before he signed it to be sent. He had worked through three letters and signed them when he began to feel light headed and dizzy. His heart rate had accelerated to well over 150 beats per minute and he felt flushed. He had a funny taste in his mouth that left an almond aftertaste, which was strange since he had not had any almonds to eat. His peripheral vision was closing in and he was close to losing consciousness. He felt a sudden pain in his abdomen and a couple of seconds later, his heart stopped and he slumped over his desk on the paperwork he was working on.

Within two or three minutes, Senator Jacobsen's new assistant slipped quietly into his office. He quickly emptied the coffee container and the partially empty cup and rinsed them both out and placed them on the table where they were normally stored. He checked the Senator's pulse and then picked up the phone and called for emergency help.

Within a few minutes, the medical staff in the capitol building had arrived and tried with no avail to revive him. Senator Jacobsen had passed away very suddenly. Everyone around him was stunned, as he had seemed to be in good health.

Within a few minutes of Senator Jacobsen's death, the President was notified. He expressed his shock and sadness to the official caller. As he hung up the phone, he thought to himself, one just never knows when one's time is up.

Right on time and on target, Jim and Sam spotted a trawler and yacht on the horizon anchored 15 miles off the Cayman Islands. They made a low pass directly over the top of the two boats and could see their three teammates waving on the stern of the yacht.

Lorenzo keyed his mic and repeated a couple of code words on a specific frequency, letting Jim and Sam know they were awaiting the drop and all was a go.

Jim and Sam circled to the west, climbed to 3,000 feet and prepared for the drop. As Jim throttled back and flew the big Herc in a racetrack pattern, Sam lowered the rear ramp and began to unchain the glider.

Within a couple of minutes, Jim confirmed they were ready and Lorenzo confirmed that he was ready as well. Sam released the glider, and as planned, the drogue chute pulled the glider out of the open ramp and suspended it in the air until the wings on the glider self deployed and the chute released the glider. At the same time, an electrical system kicked on in the glider and a signal transmitted to Lorenzo's receiver. On cue, Lorenzo began maneuvering the glider with the joy stick on his controller, and the glider flew very smoothly in big lazy circles, spiraling down towards the landing site astern the yacht.

Lorenzo executed a perfect landing on the water and, as planned, it bobbed up and down with the swells. The three team members hoisted anchor and prepared to move closer to the glider to bring it aboard.

Allison had the engines started and had begun to swing the bow of the yacht towards the floating glider when Lorenzo began to yell. "The glider is sinking! Hurry up - get me over there!"

Lorenzo quickly put on a mask and flippers and a scuba tank as Allison maneuvered closer to the glider. The dingy crane had more than enough lifting capacity to hoist the glider, but Lorenzo was going to dive in and hook the crane cable to the glider so they could haul it on to the stern of the yacht.

The glider was riding low in the water and getting lower. It was obviously taking on water quickly, but given the smooth landing, Lorenzo could not figure out why it would be sinking.

By the time they were alongside the glider, only a foot or so of the top of the glider was above water. Lorenzo and Carmelita wasted no time jumping overboard to get the cable hook into the attachment ring on the back of the glider. Despite their best efforts, the glider slipped under the surface before they could get to it.

Lorenzo followed it down as it slipped under the waves. He had descended to a depth of about 25 feet when he got the shock of his life. Coming up from the deep were six divers in U.S. Navy scuba gear. He was just recovering from that startling discovery when he looked below them only to see a U.S. attack class submarine suspended in neutral buoyancy another 30 feet or so below the divers.

The lead diver approached Lorenzo and handed him a slate board. On the board it identified he and his team as U.S. Navy with directions to assume authority over the glider. With a six to one ratio, Lorenzo didn't have much choice but to return to the surface.

Just as he stepped back on board, Allison said she received a radio message from Mac telling her that the glider was in good and proper hands and to make ready to cruise the yacht back to Florida. A crew would be sent to pick up the trawler later today, and their mission was complete.

While relieved that the tension of the mission had been lifted, they were also wondering about the change of plans. Perhaps it was part of the plan all along, or maybe they wouldn't ever know. Nonetheless, they hoisted anchor and set the GPS and the auto pilot for a cruise to Miami.

Chapter 46

A̲ll of the public communication and news services
had been notified that the President of the United
States would be holding a press conference about an
undisclosed topic or topics. The press room of the White
House bustled as the staff prepared for the conference. Re-
porters and camera personnel were passed through security
as they gathered and sat up their equipment.

The President walked onto stage and the press corps
fell silent. While there was a lot of speculation as to the
topic, it was clear that whatever it was it was of great significance.

"Ladies and gentlemen of the press, and my fellow
Americans," the President began, "I have a prepared statement and then I will take questions. Before I begin on that
topic, I would like to extend my condolences to Senator
Jacobsen's family. He served his country with distinction
and his passing is a great loss to the U.S. Senate. We will
all miss him and his contribution to the ongoing effort to
keep America safe and the best country in the world. Services will be held the day after tomorrow, and we will join
his family in mourning the passing of a great statesman, a
father, husband, and grandfather. Our prayers are with the
family in this time of sorrow."

He took a deep breath and paused with his head lowered before he continued.

"I know if Senator Jacobsen were with us today, he

would celebrate along with us all about the achievement I am about to announce.

It is with great pride I announce the deployment of new technology that will change the world as we know it today."

The press corps scribbled notes, cameras whirred and hummed and the President's word reached out across America and the world as he described the Sky Shield. His presentation was designed to point out the humanitarian benefits rather than the strategic leverage it brought America. Those issues will evolve later.

At the end of his talk, the President ushered up to the podium his scientific advisor and project coordinator, Professor Holmsby, to answer questions.

The stunned press corps could not get enough, and finally the President reassumed control of the conference podium and ended the questions with the announcement that a demonstration of the system would be held in southern Florida in a week.

Southern Florida had very predictable weather in late summer. Every day by late afternoon, the blending of warm moist air from the Gulf would create convective activity that would either become thunderstorms or towering cumulus clouds that created a hot humid environment on the ground.

The press corps and officials from around the world were on hand to see what this marvelous new technology would do. Mac, the designated spokesman from NORMA, was on hand to describe what was happening in space to create such effects on the ground. As he described the reflective shield, a noticeable darkening of the sunlight began to occur. It was as if everyone put sunglasses on at the same time.

In several key viewing spots, giant screens had been assembled that were connected to weather radar displays. On screen were the radar returns that were color coordinated to display the temperature variants aloft in the building convective cumulus clouds. In the center of the weather development, the color was a deep red that indicated the higher temperature that was at the core of the build up.

As the shadow over southern Florida deepened, the deep red of the radar display began to moderate and shrink, and the temperature on the ground began to cool.

The crowd was awed as the reality of Sky Shield settled on them and they understood first hand what this meant to mankind. Within 30 minutes, the temperature on the ground had moderated by eight degrees, and the core of the radar returns indicated more of a yellow and orange tone which meant that the convective aspect of the storm system had been alleviated. While rain could still occur, it would not be a dangerous storm with high winds and tornadoes.

The Monkey Wrench Gang was on hand to watch, and they stood together anonymously in the crowd, beaming and congratulating each other for the contribution they each made to make this incredible technology a reality.

With their covert attachment to NORMA still intact, they had all returned to their cover jobs. They all knew that in this unstable world, they would be called upon to serve again in the future, and they all knew they would step forward to help preserve and protect the greatest nation in the world.